POWER TO THE PEOPLE

A B Jamieson

Praise for *Prepare to be tortured – the price you will pay for dating a narcissist*, A B Jamieson's debut publication

'Insightful, humorous and clearly a master of observation…I wait with anticipation for his next book. A must read!'

'A great read from start to finish. At times quite funny and at others depressingly cynical'

'Thought provoking and informative'

'If you could own one book, this would be it'

ABOUT THE AUTHOR

A B Jamieson is the author of one other book, *Prepare to be tortured – the price you will pay for dating a narcissist,* a non-fiction exploration of the negative impact that narcissists can have in all aspects of your life and the strategies that can be adopted to get rid of them. Written in layman's terms and based on experience, it has been the sleeper hit on the topic of narcissism since its publication in 2018. This new book is A B Jamieson's first foray into fiction and is a twisting and turning tale of family, betrayal and morality.

Chapter 1

1979

Waltham, East Sussex. What was once described by day trippers as a quintessential English hamlet complete with church steeple, village green and thatched pub is now barely recognisable from the photos of old. The heart of the village has remained intact but represents a small part of what is now one of the fastest growing new towns on England's south coast. Population now well past the ten thousand mark and growing fast, with improved road and rail links into London explained away by those in public office as being one of the key barometers to their success in driving the town's growth forward. That's the party line. Ask the local and, for the time being, only estate agent however and you might just get a different answer. It helps of course when you can get home from your work in the capital half an hour earlier than normal, but the developers were also keen to exploit Waltham's proximity to its nearest larger next door neighbor. A Royal Borough no less!

The town had become the place to be as buyers viewed it as an affordable step before the next one up to an altogether more distinguished post code next door. Geographically it had the best of both worlds which easily explained why the developers were fighting over themselves to get in on the act. A prestigious neighbour one hour's drive to the west and a day out to the coast with the kids the same amount of time by car heading south. For those keen on making the big bucks in the capital the added bonus of an extra half hour in bed before slaving over a hot desk in the city. What was there not to like about Waltham? All this and a village pub to boot! Any wonder the one and only estate agent knew his days as a solo artist in town were numbered. He was right. Still only April, by the year end he would have four new competitors on his doorstep with yet more still to come. Bigger companies meant bigger advertising budgets and better terms for their clients. That offer he had been made to sell up kept niggling away, the wife perpetually reminding him of the virtues of getting out while the going's good.

Middle class and proud of it was what one young female voter was heard to say when the Labour party canvassers came calling. In Conservative heartlands like this anything above coming third for Labour would be judged a significant result. They may have been in office but this was the dying embers of a government destined to fall mercy to the guile and utopian vision set out by the latest opposition leader who was proving herself adept with the use of slick marketing to promote her message. The slogan, 'Labour isn't working' with the image of queues of the unemployed tailing off into the distance screamed from billboards the length and breadth of the country. That one particular advert would be the making of the Conservative Party and provide its marketing agency creators with enough work for the next twenty years alongside a knighthood for one and peerage to the House of Lords for the other. On the 3rd of May 1979 Margaret

Hilda Thatcher became Britain's first ever female Prime Minister by a landslide majority. The mood in the country was changing and Thatcher was the embodiment of this change. A grocer's daughter from Grantham in middle England, her simple message centred around adopting the same virtues that her father applied when he ran the village shop. By a combination of sacrifice, thrift and hard work material dividends would always be just around the corner. The public like simple messages. Anything that resonates with and become an improvement to the humdrum of daily life would always win favour. This was a leader in tune with those that took care of household finances.

Places like Waltham typified this swing towards greater self-reliance and the increase in living standards to be had by following the golden rule of 'looking after No 1.' The utopian vision was simple - anyone could do it! All about being in charge of your own destiny. If a girl from a humble upbringing could reach the top job in the country, then surely they could too. The prosperity of the UK had always been stronger in its southern half but with a card-carrying Messiah now occupying No 10 its future had just gotten a whole load brighter. Waltham was now on the map. The place to live and the place to be seen to live! With all the hype surrounding its desirability it could soon be giving its still more up market neighbour a run for its money. More scenic for a start! For those already there and others waiting in the wings to become part and parcel of this idyllic enclave, its residents would shortly be riding the crest of a very prosperous housing boom wave.

You need the optimism before you find the confidence to invest which then feeds through to the crucial and most important part. The workforce spending their money! Thatcher provided the former which gave business in the area the green light to make some key job creating decisions. Technology was now leading the way with job creation in the area. With shorter travelling times to the capital on offer, no point in shelling out small fortunes to build factories on the outskirts of London when much cheaper alternatives could be had an hour and a half's drive down the road.

Yet again Waltham found itself at the epicenter of all the action. The demand for skilled labour was bringing even more highly paid jobs to the area and newcomers were all looking for decent areas to live commensurate with their earning power. House prices were now rising as fast as their owners were moving in. Homebuyers were now making money over and above the dual household income. On paper at least! No matter they did not have the physical cash in their hands. Just the very fact of having made something over what they paid sure felt great. Developers could not build the houses fast enough and the local authorities were awash with planning applications. Bear in mind this was a green belt area as far as Government planning was concerned. England's green and pleasant land not to be ruined by the odd couple of thousand two up and two downs - but Thatcher wanted prosperity. Her people as she saw them had to be given the opportunity to improve their lives. Bureaucracy only stymied opportunity. Councils were pressed, some might say leaned on from above to relax the restrictions of green belt planning regulation and thus hurry along this changing face of prosperous Britain. For Waltham the green light definitely screamed Go!

But not only the housebuilder's wanted in on the act. A few others were also keen to join the action. The builders needed their supplies and lots of them so it was obvious that merchants would want sites closer to large scale projects. The microchip manufacturers favoured the south coast not only because of its proximity to the capital but the ferry terminals could be reached within a reasonable driving time cutting down on transport costs to Europe. Then came finance and insurance. If they could relocate to within reasonable travelling time to the capital but without the huge rents involved, then it had to be win-win for all concerned. Only one sector of the local economy was left to get in on the act and that was the shops!

The small High Street had enough to service the communities needs but little else. Any wonder the town was already on the radar of many of the UK's established clothing and food chains but with so little space available in the town centre this was always going to be somewhere for the long term. As such, the residents would have to make do with what they had for the time being. The one and only supermarket, Simpsons, got the bulk of the trade simply because there was no place else to go. Either that or jump in the car for a fifty-mile round trip to the larger supermarket in Sharfield but the petrol and time immediately wiped out any savings made in that area. The Royal Borough an hour away had a much wider array of shops and services but with the same problem as visiting Sharfield. How many of Waltham's hard-working families were prepared to use up practically one whole day of their weekend for the privilege of driving and stocking up. What little they had by way of newsagent, baker, florist and the odd delivery van on top of having Simpsons could suffice for the meantime. At least the village pub had remained intact. The Horse & Farrier which until eighteen months ago had been dying on its backside, had been shrewdly purchased by a local builder who knew absolutely nothing about the pub game but could still spot a golden opportunity when he saw one. Hoodwinking its current owner into believing its days were numbered, now try getting inside the place on a Friday night let alone being served. Fine if you were prepared to wait four deep at the bar for a drink then stand cramped attempting to sup a pint while being squeezed like a sardine. For those frequenting the city bars midweek in the capital, it was now something of a culture shock to come home to a relic of a pub that had obviously seen better days. The height of the new publican's sophistication appeared to be the over-priced Space Invaders machine in the far corner. Easier to queue for that than to try and hear yourself speak.

For the residents of old, time to accept that the town's High Street was now on the cusp of becoming a whole load busier. They could either embrace this change or cling onto a village way of life that looked unlikely to be coming back anytime soon. Still, they always had Armstrong's to go to.

For the incomers there would be enough new residents moving within the right professional circles to validate the murmurings about the High Street going on over the new garden fences. All they had to do was wait, but in the meantime they could enjoy the star performer of the South coast who had pride of place on their very own doorstep. A business with an acclaimed following that stretched far beyond anything that the residents of Waltham could offer. Mention Waltham's name in any form of context and the same inevitable question was always guaranteed to follow.

'Ahh, so have you been to Armstrong's?'

Waltham and Armstrong's were inextricably linked but in recent times it had been the town that learned to play second fiddle to its more accomplished resident. People came from all over the county and beyond to pay homage and enjoy a traditional English family day out. Armstrong's would be first on the agenda and it was not difficult to understand why, considering you reached the place first before driving ahead some thousand yards or so before hitting the town's edge. More out of curiosity and the prevailing attitude of 'well we're here anyway.' Visitors then drive the short distance to see for themselves a picture postcard village green complete with pond and photogenic ducks. Eccentric local complete with straw hat and sheepdog occasionally sat on a bench nearby to provide added authenticity! The very same person barred from the pub and just about every other shop in town.

Armstrong's. More often than not spoken in the same breath as 'you could not find a better location if you tried' and it would be hard to disagree. The type of location deemed too good to be true if you had brought a bunch of surveyors together, given them a map of locality then asked to pick most suitable spot to build a garden centre complete with scenic backdrop and excellent road access. Any wonder rival competitors and the local business community tended to look on this well-established family business with a large degree of dark green envy. For the patriarch of the business, Jim, there was no doubting the admiration the locals had for a man who took what was in essence his father's market garden and transformed this fourteen acre site into a family friendly complex comprising shops, café, restaurant, play area, plant section and his latest piece de resistance. An idea of his own, yet to be copied and an absolute hit with the latest swathe of incomers, the majority of who could aptly be described as hard working but complete novices when it came to garden design. A dozen completed gardens in a variety of styles but crucially the size and shape of those already being built by the developer. All the incomers had to do was select the style then buy the plants. From Armstrong's of course! The business could even do all the hard landscaping if the time pressed locals had enough on their plates already. Not cheap but swayed by the increase already taking place in property values, most residents now appeared more than willing to pay.

Jim could sniff an opportunity at fifty paces.

'Got to stay ahead of the game'

Hi favourite phrase at the bi-annual Rotary Club dinner where to not have him as guest speaker would be deemed an insult to those local business people responsible for keeping Waltham on the map! For locals of a certain vintage however, those going back far enough to remember his father, Frank, it came as no surprise when his son continued his entrepreneurial vision in the same vein.

Leaving the Army the wrong side of thirty on a medical discharge and with no real skill set, Frank's lucky break came when he found himself sole beneficiary to a four bedroom house and half acre of land after a spinster Aunt with who he had exchanged letters regularly during Army service passed away.

A consummate wheeler dealer from his time as a streetwise corporal bartering cigarettes, he set himself up buying whatever local and surrounding farms were prepared to sell. The formative early days of the business started when Waltham's latest resident, Frank Armstrong, began by selling local produce out front on trestle tables by the side of the road. From this he expanded into whatever he could get his hands on, but with money being tight he stuck to food staples and taking work out of season on the local estate to supplement his income.

Through time and with no small amount of ingenuity, the able minded Frank began to experiment by utilising the land to grow his own fruit and vegetables, with further lines being added by farmer's wives keen to earn a few extra shillings and see more of the strapping young man by selling him their home-made jam and bread. Sometimes gaining more than he expected!

With one eye on the deal and keen to grow more of his own, a couple of acres next door were added by way of bank loan, which were immediately upgraded from grazing to producing. Early days, but by sheer hard work and no small amount of guile, at a local level at least Armstrong's was finally on the map. That he would meet and marry a local lass which produced an only son, a foregone conclusion that offspring Jim would follow in father's footsteps.

Chapter 2

Indicative of the can-do attitude sweeping the country, Armstrong's was the epitome of the true family business where everyone played their part. Although as is always the case there were some that thought they pulled their weight more than others. Regularly featured in the annual list of the UK's top 10 garden centres as voted by their peers, the business had been transformed over the best part of two decades from a one-man band seasonal horse and cart operation to this slick all year round enterprise turning over well in excess of a million.

It was Frank's son Jim who really must take the bulk of the credit for this, building not only on his parents' achievements but creating the brand. First, he moved away from the wholesale side which was a whole load of work for peanuts of a return. Secondly, he did what his father should have done all along as it had been staring him in the face for years. He simply demolished the place and started all over again. Long before the house building boom kicked off with Waltham still a sleepy little backwater, Jim had a hunch they were sitting on something special. The views out the back were enough alone to make people come visit. Build something that kept customers here for longer and they could be sitting on a goldmine. The new bank manager, eager to make a name for himself, agreed and the rest as they say is history.

Tall and slim, rakish even, unless you knew Jim and who he was, you could be forgiven for mistaking him as some

Headmaster or another having a browse around the plants on his weekend off. He looked distinguished. At the very least you would swear he came from the professions. Any lack of discerning weight gain for a man of his years attributable to self control, good genes or more than likely the odd decade or so of financial stress. Now in his late fifties and the elder statesman of the business, his days were spent patrolling the site to show face which effectively meant keeping the thirty odd staff or so on their toes. Nothing up with a bit of genial intimidation he would tell his protégé Joe. Everyone has to know who's the boss. A good man by nature, quite simply he loved what he did. gardening was in his bones. Ever since childhood when father Frank had taught him how to plant seeds then watch nature take care of the rest he'd been hooked. Still as passionate about gardening as ever Armstrong's had long since become a labour of love from which he was simply unable to break free.

Always some customer or another waiting to pounce as he did his early morning rounds!

'Aye you'll be a busy man these days counting all this money you're making Jim.'

The kind of question dispensed from those of envy, but poorly disguised through humour.

'If only that were the case. It's not as easy as you think. There might be money but look around you at all the wages I have to pay.' [Closing his fingers together] 'I just get that teensy weensy little slice that's left over once everything else has been taken care of if I'm lucky.'

'Oh, come on Jim. Do you think I was born yesterday? We all know you must be one of the richest men in Waltham right now. You must get offers to sell up every other day.'

'Good God no! Where are you getting that from? Never sell this place in a month of Sundays. I would not know what to do with myself for a start and besides there's his Lordship the other side of town who has that title all sown up for himself. I wish I had a pound for every acre of land that man owned.'

'Looks like I must be listening to all the wrong people then. You keep your cards close to your chest I'll give you that.'

'Well, if you want me to stay that way then you'd better keep dipping your hands in your pockets. Have you been to the restaurant yet for your breakfast? You won't get a better one anywhere else at that price and in fact it's where I'm heading right now.'

Jim would be right on both counts. First off he did receive offers to sell up not every day of the week but with increasing regularity for sure. Those just chancing their arm a few years back had now become some well-known competitors looking to develop a bigger presence in the more prosperous south. But he was not for selling. Old Frank would have turned in his grave if he thought his son were even to contemplate selling the family silverware. His Lordship in his stately home along the road and himself a keen gardener and regular visitor to Armstrong's also sang from the same sheet.

'Investments come and go old boy but the most stable one of the lot we just so happen to be standing on right now. My own family had been interested in this plot long before your great Aunt popped up, but she was quicker off the mark. Fair play to the old girl! I think you could multiply this sites value at least twentyfold, James.'

By the time of Jim headed for his ritual afternoon nap his resolve would be tested to the limit. What his Lordship failed to mention was that in life there are offers worth consideration and others deemed extremely foolish to turn down. Jim may have had so many of the former in the past that they may blind his judgement of the latter when the opportunity came calling which it was just about to do.

His second point more relevant to the here and now was that Armstrong's really was the only show in town when it came to breakfasts. There were no end of travelling reps or van drivers willing to take the four mile detour off the M11 in order to replenish their digestive tanks. A far cry from the early days of wife Ann tending to her husband and three children on an evening before burning the midnight oil making food for the café once all four had gone to bed. A glorified shed that had masqueraded as an early days garden centre café had six tables, a corrugated roof but no toilet.

She was Armstrong's cook, waitress and solitary cleaner until the weekend came along and the kids were roped in to help. Photographs of those early days still adorn the odd wall or two but the latest upgrade to the most profitable part of the business stood testament to wife Ann's determination to move with the times. Much against her husband's will the cheque book had been prised apart even further to create a one hundred and twenty cover family restaurant that competed with the best any of the larger chains had to offer in East Sussex in terms of décor or value for money. Not the cheapest by any stretch of the imagination, but by God Ann knew a thing or two about giving the public what they wanted. With traditional Sunday lunch roasts now bringing the newcomers to the town through the doors with a vengeance, weekend bookings were required now at least two weeks in advance. The back of the restaurant was one long bank of sliding glass doors revealing the spectacular backdrop of rolling English countryside! These then opened as soon as Jim could smell spring in the air This gave more covers on the attractive terrace. Add on the children's play area and ice cream bar and it became difficult to describe this place as anything other than the ultimate money spinner.

If Jim was the metaphorical Chairman of the business, then the golden child and eldest son Joe would be its Chief Executive. Dispatched to University to earn himself an Economics degree, the favoured one had returned and at still only twenty two the father's protégé was destined to be the next generation of Armstrong driving the business into the twenty first century. He certainly looked and acted the part, although the term 'arrogant little shit' could be oft heard in the staff room. He had his father's looks but much stockier and always immaculately turned out. Joe belonged to the 'say it as it is' persuasion rather than the genial coercion employed by his father to get the best out of people. With an almost pathological obsession with appearance, woe betide should anyone forget their name badge or have creases in the staff uniform but that was just his thing. As the majority of the staff had long figured out, to massage his ego or simply agree to just about everything no matter how ridiculous the instruction, meant the days passed a whole load easier.

Unlike Joe who was that enviable species where the clothes fitted rather than hung, the same could hardly be said for the youngest of the three siblings and scapegoat of the family, young Mike. Five years apart but chalk and cheese in terms of confidence! Even when he was young Joe was still a confident kid. Owned a car as soon as he could, captain of the school rugby team and even back then he still had no shortage of female admirers. Good grades, though not enviable, were still enough to justify packing him off to university to take advantage of the opportunities that had escaped his parents. Any wonder he returned home as the natural successor to his father with responsibility for running the show more or less from day one.

Compare these attributes to his younger brother who had recently left school, a practical kid more than academic but perceived by everyone else on site as simply making up the numbers. A crippling lack of self-confidence which his parents simply put down to living in the shadow of his more accomplished, better looking and talented brother! Correct to a point, but there was no doubt in the early days that his father had a favoured one when it came to the distribution of tasks around the site. The more menial always being directed to the son who seemed to prefer his own company than that of others.

The final jigsaw piece of the family quintet was rebel and renegade, Carolyn. Studious and single minded, the middle sibling would not be pursuing a career in horticulture anytime soon. Especially as it would only have ever meant playing second fiddle to her infinitely more accomplished elder brother. Resentment about this favouritism festered in the younger of the offspring much deeper than their parents realised. It would be the field of law that would win her affection but at the same time her father's disdain.

'Where's the job satisfaction in spending your life drawing up someone's last will and testament for heaven's sake?'

'I think you'll find there's more to it than that dad.'

'Such as?'

'Ehhh…such as criminal law for starters! Then there's family law, corporate law, international law, Human Rights, employment law…do you want me to keep going?'

'Employment law?'

'Yes Dad - employment law. Just the kind of thing required that keeps the likes of Joe in check but that's not to say I want to be an employment lawyer.'

'So, just what are you going to do with this degree of yours when you get it then?'

'No idea…yet! But rest assured Dad, when something jumps out at me you'll be the first to know!'

'I think you are making a big mistake. The legal field is a man's world. How many female lawyers out there do you ever see?'

'Round here, none that I am aware of but I never knew you were so knowledgeable when it came to exact numbers of women working in the legal profession.'

'Why do you have to be so damn sarcastic Carolyn I'm only asking civil questions!'

'No, you're not Dad. Your stating fiction as fact which is why I want study something based on fact rather than just hearsay. For what its worth in my class at Uni half of the students are girls. If nothing else at least that means there's going to be an additional twenty women added to the minuscule amount of female lawyers that you claim there to be!'

'You've always got a smart bloody answer I'll give you that!'

'I wonder who I got that from then?'

The trouble with Carolyn was that out of the three of them she was the only one that her father couldn't handle! Simply too smart and he knew that she knew that too. Young Mike had already been criticised into oblivion so the odd simple stare could more than suffice when it came to kicking him into touch. Joe would be charmed and cajoled, reminded of his brilliance for one so young, but Carolyn was a different story altogether. She knew her own mind and was not one for following company orders.

'You're too alike that's the problem', declared a wearisome Ann. Carolyn had the knack of getting under her father's skin and Ann could always tell by his body language alone when he came through the door after a bust up.

'I'm nothing like her at all. She never gives an inch!'

'Oh, really! Well,, I must be living in a different house to the pair of you then!'

'She's worse than me. There's been a great career sitting here waiting for her after school, but no off she goes and studies for something that will take years before she makes any money at it. Have you any idea how long these new starts stay at the bottom of the pile before they get a leg up. The legal profession is Britain's worst for the old boy network. It's all about who you know.'

'But you never went out of your way to stop Joe from going to University.'

'Yes, and that was because it was a business course. Economics is all about business, Ann. Look at what he's done already. The place is already more productive and it's all down to him. A degree that's going to pay itself back several times over unlike Carolyn's! We've already done our Will so not as if she can even help us with that!'

Jim should have left it there. With lunchtime fast approaching the three children would be converging in the direction of their mother's kitchen just about now. Young Mikey was the first to make his way there. What he lacked in academic nous he made up on instinct. The very same thing that told him to pause the other side of the kitchen door before entering! Perfect timing! He was next on the father's hit list.

'Son and daughter taking care of the business with us in the background! What's wrong with that? That was always the plan Ann, but it's not working out that way is it? Thank God we have Joe. We'd be well up shit creek if he wasn't around.'

'There's still Mikey! He's only young but come on...still plenty time.'

'Nah...don't know what I'm going to do with that boy. He's not cut out for this. Too much of a shrinking violet! He's still to find something he enjoys doing but it won't be in this line of work. I could do with another young Joe instead of a timid little mouse that wouldn't say boo to a goose. Three of them and only one that's any bloody use. Where did we go so wrong?'

'We never did anything wrong. We treated them all the same so don't be so hard on yourself. It's just the way things work out sometimes. Anyway, who's to say Carolyn won't be involved in the future? A daughter that's a lawyer is always going to come in handy is some way. It's young Mikey that we have to figure out what to do with and give him some kind of direction.'

For someone so young and impressionable nice to know when your parents are thinking so highly of you.

For the head honchos of East Sussex County Council, this afternoon's lunch at The Dorchester was destined to be a more pleasurable and salubrious affair than the battle due to commence over Ann Armstrong's kitchen table. His Lordship's advice to Jim was proving less substantive by the minute.

For the newly appointed Finance Director of the aforementioned Council, lunch invitations these days were hardly uncommon. As self-appointed Strategic Development Director, the brief was to encourage as many high-end global entities into the area as possible. The theory dictated that their mere presence would then encourage others to follow suit. Glenn Daly was a man who knew his numbers. Just like young Joe he was a man of economics but that's where the similarity ended. Unlike the favoured one, here was someone with a first from Cambridge alongside a couple of decades experience spent putting the theory into practice. Only in the job a year since being headhunted, Daly was not the type afraid to ruffle feathers as and when required. A few had already taken 'early retirement' after being shoved out the door since his arrival. So, here he was with his trusted cohorts for a three-course lunch at The Dorchester. The expanding waistline may have highlighted the number of free meals enjoyed already, but as for being invited up to Park Lane well, for a guy that came from such a humble background as his, testament to the fact that at long last here he was finally trading in the super league.

In Glenn's case it was quite simply a case of sheer determination that had gotten him to this stage in the first place. With no desire to follow in the footsteps of his bus driver father or factory worker mother, their self-sacrifice would be the impetus that drove the young Glenn on. At University he developed a reputation for always being the first into lectures and the last to leave the library on any given night. With many a slacker that never pulled their weight discarded along the way, Glenn was a shining example for what could be achieved with a modicum of talent but a whole load of effort. As if the feet were not already planted firmly on the ground, the good wife did ask that he pinch an embossed roll of toilet paper from the probably very plush loo. The request brought a smile to his face as the three of them sat waiting for the opposing delegation that were noticeably late for the one o'clock lunch already. Deliberate ploy! Quite possibly, but Glenn was becoming used to the myriad of different tactics interested parties now deployed. The more that was at stake, the more likely it was that gamesmanship would figure somehow. Now half an hour late but little sign of the maître d' displaying even the slightest concern. Not that places like these have to worry about turning the tables over three times in a sitting. A bloke like him must see this all the time.

The sound of someone's stomach grumbling temporarily lightened the mood!

'Is this just a coincidence or are they keeping us waiting to try and soften us up and hope we forget our lines?' Alan the lawyer - true to form regularly the more suspicious one of the group!

'Maybe they are but I don't know why. We are holding all the cards. Who approached who here? They need us more than we need them. If they take that stance it's because they're so well known in the States! Are these guys really so arrogant as to think we'll just roll over and welcome them at any cost?'

'So, how long do we have to wait before ordering then? My belly growling was a good indication of just how fucking hungry I actually am.'

Glenn checked his watch more for effect than necessity. He'd had his eyes religiously peeled on the clock above the maître d's desk since they sat down.

'So, what time is it now? Half one! What say we give them another twenty minutes! If anything serious had happened someone would at least have phoned through to the hotel. Ten to two and we call it a day.'

'We order.'

'Do we fuck! It's them picking up the tab for this not us. You think I'm playing those prices for a bloody work of art on a plate.'

'Well, - wait no longer - looks like someone's here.'

Unlike their own rather staid awestruck arrival, the two late entrants to the show finally appeared and immediately immersed themselves in conversation with the maître d' like long lost friends. No need for them to scour the restaurant in search of invited guests as they had been briefed already. If only Glenn and his team had paid more attention to the couple dining immediately to their right, they may have picked up on the fact that here were two people managing to see their way through the entire set course lunch without actually speaking to each other. Clocked as she walked past their table, presumably on her way to the toilet, the eyes failed to follow her path out of the restaurant and back into the lobby for the pre-arranged five-minute brief with today's lunch hosts. The task was straightforward enough. Who looked like they were in charge, who became agitated first and most importantly who had the roving eye. Make their lives a whole load easier if it was the top dog. Blissfully unaware that that they were already being vetted, today's lunch guests failed to notice their hosts appearing at precisely three minutes after the attractive diner had sat back down.

'OK we're on. Here they come. Bet you five pounds the one on the right is the smug bastard. He just has that look about him.' George, Director of land estates and valuation and the one marked down as having the roving eye. The correct call! Only forty two but just so happens that he's already on his second marriage with four kids between them and an appetite for the chase that showed no sign of abating anytime soon. With no outward sign of appearing as pissed off as they sounded, they stood to greet their hosts. Still no harm in Glenn including a little side to his introduction!

'Gentlemen - nice to meet you. I should really say at long last.'

'I...we really do apologise. First time back in London in over ten years and boy your traffic situation has sure gotten a whole load worse. Either that or our cab driver took us the long way round for a few extra bucks.'

'No, it's the traffic believe me. I don't think the taxi driver...'

'Do forgive me - I forgot these guys have a different name over here.'

'No, your fine! When I'm over your neck of the woods I still address them as taxi drivers. At least you're making an effort to integrate. Next time to avoid the congestion you may just have to do as we do and get up at a ridiculous time in the morning which probably explains the baggy eyes all round.'

Back-to-back remarks in the space of less than thirty seconds highlighting Glenn's obvious annoyance, though at least sugar coated in a subtle way. Already noted in Don Walsh's head! For the visiting Chief Executive of global behemoth, 'Be-Smart Inc', Mr Glenn Daly was clearly not destined to be a pushover as others of his ilk stateside had been in the past.

'Well, gents, you've been sitting here longer than I have and I guess the sight of all these people enjoying the Dorchester's fine cuisine has been enough to drive you crazy. Neither of us would have been offended if you had started without us trust me. So, let's eat.'

'I'll drink to that' from a jovial George. His morning improved immeasurably with the thought of some haute cuisine about to enter his stomach alongside the glances exchanged with attractive middle-aged female dining immediately to his right. If only he'd known that this unofficial observer had already decided in advance which two girls would be best suited for a night he'd never be allowed to forget.

Not quite as refined as the five langoustine, ravioli currently sat awaiting chef's approval at the kitchen pass but horses for courses. Four hours spent working in the fresh open air would always provide the need for something more substantive than that about to be eaten under The Dorchester's finest crystal chandeliers. With only two ravioli per portion and having skipped breakfast on the way here, it did cross Day's mind that if this was the sign of things to come the trio from East Sussex could find themselves making their way towards the Burger King at Victoria station before the two hour trip home.

No such issues for matriarch Ann's family back in Waltham when it came to the feeding of the hungry masses. There was always the main restaurant or staff canteen from which to choose but lunch was at her insistence religiously a family affair. Always 12.30 pm every day. Time set in stone by Ann as was its duration. Forty five minutes for all and that included the same generous allowance given to their staff to avoid accusations of prejudice or bias. Much as she looked forward to having her family together as one, in the summer months when Carolyn returned from Uni, she was acutely aware that the joyous times were now probably all but a thing of the past. The kids had gotten older and personalities had become stronger. Harmonious was about as good as it was ever likely to get with the majority of her time now spent acting as a form of peacemaker between the two strong willed offspring vying for position as official number three in pecking order. One by the use of intellect and the other by sheer force of personality! The young Michael never really stood a chance. Predisposed to watching from the sidelines as brother and sister jockeyed back and forth, it was entirely predictable to this young man that his father should stand shoulder to shoulder with elder brother. His mother's presence on the other hand was all that was needed to provide his sister with the ammunition to give the opposing side a run for its money. Yet all the while what this lack of inclusion actually meant, and his parents should have realised, was that here was a kid who's confidence had slowly ebbed away. The timid little mouse was primarily of his father's making and at this stage of the proceedings undeserving of the very same kid's enormous sacrifice that would follow. Unable to see the wood for the trees, what their youngest had needed all along was even plain to see for some of the workforce but alas not its owners. Here was someone lacking a sense of purpose. Unbeknownst to the young Michael seeds in this area were already being sown.

This lunchtime Joe would be first to bat.

'Tell me what you think about this. At weekends I've been keeping an eye on the play area and I can tell you that some of the kid's games are hardly being used.'

'Ok', said Jim, 'but that's not so unusual is it?'

'No, but it's no longer enough just to have a slide, some swings and a roundabout any more. Kids want more than that. A lot more.'

Jim nodding in agreement with most things his protégé has to say.

'So, - my point is to bring in more activity games that kids will definitely want to use but this time they pay for the privilege.'

His arch nemesis Carolyn ready as always to see any suggestion from both sides.

'So, we become a glorified theme park? Forgive me I thought we traded as a high-end garden centre.'

'No, don't try and twist things, Carolyn. No I'm not saying we become some kind of amusement park. I'm just looking at additional ways for us to make money. Kind of keeps us in business don't you know.'

'And do you not think the public will feel we're getting greedy? All sounds a bit too tacky for me. By the way, this soup's gorgeous Mum.'

Ann secretly enjoyed her daughter's style. Joe would always go for the 'all guns blazing approach' whereas Carolyn was infinitely more the iron hand in velvet glove. She could mix it up when she needed to. Joe was more a one trick pony.

'And since when did you start taking such an avid interest in this place then Sis? Not as if we see you regularly getting your hands dirty, is it?'

'What do you think I've been doing all morning then? While you've been twiddling your thumbs watching the kids' play area I'm covered in shit having spent all morning tidying up the compost.'

Headmaster Jim yet again forced to intervene as the two lock horns.

'Mikey you're quieter than normal - what's up?'

'Nothing, I'm fine but you might have more than kids play areas to worry about in a few year's when the Americans get here.'

Joe practically half choking on his soup lightens the mood and it's a case of laughs all round.

'What are you talking about little bro? Are the Red Indians coming then?'

'I knew you'd say something like that. You should read some of the gardening magazines Dad gets about the way people buy their gardening stuff in the States. Some of the magazines are saying it'll happen over here.'

'Oh, yeh, so what do they say then mister font of all knowledge. Is this what Carolyn's told you to say?'

'Nothing to do with me but be nice to hear someone else's voice for a change.'

'Let him speak Joe', his mother at least allowing her youngest an opportunity to express himself in some shape or form.

'It's what two of the magazines said. Go and read them for yourself. You don't need to take my word for it.'

'So, just tell us then Mikey. What do they say?'

'I can't remember their names, but they said in America there are some garden centres that are just so big the staff have to drive around in little buggies. It said they sell plants and things at prices that small stores can't even buy them at. I don't know what it is in our money but they do full meals for ninety nine cents and sell thousands a day.'

'So, what are they called?'

'Don't know, can't remember but it's all in last months gardeners World in the office. Said they want to come to the UK. Quite a long article - thought you would have read it Joe.'

'Whereabouts in the UK, Michael?'

When Jim addressed his youngest by the full name it was either due to impending scalding or concern.

'Go little Mikey…suddenly got a crystal ball in front of him with retail trends. Never work over here in a million years.'

'Says who Joe?' Carolyn unable to resist that one! Scenting blood, time to go for the jugular!

'Because things are just different over here! garden centres in this country go back decades. You think for one minute someone just opens up with a completely different concept and it's going to take off just like that. I also happen to know a bit about economics, Carolyn. Selling stuff at cheap prices might bring customers through the doors but who says they're making money.'

'Well,, if they're that big and want to open over here they must be doing something right. What do you think Dad?'

'I'll take a look at that article but Joe's right. Most overnight successes are twenty years in the making so I can't see anyone being able to replicate what all these family businesses up and down the country have taken decades to perfect.'

'Why don't one of you go over to America then and see how they do things?'

'Ehhh Mikey just drop it ok. You've made your point. Put as much effort into working here as you do reading about garden centre trends and you might actually begin to be thought of a bit more highly by the staff than you are now.'

'What are you talking about? I do my fair share.'

'Glad you think so.'

'Unlike you of course! You criticise me and Carolyn but all I ever see you doing is chatting up the girls that work here and wandering around with bits of paper.'

'Watch your mouth son. Don't overstep the mark.'

'Ok, so now he's not even allowed an opinion' as sister senses elder brother now on the ropes.

'Will the pair of you just pack it in. Everyone's made their points so let's just drop it. Michael - well done for making us aware of something your father should already have known about and I don't care about the economics of it all Joe, whatever happens in the States is bound to come over here sooner or later. Let's just hope it happens on someone else's doorstep and not ours. Jim, I want to read that article Michael's talking about and soon.'

'Message received and understood.'

'So, getting back to my point about the play area then? What about it, Dad?'

Jim clocked Ann who he just knew would be giving him an ear bashing once this was over. He wanted this lunchtime over and done with before something else kicked off.

'I need to think about it, Joe. How much it costs for a start.'

'We can just rent. You can have free trial periods. Nothing ventured and all that.'

God, how he wished his favourite son would shut up. So, wrapped up with his latest project and completely oblivious to the atmosphere created of his own doing.

'Ok, do that then but I want to see what sort of thing you have in mind first. It makes sense if we want to stay ahead of everyone else that we must keep evolving somehow or another. Agreed?'

Ann and a reluctant Carolyn nod in agreement. Young Michael without so much as even receiving a glance. He knew which side his father's favour lay on.

'I'm only going by what you keep telling me Dad. I'm only trying to follow all your great advice over the years.'

This was Joe, having learned to pick up more than just the odd business snippet from his father's repertoire of forty years' experience. He had now mastered the art of flattering his father's ego in order to turn the argument around in his favour. Charm offensive over, it was now time to return to playing Dr Jekyll with young Mike!

'Mike did you sweep the front car park this morning?'

'You know I did.'

'Well, do it again then. You never made a very good job first time around!'

'Who says I never did a good enough job?'

'Me and I'm telling you to do it again.'

'Why is it always me that has to do these jobs? Not as if there's no one else?'

'Because they're busy doing other things, that's why.'

'So, I just keep getting the crap jobs then?'

'All you deserve. Maybe stop you reading magazines in company time.'

'So much for fairness' chipped in Carolyn. 'How is Michael meant to learn anything else if you just keep giving him menial jobs? Not as if you lead by example is it?'

'Says who? I've done it the hard way, more than you for sure and what's all this about anyway. All of a sudden become our little brothers defence lawyer?'

'So Dad, why do I keep getting the same crappy jobs? Can't I do something a bit more creative just for once?'

'You will but not yet. We're too busy just now to have the time to teach you anything but you will in due course.'

'Yeh if you say so.'

'Don't speak to me in that dismissive tone of voice of yours Michael. You only get out of life what you put in and right at this minute in time your inputs are questionable. Take a leaf out of your brother's book and put in more effort and you'll soon see the results.'

'Also helps if you're given a chance!'

'Carolyn - just for once give your father a chance.' Rare intervention from Ann!

'Try and give him some support instead of continually deriding everything he says.'

'All I'm trying to point out...'

Saved by the sound of the doorbell providing temporary respite from what looked like yet another eventful lunchtime from which Ann had just about had her fill. Much as she could never admit, young Carolyn's absences to University mostly proved a more serene dining atmosphere albeit with one of the remaining four regularly being sidelined.

'Mr Armstrong. Sorry to disturb your lunch break but there are two men at reception wearing suits asking to speak to you in person. They said it's important.'

'They're only asking to speak to the owner in person because it's what sales reps do, Frances. I thought I had told you that already.'

'They did say, Mr Jim Armstrong. I know what you said but these guys just feel different. They said you would understand after they introduce themselves.'

Inland Revenue he thought, but everything was in order and had been for a while. No missed payments and no extensions requested in years. A new larger firm of accountants looking after the books tended to deter surprise visits these days.

'They said they would like to speak to Jim and Ann Armstrong. It was just a gut feeling I had Mr Armstrong, but I can put them off if you like.'

'Looks like you're not important enough yet Joe' from a mischievous onlooker.

'Carolyn, no more please.'

'It's ok Mum we all know where Carolyn's real loyalties lie and it's not here.'

Words that would return to haunt Joe in the very near future.

Not for everyone were the good times rolling in East Sussex. For twenty-two-year-old Rachael Compston just keeping her head above water was as good as she could expect things to get. An attractive girl who, on the face of it, should have ended up with the cream of the crop had alas paid a heavy price for choosing looks over substance. Now with two failed relationships under her belt and a child by each, the ingrained conclusion was that men simply could never be trusted. From now on fending for herself had become the order of the day.

Since the last split, to stay in Waltham was an unaffordable pipe dream unlikely to come good anytime soon. Forgoing the safety net of staying with her parents, Rachael as a young single mum had gone straight to the top of the queue when it came to allocation of local authority housing. A small two-bedroom end of terraced semi was secured in the distinctly unfashionable enclave of Fairfield some twenty minutes by bus from Waltham and most importantly her job with Armstrong's. Fairfield itself was made up entirely of some two hundred odd purpose-built local authority houses. A burgeoning munitions depot during the war, the warehouses may have long gone but the houses could at least be salvaged for those lower income families of limited means. The daily routine consisted of her mother arriving early to take the eldest to school before returning to look after the two year old, while Rachael headed off to catch the early bus to work. Eight months in so far and now working six hours a day for four days of the week. Just enough hours to ensure she met her subsidised rent and a pittance of family allowance from the Welfare to keep some clothes on her kids' backs. Sad reality was that parental handouts were keeping her afloat and that's not to say her Mum and Dad had much spare cash either. It prayed on her mind. Money was needed, preferably fast cash and options were limited if she were to play by convention. She had a friend in similar situation making more in a night than Rachael did in a week. Or so the friend said!

Starting off in the garden centre, she knew absolutely nothing about plants but the sight of her legs and Joe's imagination at the interview meant her employment would be a foregone conclusion. Time spent carting plants from A to B proved minimal as even Jim accepted her looks would be better served behind the counter someplace else in the store. Anyone that proved easy on the eye he knew would always make customers gravitate in their direction. She very quickly came out of overalls into something infinitely more appealing behind the counter in the coffee shop before progressing to work on her own in the newly built farm food shop. This was until Jim decided that her reliability merited her becoming Armstrong's very own daily cashier, thus relieving Ann of some the daily monotony of the business to enjoy more free time at home.

Everyone liked Rachael but she was nobody's fool. At each stage of her ascendency she picked up little snippets on how father and son ran their business but paramount to her perspective was that as a cash business there were next to no daily controls. She needed cash and with thousands being banked on a daily basis what was the likelihood of the odd five and ten pound note going missing to create suspicion. As Jim always told her!

'If it's just a small amount you can't balance, just stick it in the ESP file.'

'The ESP file?'

'Yeh, Error Some Place!'

Yes, everyone liked Rachael and what Joe would have done for some time alone together. Not for the want of trying but she'd had her fill of the Joes of this world. As easy to read as a book at one time she would have dived straight in, but this time around best left alone even if his parents were minted. She was learning fast and knew he had a darker side. Much as the best way to deal with Joe was to massage his ego, get on his wrong side and your hours and thus wage could be cut dramatically. She knew of one girl who had already paid a heavy price for jumping into bed and subsequently discarded once her purpose had been served. To keep Joe at arm's length, the cover story stayed the same. Rachael, as far as he was concerned, had a long-term partner who was going nowhere fast. She was also going nowhere soon, that extra fifty pounds a week siphoned off from the takings proving extremely useful when it came to keeping the wolf from the door. Incredible with so much money passing through the cash registers, how many of them had till rolls missing when it came to cashing up. Were others in the busy restaurant also already in on the act? Not for her to ask. She simply concluded that the business was making so much money these days no one noticed. Now affording to pay another friend to babysit tomorrow night for a couple of hours, it was time to throw even more caution to the wind. Her self-confidence now growing by the day! No harm in trying this out. By 8 pm she would be seeing her very first client!

'Have to say, much as I enjoy fine dining, my wife and I never tire of your English Fish and Chips when we are over here.'

'You should have ordered them off the a la carte' quipped Glenn, 'though not quite the same on a plate. Wrapped inside a newspaper wins hands down every time.'

'Am glad you mentioned that. So, why newspaper?' An obvious rapport growing between the two!

'I don't know why now you come to mention it. It's been that way ever since I was a child. I strongly suspect it was just economic in the early days that using up old newspapers was a damn site cheaper than forking out for wrapping paper. Good insulator as I well I seem to recall. It's been a while since I had some myself so well done you've planted a seed. We can draw straws to see who pays on the way home.'

'Forgive me – 'draw straws'?' Laughs all round from the British contingency.

'It means to take a chance. You cut a straw into different lengths and cup them in your hand. Whoever draws the shortest length has to do a job that nobody else wanted to do or usually it means the loser ends up paying for everything.'

'I see.'

'Oh, the English language is full of them. We could be here all day.'

So, far so good, but everyone present aware that the time was about ready to get down to business. Apart from food analogies the conversation up to now had mainly centred around newly appointed Prime Minister Margaret Thatcher and her love of the free market. Music to the ears of Don Walsh as it sure helped contribute to B-Smart's spectacular growth over the past decade. So,, time to break cover and it would be Glenn going first albeit in a softly-softly kind of way.

'So, what type of volumes do you achieve stateside with your sites?'

Don and his sidekick Lee otherwise known as B-Smart's Chief Operating Officer exchanged a glance before Don gestured Lee to take over with the detail.

'On a daily basis during the week, three to four thousand, at weekends double that figure. Bear in mind our stores are what we now look on as destination sites for families where they come for the day rather than just a segment of that day. For the site we have in mind for your county it's difficult to come up with an exact number of visitors but our price advantage is clearly a big draw in bringing people in.'

Lawyer Alan being a bit of a socialist at heart prised his head above the parapet.

'Then there's the argument that because your cheaper than everyone else you end up with a captive market because smaller competitors eventually all go bust.'

Two lawyers now going head-to-head! Not that he was likely to admit it, but his opposing adversary guessed this was coming and had prepared the script well in advance.

'Actually, no Alan. What you find is that our competitors become more specialised because frankly we're just too big to be able to give the personal touch. We are a volume driven business, but other smaller independents not only survive but prosper on our coat tails because they operate in areas that are just not economical enough for us to do that. Visit any B-Smart and you'll always find at least one independent really close by.'

Water off a duck's back so far for Don and Lee! Now Glenn's turn to chip in.

'Now I'm just going by reports in the media and a bit of hearsay, but it's been said that you've been known to hold suppliers to ransom and not the fastest in the world either when it comes to paying them.'

'Well, how about I…we give you a list of the main ones we use and feel free to call any of them. Don't just take my word for it. We spread our suppliers across the board from workshops to multinationals and terms for each are the same. We try and pay within thirty days but never any more than forty five. No ifs or buts.'

'And how many staff employed per outlet.'

'Kind of works out about between fifty to sixty full-time, then half of that part time. Then of course you have the support network who increase the staff count by at least another twenty-five per cent.'

George's turn to chip in! Attention up to now seriously diverted by the blond at the next table who appears to be stuck for conversation with her dining companion. Actually, she was but not for the reason George would ever suspect. The poor bloke was just a good-looking stooge hired for a few hours under the premise of a half decent lunch and a hundred quid for his efforts.

'So, where exactly in Sheast Shushex did you have in mind?'

Oh, shit, the first to let slip that the three bottles of wine and two single Malts consumed had affected some more than others. With nothing other than a wry smile Lee carried on as if the question were asked in perfect Queen's English.

'Our scouts have located one site that appears on paper at least to tick a whole load of boxes. Proximity to the town of Uxbridge if that rings any bells. Great road links. We've done our homework with customer demographics and it sure is the kind of place that would be of mutual benefit to us all.'

'Actually I know that area very well. Very green belt when it comes to future large-scale development. A lot of the land is council owned which, if you've done your homework as well as I expect you, then you'll know that already.' Glenn chipping in alongside a slight tapping of George's heel under the table to now keep schtum.

'Sure - which is why we invited you here today to see what room you guys thought we had for manoeuvre. Providing you're interested in having us of course. Where we go other well known names tend to follow but Glenn just like our side, you've obviously done your homework on us and I think...somewhere there's a deal to be done. What I think would help put your minds at ease is how about you come over and pay us a visit. See around our stores, get a feel of them and heh, you can visit mom and pop independents nearby and ask them what we've done for their businesses. It's just a suggestion but I really think it would help. Better still if it's us that picks up the tab…flying second class of course!' Laughs all around!

'Don't see why not. A change away from this damn weather might be no bad thing. I think Don we may just take you up on your kind offer.'

None of them noticing the discreet signal Lee had already made that it was time Andrea and her hired companion made their exit. She already knew which of the three she wanted when the time duly came.

'Good. In which case we've recently opened a new store in Florida and take it from me the East Coast has the best seafood restaurants the States has to offer.'

'Selling fish and chips?'

'You leave that with me.'

Successful outcome indeed! A business trip to Florida and some female delicacies the likes of which the trio will never have tasted before.

Carolyn was right and it irritated the shit out of Joe that here he was only looking in on his parents' discussion with sharp suited gents at the back of the main restaurant, an outsider rather than being in the thick of the action which he thought his position at least deserved. It was him that ran the place and to listen you could be forgiven for thinking it was him that had also built the place up rather than his father's three decades of hard graft. In the meantime, there was a score to settle and the recipient of his venom conveniently happened to be heading right his way.

'Mikey do you have a minute. I need you to help me with a lift.'

'Thought you wanted the car park swept again.'

'I do but come on. Only take a minute.'

Bait taken, young Michael followed his brother along to the wooden storage shed and then into the lions' den.

'So,, what do you want lifted.'

'How about this?'

'What? Urrggghhhhhhh.'

Wind completely knocked from his sails. Direct punch on target straight to the middle of the stomach! Wasting little time his brother has him immediately picked back up by the throat with his left hand and frog marched the remaining few steps to the back wall where the right fist is now clenched firmly against his younger brother's face.

'You ever fucking embarrass me in front of anyone ever again and this goes down your fucking throat, do you understand?'

Still breathless, the faintest nod of approval.

'You fucking little prick, who do you think you are with all this bullshit about the Yanks opening up. I ever hear even a squeak about this and your mincemeat son. You hear me?'

Yet another couple of quick nods of the head in succession! To speak he reckoned simply incurred more of the same.

'You really piss me off, you useless little cunt. The sooner you fuck off out of here the better.'

Frozen in terror Joe unleashes one last knee to the groin for good measure. Still only 2.30 pm, the remainder of the day he'd already decided would be best spent elsewhere but who to choose. As one of Waltham's most eligible these days there would never be a shortage of offers.

'Bloody Sheest Shussex George what were you playing at?'

 As expected, the Burger King at Victoria station proved to be as much to soak up the wine as satisfy late afternoon appetites.

'That's what three bottles of wine on an empty stomach does for you. The size of the bloody portions I was still starving by the time we'd finished the world's smallest lemon soufflé. I rest my case.'

Gesturing towards the feast of three quarter pounders with cheese, triple fries and cola spread across the carriage table of Coach D in second class. Another hour and the likelihood of being seated together on the 5.20 pm commuter home were less than negligible.

'How much do you think that cost?'

'Not as if they'd be paying for it is it? The company credit card and offset as expenses somewhere or another.'

'I am so bloody enjoying this even if half of its going down my shirt in the process.'

'Just hope the portions are bigger in the seafood place they were talking about or else it'll be Burger King USA here we come.'

Here were three guys who irrespective of position actually got on very well and like three good mates the American trip was something that could not come around quick enough.

'George, they said they had their eye on Uxbridge. When you think about it? It's actually a pretty good spot to build on. I mean it'll piss off the residents but no real opposition from businesses in the area. Not as if they're stamping on anyone's toes.'

'Apart from just one business I think will be seriously pissed off.'

'Yeh who?'

'Armstrong'. You know the garden centre in Waltham no more than six miles up the road. Probably hammer them big time but like he said, independents get to ride on their coat tails, so maybe an impact short term then ease off.

'Oh, come on George you never surely don't believe that bullshit?' Alan the socialist lawyer not so convinced! ''Full credit it was a polished mini presentation that those guys must have performed a hundred times.'

'So, what are you saying?'

'I'm saying how much do we actually need them? Quality of jobs created unlikely to be well paid and I don't believe the full time figure he was on about either. Come to think of it I don't believe much of anything they said …but that's not to say we look a gift horse in the mouth passing up on a free holiday when it's presented on a plate.'

'Take your point' from Glenn. 'I'm somewhere in the middle with this. If we don't take them then somebody else gets their business and big names are what we need.'

'What we need or what you want?'

'Listen, I'm prepared to say no…but I'm not prepared to pass up on a few days free holiday to Florida. Beaches, bloody sunshine and seafood! What more could a man ask for?'

That vital other missing ingredient would be left to Walsh & Co to take care of!

Number two, Lee Trenchman already had the itinerary worked out by the time Walsh and his mistress/company hooker, Andrea rejoined him in the Champagne Bar. The room had already been booked but its use required a few hours earlier than planned as successful outcomes had this funny habit of giving Don the horn. By the time Glenn and co had settled in the black cab Don already had her pinned against the inside of the lift and her pounding would shortly follow. Now a more casually dressed and visibly relieved Walsh and companion took their seats alongside for what would essentially be a rubber stamping on impending blackmail job for trio now dubbed the East Sussex Three.

'I like Daly. He's smart, confident and in control' observed Don. 'The lawyer is also good but he's not on our side and I guess on the train home he'll be picking holes in our plan already. The other one's just a fool.'

'Never took his eyes off me the whole time' quipped Andrea. 'He's easy.'

'Yeh, we don't need to put a whole lot of thought into that one' added Trenchman.

'Bear in mind I want this site at a bargain basement price, so he needs to be in real deep.'

'Two young chicks then' suggested Andrea. 'Have it so he not only craps himself about the wife but the adverse publicity too.' The others agreed.

'I'll take Daly myself.'

'Fancy him do you' added Don.

'A bit! You're not jealous are you?'

'What do I have to be jealous about if someone's younger and better looking than me?'

'Slightly thinning on top and putting on a few pounds' she replied, 'but he's one of those that strike you as being honest and principled.'

'Yes, I certainly got that impression as well' added Trenchman as if to reinforce this is the nut likely to prove hardest to crack.

'He won't need flattered but given enough attention most men always buckle one way or another.'

'And he won't remember you from this afternoon?'

'Well, first off the wig's gone.'

'Good point.' Yes, the blond wig had been dispensed with and if anything the brunette in her managed to turn heads even more.

'I was watching the whole time and he hardly glanced. He's happily married. Doesn't need to look! It was the other one, the fool, what do you call him, George that was practically salivating second time I walked past.'

'So, that just leaves Alan. What type do we invite along to introduce to him?'

'I'll need to think on that one' suggested Andrea.

'Someone mature, confident and a bit about them when it comes to conversation. If all else fails someone so stunning they're simply impossible to resist.'

'Remember we don't need a hundred per cent success rate here. Ideally, yes, but I'll settle for two out the three. One's already in the bag but of the remaining two I'll take Daly. Andrea you just gotta pull out all the stops with this one.'

'I will my darling.'

Actually, she really wanted to. Don was the proverbial sugar daddy who gave her the kind of lifestyle unattainable by any other means. He was also sharp as a tack and extremely rich. As good a reason as any to stay attached given how quickly her birthdays now seemed to be coming around. But he was well past his best and only his ego prevented him from believing the howls of satisfaction had more to do with her acting skills than male prowess on top of the kingsize. Affected by Walsh, her scruples were now quite plainly as corrupt as her paymasters. Here was a good family man being targeted for seduction before his infidelities were brought back to haunt him for a thoroughly unscrupulous businessman's personal gain. Like many a mistress she traded off the reflected glory of association. Walsh was seriously flawed but he could be manipulated as well as he did others. Truth told she seriously fancied Glenn. This could be one of her more satisfying entrapments.

Trenchman continued. 'So, I have these dates. Here for five days. First day we just leave them alone. Too much too soon and they're still in strict business mode. Let them relax in the hotel and take in some sights for the first few days. It softens them up a bit.'

Walsh always smiled at this part of the strategy. He got off on the idea of gullible civil servants being lined up for the kill.

'Day three we show them around the store. I'll take care of setting up the fake plant store in the industrial yard nearby. Next day a trip to Hedgeways for some meet and greet supplier interaction then dinner at Regalo's Seafood on the Pier on the evening. This is where you come in

50

Andrea as an invited guest and bring someone along for Alan.'

'Will do!'

'Day four I'll suggest at breakfast they go see another store or by this time if you've worked your magic they may want to spend some time with the girls instead. I'll have the jet on standby just in case.'

'Excellent Lee. Find out when you fax whether Daly or even the other two play golf. Could maybe do that one early on. We suggest a store visit and just as a matter of course or a round of golf. I think I know which one they'll go for.'

'Good point. Now this is the first time there's been three of them and I've only got two rooms set up with cameras so you might need to be a bit logistical Andrea when it comes to who has who and when.'

'Certainly some variety but am sure I'll cope' she replied.

'I want Glenn Daly in the bag, Andrea. The other two give it your best but in business you have to bag the guy that calls the shots. If not, it sure makes everything else a whole load harder.'

'It won't be for lack of trying honey.'

'Sheeez, that's a lot of money.'

'Our client thinks it reflects a very generous market appraisal of your business, Mr Armstrong.'

'Who is?'

'Not at liberty at this stage to say other than it comes from one of the UK's most prominent leisure centre operators who are looking to diversify into other high margin areas. garden centres have been identified as being on the ascendency and our clients have enough money to get in on the action at the top end saving them the hassle of starting afresh. As part of the package you'd be expected to stay on as consultant for at least a year to help their management team get up and running.'

'Yes I get that' nodded Jim.

'That was a very corporate speak speech if you don't mind me saying so' added Ann.

'Yes it was actually Mrs Armstrong, so forgive me. It's just the way we're used to speaking when we dress this way in shirt and tie. So, basically yes, they realise you have a blue chip business here and want it all for themselves. They also would like to incorporate other features but don't ask me what they are. I really don't know. It's a very, very good offer. I personally have never heard of any other garden centre going for anywhere near that.'

'Neither have I' added Jim 'and I have been around a whole load longer than you. Two million pounds but bear in mind I have loans.'

'Of how much if you don't mind us asking?'

'Long term loans of three hundred thousand which was the upgrade of restaurant, farm shop and visitors' centre, so it brings the figure down a bit.'

'Completely understand.'

'Still a heck of an amount' chipped in Ann. 'I know what I want to do. Can I ask who you are?'

'For sure, nothing sinister about this. We simply go around the country looking for great sites for various businesses. We're both surveyors by trade. Nothing technical about what we do.'

'I'm flattered but you understand it's not something I can just give an answer to straight away' said Jim.

'How long do we have?' as if Ann was ready to agree there and then.

'Well,, as a rule of thumb to avoid wasting everyone's time I think two to three weeks is fair. Save's it all becoming a long protracted process. If the answers a positive one, then a very brief process of due diligence will take place.'

'Forgive me again' asked Ann. 'What's this. Sounded a bit double Dutch.'

'It's simply us running over your books. Just make sure there's no hidden Gremlins which we know there won't be.'

'I see.'

'Well, thank you for coming' added Jim 'and I'll get back to you when we make our mind up.'

'I hope it's a positive one Mr Armstrong, Mrs Armstrong. As the saying goes, half the battle is knowing when to pull out.' A line that this silver-tongued middle man frequently used to great effect time and time again.

His Lordship's words were now ringing in Jim's ears. 'The most valuable asset you're standing on right now.' One point seven million net cash in the bank might be a nicer asset to have when you're past sixty though.

But a stone's throw away young Rachael was doing the rounds collecting the cash while even younger Michael was feeling bitter with everything his family and garden centre had to offer. Yards apart and without knowing, each closing in on the other fast. With coffee shop and farm shop the first to shut up shop early on the quietest day of the week, she separated the cash float from the takings, then placed excess notes into her low security linen bag. Job completed, she made her way back to the small cash office which in essence was a glorified cupboard next door to the main office adjacent to the house. A short cut through the timber yard and well out of sight of prying eyes! In between pallets of fencing panels, she dipped her hand back into the linen bag to bring out a single twenty-pound note which she folded and slipped into trouser back pocket. Dusting herself down she turned to retrace her steps back out...and there he was. Talk about being in the right place at the right time to catch a thief.

'You gave me a fright Michael.'

'I guess I did.'

'Is this where you tell your parents and I lose my job?'

'No, it's not'

'What is it then?'

'It's where I say you owe me one.'

'Why?'

'Never mind why.'

'Please say you won't say anything? I need the work.'

'I said I won't'

'And I believe you Michael.'

This would be the precise moment in time he would recall years later when wedged between pallets of wooden lap fencing while facing a thief stealing from the family business that he first implemented one of life's valuable lessons. Always pays to play the longer game than its shorter version.

Chapter 3

'You cannot be serious!'

'Who do you think you are? John McEnroe?'

'Why would anyone be daft enough to ever give it a seconds thought? A complete no brainer. Take the money and run.'

'Your mother and I are just sharing this with you to see what you think. You're the legal brain among us Carolyn which is why we wanted you to come at it from all the angles.'

'Nope! No angles needed. Screw everyone else. You've worked hard enough all your life to get to this point in time so just take the money and go lots of holidays.'

'And then what are we all left to do with the rest of our lives?'

'You mean Joe what do you do with the rest of your life. That's your problem. This is not about you. It's about your parent's retirement.'

'It's more than that Carolyn. My father left me this place. I'm not sure I can face giving up on his legacy.'

'Oh, please Dad! What to you think Grandpa Frank would say to this? Bite their hand off or something along those lines.'

'And who says two million is all this place is worth? Did you ask for more?'

'What do you mean? Why would we ask for more than that? Neither of us are that greedy' Ann somewhat shocked by the mere suggestion.

'But Joe certainly is.'

'Oh, Carolyn shut up please. I'm putting my Economists hat on here. Why did you not ask for more? I mean not as if you're not allowed to.'

'Never crossed our minds.' said Jim.

'Put the shoe on the other foot. If it was them selling and you were the buyer do you think for a second this all they would be asking for? You should always ask for more. What's the saying about there being no such thing as a final offer?'

'He's got a point Ann.'

'No, he hasn't' replied a furious Carolyn. 'This is Joe doing what he does best playing mind games with the pair of you. Pack it in. He's only worried about what he's going to do when this new bunch take over.'

'They might keep him on.'

'Why would they be daft enough to do that?' His sister loved that one!

'Why would I want to be kept on anyway? Dad all I'm saying is look longer term. Five years down the line from now the way profits are going it could be three or four million we're talking about. Who's to say?'

'And who says your father or I will still be around to enjoy it all Joe.'

'Excellent point mum.' A line her daughter had wished she'd come up with.

'I need to think about this.'

'This place gives you a good living and you love being here Dad. All I'm saying is look at the bigger picture.'

'That will be Joe's picture. You're beginning to make me feel nauseous.'

'Heh sis it's obvious you're good at talking the talk and you've obviously got some kind of agenda and that's fair enough but it's not you that lives here permanent is it? This is all our lives as a family and sure I love being here as much as my father. No point in denying it. Don't go biting their hand off just yet. If it happens in a few years then fine but not now Dad. We've too much unfinished business to work on.'

'Round of applause for Joe.' As his sister slow hand claps to his increasing resentment.

'Well, we wanted to discuss it through with you all and we have. Now let's just leave it at that.'

The discussion did have one notable exception and he's had enough.

'Can I be excused?'

'Sure Mikey are you feeling OK' his mother enquired.

'Just need some fresh air.'

'When you're out there can you finish off sweeping around the compost Mikey' said Joe. 'Your sister only managed half a job.'

'Will do!'

Last week proved to be yet another fruitful one for Rachael. Her regular seventy two pounds official weekly wage from Armstrong's plus another fifty creamed off on top. Then there was yet another forty from her client for a half hour's service and a five pound tip as she'd stayed an extra ten minutes. All in all just short of a hundred and seventy pounds for the week on top of her housing allowance and benefits. Thing was, with a bit of experience now under her belt she knew she could be out there making a whole load more.

Up to now he'd kept his word. Not a squeak but not to be seen either. If something had been said then surely Joe or his Father would have had her in the office by now. Then the very same person seen from the side window of her glorified cupboard of a cash office busy tidying around the compost. Others milling around in conversation but young

Michael as always keeping himself to himself. The way her little sideline was going she could do with some help but trustworthy mates were proving thin on the ground. She was finding out fast that people tend to have loose tongues when the topic of conversation had anything to do with someone making an extra bit of money on the side. The young lad she thought never came across as someone who prejudged or held a stigma and they were of similar age but the resemblances ended right there. Whereas Rachael was bright with a bit of spark Michael was dull as dishwater but he kept his word and he had a car albeit a very old battered mini which was saved for from his derisory wage packet and kept out of sight at the back of the house. Compare that to his brother's brand new Range Rover taking pride of place in his very own reserved spot in the Customer car park. Not that Joe had to pay for the privilege of running his more up market mode of transport. His went through the books, perk of the job of being in charge even when appearances were sporadic. She was gradually working the young Michael out. More an excluded member than being the black sheep of the family!

If nothing else Rachael had at least one thing in common with the Armstrong family in that she was prepared to take a risk. They had money to burn whereas she had absolutely nothing to lose. When you're on the lowest rung of the ladder why worry about failure. This was Rachael's very own warped justification of theft and prostitution rolled into one. Time she put her hunch to the test.

'Hi Michael'

'Rachael'

'Thanks'

'For what? Keeping my mouth shut?'

'Well, yes. I can't think of anyone else round here that would have.'

'Like I said you owe me one.'

'And how do you want me to repay you?'

'When I think of something I'll let you know.'

'Why did you not spill the beans to your parents or brother who would have sacked me on the spot? I'm curious?'

'I have my reasons and these days they can afford to lose a few pounds here and there.'

'I can't believe you're really talking like this. I just don't get it.'

'You're not meant to get it Rachael. One of these days I'll explain.'

'Are you doing anything tonight?'

'Not a lot.'

'Why don't you come over?'

'Where?'

'To mine you fool. Where do you think? I live at Fairfield. The kids get put to bed around eight. You can come then if you like? If you can get away?'

'Well, of course I can. I'm not a kid even though they treat me like one.' Another clue for Rachael to unravel!

'Eight o'clock then. Number two Green close! Take two rights then a left as you enter the village. It's not that big a place.'

'OK. Eight o'clock.'

Suck on that Joe! When did Rachael Compston ever invite him over for tea and biscuits? Joe would have been as green as the turf on sale at the store entrance if he knew the proposition Rachael had in mind.

'Are you sure this is a business trip? Bears all the hallmarks of three friends flying off on a bit of a jolly holiday to me! So, are you taking your clubs as well?'

'No way! That part just came through by fax this morning enquiring if any of us were golfers as apparently the silky smooth Lee Trenchman has a single figure handicap. He actually looks just the fucking type that's good at every sport he turns his hand to. No doubt out to show his prowess and kind of rub our British faces in it at the same time. I doubt somehow that it's going to be all golf.'

Clair rolling her eyes but underneath seriously proud that all his hard work and sacrifice were finally paying off! Here was her handsome husband of fifteen years in part responsible for the future prosperity of her home county and the perfect loving father to their two teenage girls. Who was she to begrudge him a transatlantic freebie considering the demands of having to spend each and every weekend with three women under the same roof! Clair loved him dearly and she knew the feeling was more than mutual. He worshipped her. Never a day passed without him calling her at some point and yes, even returning home from Park Lane as requested with two embossed rolls of toilet paper in his briefcase albeit taken from the Gents. This was his secret that day. Even his two accomplices were kept out the loop. Humorous anecdote for the next dinner party upon his return!

'So, what else is on the agenda apart from golf and fine dining?'

'Well, we're going to get the full works that's for sure. Everything will be painted as rosy and no doubt we'll only be introduced to a carefully selected band of people. We're under no illusions and Alan's ultra cynical about that side of it. We just have to try and cut through the smokescreen and draw our own conclusions. See it as how we think it is. We don't have to give them planning permission but you know me. Always open to new ideas and to be fair they are the world's biggest garden centre operators so they must be good or else they would never have lasted.'

Quite correct Glenn they were the world's biggest but also one of the most ruthless operators when it came to being in their employ or waiting to be paid. A struggling outfit of eight units a decade ago had been taken over by master marketeer Don Walsh and rebranded as a pile it high sell them cheap all things to all people glorified leisure centre before embarking on a swashbuckling acquisition trail that would leave competitors trailing in their wake. In a nutshell put everyone out of business then hike up the prices but still market yourself as something your patently not. His prime time adverts bore testament to this. Floated on the NASDAQ some five years ago those adventurous enough to take a punt would have seen their investment multiply six fold with some well known names now on the list of major shareholders.

The name of the game was to secure the land at as cheap a price as possible through debt which would then be refinanced by some gullible investor or another at its higher valuation with the difference somehow or another feeding its way through to the bottom line as profits. Notwithstanding the odd hundred thousand siphoned off along the way to feed Walsh's addiction to women and keep his prize hooker sweet.

Sales were everything to maintain the charade and the UK was now proving itself ripe for some garden centre Stateside razzamatazz. A certain person's ego may also have had something to do with it. Walsh had learned a while back that expansion when reliant on the bureaucrats at City Hall could prove to be a protracted and ultimately expensive affair if left to their own devices. By fair means or foul play he would always say and his latest tactic of success by entrapment was proving to be highly effective. It certainly helped speed things along with the money shelled out in the interim sure paying dividends in the longer term. No end of fun to be had watching girls go about their business in the process.

So, yes Glenn they were indeed the world's biggest but also known to run fast and loose when it came to operating within the guidelines of the Queensbury rulebook.

'So, what if they come over here and ruffle a few feathers in our genteel part of the world' said Glenn. 'If it makes others raise their game then I don't have a problem with that.'

'Armstrong's won't be happy that's for sure.'

'Christ you're the second person that's now mentioned that place. I don't know the slightest thing about them. Who the hell are they?'

'Biggest garden centre in the South Coast! They do fantastic afternoon teas. We should go there for some ideas for our back garden which you said you were going to give a makeover to once spring had passed and the drier weather came in.'

'Did I?'

'Yes you sure did!'

'Well, maybe we wait till B-Smart opens and I'll get everything at half the price.'

'Ah but will they actually know anything about plants?'

'Of course they won't but how much does anyone need to know apart from will this plant come back again next year.'

'You're impossible. Just make sure and behave.'

'You don't need to worry about me...or Alan for that matter. I think at our age our nightclubbing days are well and truly behind us.'

'And George?'

'Haha...George? Lock up your daughters. If nothing else, he'll brighten the place up.'

Prophetic words indeed!

'So, what's it to be then Jim?'

The first time they had sloped off down this way in years and yet right on their doorstep. That idyllic view from the restaurant veranda! Well, somewhere down there, but two dots on the vast expanse of Sussex greenery below walked Jim and Ann here to settle once and for all probably the last major financial decision of their working lives.

'I know you don't want to sell and if that's how it's going to be then there's not a lot I can do but I don't want us to be going on forever Jim. We both know too many people whose health has suffered by outstaying their welcome. It's time we put ourselves first. The kids are old enough now to take care of themselves. Not as if we won't see them alright financially. We'll still have the house ...won't we?'

'I should have asked them that one. There was too much to take in to make me think of something so obvious now. We'd have to sell it Ann. Never on God's earth would I want to live next door to what's been the best part of my adult working life. But we were given this house so what right do we have then to sell it?'

'So, you want to hang onto the family heirloom ad infinitum?'

'I don't know what I want right now.'

Ann smiling. ''An offer of two million pounds and here you are turning into a quivering wreck.'

'In a way it's something that I wished had never happened. Does that make sense?'

'Of course it does. It's thrown the cat amongst the pigeons for all of us and I can understand why Joe's petrified at the thought of leaving this place. Or he could use some of the money to go ahead and open another garden centre?'

'Or he could just keep this one and make it better.'

'So, what about the article young Michael mentioned? I take it you did actually read it?'

'Of course I did.'

'And?'

'Doesn't affect us in the slightest! So, in general terms one of their big operators wants to come over here and open up but do it in a discount kind of way. Fair play and they can open up wherever the like but that's not our market. Do you honestly think that style of operation would work in this part of the world? If they do come over something tells me they won't be looking to open up shop in this, one of the most affluent parts of the country.'

'So, why not?'

'Because people here would just stay away from that kind of place in their droves. It's been tried before and went down like a lead balloon. Residents here want something that befits their status in life and you don't get that by visiting somewhere that sells three course meals for a pound.'

'Fair point.' It did make sense to Ann or at the very least she was doing her level best to talk herself round to it all making sense. Although she knew only too well in the unlikely event that a huge corporation ever did move in to their patch, Jim would very likely be quaking in his size eleven boots.

'Well, you now have only a couple of weeks left to make up your mind.'

'Our mind.'

'No Jim, your mind. I know what your like. I've been married to you for long enough. I can tell you this though, whatever decision you make you do it and then that's it. I don't want to hear any more about it once the matters resolved. Is that part understood?'

'Loud and clear.'

Only one way to describe somewhere like Fairfield and that would be bleak! When the MOD went about building their munitions depots here during the war they either dug up or flattened everything within a three mile radius leaving only a vast expanse of nothingness. When the time came to pull out along came the local Council to take the land off their hands and immediate access to some much needed housing albeit of the breeze block variety of dubious quality and characterless design. What was meant to be temporary accommodation for a storage depot's workforce subsequently became something altogether completely different! The concrete pillars and eight feet high perimeter fences were still intact and visible from the main road giving the impression of somewhere resembling more a young offender's institution than a low grade social housing project. No one ever moved to Fairfield through choice. A stop gap until the Council found something better and a choice between this or else living on the streets.

The Council had Rachael on their radar when it came to being re homed. The only consolation of the abundance of draughts in what the locals had dubbed Lego brick land was that it at least kept the damp at bay. Acutely aware of the impact on two young children's physical wellbeing, she was therefore one of the top priorities in when came to being reallocated but no point in relying on the efforts of the bureaucrats alone. Just like the sharp suited crook across the pond she was aware of just how ponderous and slow the whole process consistently proved to be. To rely on the efforts of others was to stand still. It was the making money of her own accord that would be key to getting the hell out of Fairfield and making something of her life albeit with two young kids in tow. She had the looks and highly likely after tonight the helper. If he turned up at eight which she was sure he would to the second she'd definitely be looking her best! Young Michael, snared twice in the space of less than a week but this one infinitely more pleasurable than the first. The way his face looked most days she thought it was about time the boy got a treat and just as she expected with only seconds to spare guess who's little car was spotted driving slowly around the corner. The flaked paint and rusting metal framed windows bore testament to what lay ahead for Michael on the inside which inevitably lived up to expectations. Did he care? Not a jot! Freedom at last from the Gulag in the company of a girl at least several leagues higher up the dating ladder and now only inches apart on the settee. When had this ever happened to him before?

'Michael I'd like you to do me a favour?'

'Shock horror! So, that's why you invited me over.'

'No, it's not.'

'Yes it fucking is. How daft do you think I am? My family all think I'm stupid but there's not a lot I can do about that.'

'I'm only asking Mikey?'

'I like Michael better.'

'Wow you are just so angry. No wonder you keep yourself to yourself in that place. Maybe its best if I don't then.'

'So, who are you going to ask instead? My brother?'

'I don't like your brother. Nobody likes your brother. The only person that likes him is himself…well your parent's right enough. Your dad absolutely dotes on him.'

'You got that part right. I thought it was just me and my sister that thought that.'

'No, Michael you've got that wrong. The last person I would ever ask for anything is Joe.'

'OK, ok so what's the favour then? It must be a big one for you to ask me over?'

'No, it's not that big, just that I have another job and I need someone to drive me now and again seeing as I can't drive and the buses are rubbish. It was just to ask if you could do it for me that's all…Well, I also want this to be just between you and me and I figured after a couple of weeks ago that I can trust you. I don't want anyone to know this. Just me and you!'

'Yeh ok…so when do I do this?'

'It'll probably be at nights.'

'So, I drive you to your other job at nighttime?'

'No, it's not like one job! Listen Michael I've started doing massaging ok and I need someone…well you to take me to see clients, wait on me then bring me home. I mean it's not every night just now and again. I just want to know if you can help me as there's no one else round here I trust and I don't want anyone round here finding out ok!'

'Right...Christ...fuck! That came out the blue. You of all people!'

'I need the money. I've got two kids upstairs and I want out this place. You think I like living here? I want to come home to a decent place at nights instead of this dump. It's like living in a bloody prison camp.'

Not that young Michael was paying much attention to anything other than this gorgeous specimen of femininity sitting inches apart. As if his answer was not already a foregone conclusion.

'Yeh sure. Why not? I just never expected it that's all.'

'Does that mean you're ashamed of me?'

'Don't be daft. You do what you have to do and don't worry, I won't be saying anything.

'Thanks you've no idea how much I appreciate this. I was relying on you saying yes and would have been screwed if you hadn't.'

'So, when is our...I mean your next appointment then?'

'Ehh tomorrow. Is that Ok?'

'Yeh of course.'

'Only one thing we have to sort out now. How I pay you for helping me.'

'Don't worry about that. I'll just do it. It gets me out the place at night and no one's interested in what I do anyway.'

'Have you ever had a girl Michael? I mean really had a girl?'

He was hoping she would never get round to asking that question. Not that it was a warm house but his face sure as hell felt like it had suddenly gone on fire. Not that Rachael would ever let that show. With his self esteem on the floor and still finding the time to help her out maybe now's the ideal time for one good turn to deserve another. Also cheaper paying him this way! Needless to say deadly silence.

'OK Michael! I have a proposition but I want you to remember one thing and it's important you do. I don't fancy you and I'm never going to fancy you so don't go getting any ideas Ok. If you do then trust me I've been fucked around by so many guys I'm prepared to just walk away and I don't care if that means you also get me fired. This way everybody wins. Do you want me to go on?'

Successive nods of the young man's head compensated for his heart racing at such a speed it rendered him utterly speechless. He should have been excited instead of being nothing short of utterly petrified.

All that was needed was the obligatory make up and some lighting and the scene could have been plucked straight out of any midweek TV drama. Sombre cast sit with baited breath awaiting verdict from the foreman of the group who also just happens to be their dad! Ann already knew what was coming but managed to hide it well. The older two both quietly confident the big decision would be the one that went in their favour but the youngest the only one just like his mother to know for certain. May just have been two inconsequential things but being the first to pick up on something of such relevance in a gardening magazine and then to call out and end up getting into bed with one of their most valued employees had done much to lift the young lads esteem well up off the floor. That he could read people and events his father's decision would either shatter or validate just how intuitive he thought he actually was. To add a bit of drama given his father's love of attention Jim stood to address assembled audience.

'Heh Dad you come across as a defense lawyer about to begin his summing up.'

'Good old Carolyn. Never one to miss an opportunity at introducing the matter of law at every conceivable opportunity!' snapped Joe.

'Let your father speak. Jim just hurry up and get on with it before we get a repeat performance of last week' from a somewhat tetchy Ann.

'Ok so what I...'

'Sorry Jim...and you two. Whatever your father says I want you both to just accept it and no more sniping at each other. Is that understood?'

'Fine by me' from Carolyn.

'Joe...understood?'

'Yes mum I hear you.'

'I'm ok with it all too mum just in case you were worried that I felt sidelined.'

An unexpected piece of sarcasm from the normally reticent Michael raised at least one of his parent's eyebrows and a large grin from his sister. Amazing what a shag with a good looking girl can do to a young man's self confidence.'

'Right Jim just get on with it.'

'Thank you dear......I will if people would just allow me to speak that is. Well, we talked about this last week where everyone had the chance to put their opinions across.'

'Apart from me!'

'Michael will you please not interrupt your father when he's speaking.'

'He does have a point.'

'Oh, Carolyn don't go off on one yet again' Joe interjects.

'Will you please all stop arguing' shouts a now exasperated Ann.' Don't you all realise how stressful enough it is for me and your father. Jim just hurry up and fucking tell them.'

Whoops!! Now for Ann to swear that really is something and a deathly silence ensues.

'We're not selling. That's the bottom line. Joe actually had a valid point which swung the balance in the remain camp. Carolyn…Michael…this family works as one and we're all in this together. You may not agree with what your mother and I have decided but there's still a lot of unfinished business lying ahead as Joe has quite correctly pointed out. With this in mind it's about time I took not just a bit of a back seat but withdrew from the scene completely and gave more of my time to your mother. Carolyn we both took on board your point about holidays and that's what we intend to do. We'll still be here for the foreseeable future but as of now, right now, the running of this place, lock stock and barrel is in Joe's hands so it's over to you completely. Your mother and I are to be used for emergencies only nothing else. Now one final point! This was our decision which we believe to be the right one so I want this to be the end of it. No more arguing and backbiting. We are a family and we're a team. Is that understood?'

'Is it worth me saying anything at all' enquires Carolyn.

'No, its not' snaps her mother.

'Listen to your mother Carolyn. That's the end of the matter and for the sake of your mother's health and mine I want this to be the last time it's ever mentioned. Agreed?'

'Ok agreed' from a visibly dejected daughter.

'And you Michael?'

'Yes dad.' Not that the young lad was too concerned about any of this. More pressing concerns on his plate!

Not in Joe's nature to resist one final dig.

'Sorry about that Carolyn! I guess the better argument just won the day.'

Bookings had already jumped by the time he reappeared on her doorstep exactly twenty two hours later.

'Mum's here to babysit. I've told her we're going on a date ok.'

'Are we?'

'No, you fool' she whispered. 'Of course we're not. It's just the cover story why you're here.' God this boy had a lot to learn but better having someone she could mould around her own way of thinking than a renegade with their own agenda. Perfect cover story and someone for once who her mother would finally approve of even if she was not the only one who saw him as a bit of a damp squib! Actually she had a thing about his brother who like many in the town had considered a real catch only to be shot down in flames.

'Mum, don't even go there.'

The story would do in the meantime as long as mother followed daughter's strict orders of keeping it all hush hush especially when it came to visiting a certain garden centre for Afternoon tea with the girls. The name of the game was having as few in the loop as possible and as it stood Michael and her mother would more than suffice.

A quick debrief in the car which hardly came across as especially romantic from where her mother was standing, peering as she always did from behind the net curtain! It just seemed to be Rachael doing all the talking with her date for the evening simply nodding his head whenever instructed. Good job his family had money she thought as there was bugger all else going for the lad.

'I've got a repeat booking tomorrow as well now. So, that's tonight, tomorrow and Saturday as well. Is that OK?'

'My God! That's a hell of a lot of guys out there looking for massages. Maybe we should open a massage room in the garden centre.'

'Michael. Are you for real? Is this a bluff?'

'What?'

'I mean are you double bluffing me?'

'I don't know what you're on about Rachael.'

'You're bluffing me?'

'With what?'

'No, you're not are you!'

'What on earth are you talking about Rachael?'

Not that she could ever fall in love or even remotely fancy the guy in a month of Sundays but he sure was nice if not occasionally utterly naïve.

'Right I can feel my mother's eyes on us Mike, drive off.'

He preferred Mike. Had a grown up ring to it which none of the family even Carolyn had considered applying now that early adulthood had finally arrived. Still young, still wet behind the ears but events conspiring elsewhere for the lad to speed the whole maturity process along! Tonight's booking would be repeated tomorrow such was Rachael's level of service so the same hotel car park twice for the young man's old relic to sit there for the odd half hour or so looking distinctly out of place. Nothing to do but conspicuously count the minutes till they made their escape but why would anyone want a massage two nights running? Did seem a bit odd?

A two day break before Saturday came around and a good half hour's drive to Uxbridge and a home visit for an hour. One of the more established well to do areas and the odd stare from one or two of the locals at the sight of an old mini driving slowly around tree lined suburban streets. Either lost or else attempting to see for themselves how the other half lives. Nothing to go on if the name of the street continued to prove elusive! All she knew was that the bloke called himself George!

'This is the street. Just stop here and I'll walk down. Best you go and park up somewhere and come back for me in an hour.'

'Great minds think alike. I can feel the fucking eyes on us already.'

'You've got the easy job. They'll be watching me to see where I go. Give me a kiss so it looks like we're a couple. Make them think I'm just visiting an aunt or something.'

Another first! All this cloak and dagger stuff was proving exciting and good experience for what was destined to lie ahead a few decades later. Pennies were also beginning to drop. Slow on the uptake but figuring out what she meant from earlier on. He kicked himself for being so green. My God! Given his mother's performance at lunchtime any inkling that one of her sons was up to something like this could quite possibly finish her off. He'd figured out the long game so now time to practice discretion and keep Rachael in check.

Never knowing quite what to expect when the door opened this evening's booking proved to be one of the best yet! Good looking, mid to late forties and in reasonable shape. Seems to have done well for himself given the house and size of car in driveway. Confident and relaxed he bore all the hallmarks of a man who not only enjoyed the company of women but was also pretty much used to engaging in this kind of activity. Chatty which made a pleasant change from the few up to now who barely gave her the time to draw breath before it was straight down to business. Two glasses on the coffee table along with bottle of wine underneath which sat her fee in twenty pound notes. What a pro!

'A quick drink before we head upstairs?'

'Yeh. Why not! That would be lovely. Take it you don't live here by yourself?' Her head nodding in the direction of family photos on the mantelpiece.

'Good God no! I'd never last on my own for more than two minutes. They've all gone off to my mother's in law for the week while I head off on business in the morning.'

'Ahh so I'm your little treat? Treat yourself often do you?'

'Whenever I can! When the wife's away men like me always tend to play.'

'I see and I bet you do!'

Just a single line can be all it takes for a woman to pigeonhole a man and this was obviously the type that seemed to be getting off on his unfaithfulness. Two camps of clientele she'd learned when it came to paying for her time. Those that need sex but want it over and done with then get the hell away from the scene of the crime as quick as they can and those that seemed to revel in the risk taking. No prizes for guessing which camp George here was in. Could easily have been clocked by the neighbours and no effort to disguise the fact there were others in his life likely to be affected greatly by what he was just about to get up to atop the marital bed. Not that she was going to lose any sleep over it and sixty quid for an hours work would be the envy of many a single mother on the Fairfield estate but underneath she seriously despised guys like this. After all, two of them in her life had already been and gone leaving her with double mouths to feed but no looking back. That being said repeat business in this line of work was everything and who's to say tonight's visit would only be a one off.

'Cheers. Sorry I forgot what your name was again?'

'Cheers. It's Raquel.'

'Haha. Raquel I like it! Well, Raquel here's to an enjoyable time!'

'Oh, I think that's a given don't you'

'Shall we?' As he gestured her towards the door.

'Why not?'

There he was parked up on a dirt track off the B705 Uxbridge to Alfriston road. This was the life of a working girl's accomplice. Two hotel car parks and now sat the other side of the entrance to a potato field. Hardly rock & roll! Only fifteen minutes in and it briefly crossed his mind what stage his friend would be at back at the bloke's house. Clothes must be off by this time for sure. Not that he wanted to dwell on that part of tonight's show. As good a time as any to reflect on his father's announcement and the ramifications of it all. Nothing was likely to change other than brother Joe now doing his damnedest to get younger brother and sister out of the place. Likely him first as Joe was that bit warier of his sister. She'd probably just go of her own accord and find something else to occupy her time when the Universities broke up for the holidays. Whatever she did rest assured Joe would still be taking the credit for having forced her hand.

Maybe time to bite the bullet and move on himself! Patently obvious he wasn't wanted. His father having said as such when he eavesdropped on his parents chatting before lunch a few weeks back. No matter what he did it would never be enough and now that his brother was number one he'd be surrounding himself with his favourites from site none of which Michael particularly liked. Doing this at least got him out the house and Rachael certainly brought much needed colour into his life but just like she said, it was never destined to come to anything so high time he took a leaf out her book and showed some initiative. For some reason he'd always fancied trying his hand at plumbing. The local guy that came on site always appeared to be rushing off to his next job somewhere and no end of pipes leaking in the wintertime. Best of all it meant working alone with no one around to interfere. That's the game plan then. Best get onto it as soon as because his cards were already marked.

'Shit.' That's what sitting thinking does for you. Eats up time and Rachael was due collection in ten minutes. Her stay though was now about to be unexpectedly extended and not because of the first thought that springs to mind.

'Tea or coffee before you go?'

'Eh...yeh ok. Quick coffee. Think I've still got ten minutes before I get picked up.'

'Boyfriend?'

'No, I don't have a boyfriend. I live on my own. It's just my best friend who drives me around the place when she's free.' A lie used frequently. She'd been told that men prefer to think of their 'girl' as being single and available. Does wonders for repeat bookings.

'So, when are you away on business?'

'First thing in the morning from Gatwick! Going over to Florida to look at garden centres of all things!'

'Garden centres?'

'Yeh, one and the same! The biggest operator in the States wants to come here so a few of us are just going over to have a look and see how they do things and whether or not we think what they do will fit in to our neck of the woods.'

Not that a twenty four year old girl on the game posed any kind of threat to a man of some local influence with a very loose tongue.

'I never knew that. What are they called?'

'B–Smart. Heard of them have you?' asked in a sarcastic kind of way.

'No, cheeky bugger of course I haven't. So, is it you that decides if they come?'

'Just to a very minor extent! I'm just part of a three man delegation that gives their operation the once over then looks at the site they have in mind this end.'

'So, what about Armstrong's in Waltham? Do you think it will affect them?'

'Oh, so your familiar with them?'

'My mum goes there for her afternoon tea.'

'Hate to say it Raquel but I wouldn't want to be in their shoes however it's not all lost. I can give you another update when I book you again. I never thought a good looking girl like you would be that interested.'

'Well, I am if there's any jobs going. I don't want to just do this all the time. I like a bit of variety.'

'You might be in luck then because they want to open up right here in Uxbridge.'

'You're kidding me?'

'No, I can assure you I'm not. Sure I could put a word in for you nearer the time if it goes ahead.'

'Would you?'

'Course I would. One good turn and all that! This way I get to see even more of you.'

'Wow that would be good.'

'Only thing is then you'll have to tell me your real name when it gets round to being invited for interview.'

'That's fine. I'll let you know when you need to. I'll leave it in your capable hands then. I guess you'll be seeing some girls in Florida as well naughty boy.'

'What's the saying Raquel. Old habits die hard.'

'Right I best get going. Give me a call when your back if you want to hook up for some more fun.'

'Oh, that's a given.'

Now if only George had such a thing as a crystal ball because seeing call girls when he got back would be the last thing on his mind. Self preservation more like.

Not a run exactly but teetering on the edge. Somewhere between that and the briskest of walks she came towards the mini as if desperate to escape. Easily the most agitated he'd seen her yet. Curtains bound to be twitching and the guy at number 42 did have a bit of a reputation. Matters hardly helped when the bloody passenger door was stuck. Talk about prolonging the agony.

'What's up? What's happened?'

'Mike you're not going to believe this!!'

They arrived on the Sunday afternoon being left alone to recuperate in the splendor of the Breakers hotel at Palm Beach.

'Heh this is a bit of alright' proclaimed George on checking in. 'The Dorchester and now this place!'

'It's called being seduced George' from easily the most cynical of the three! 'Softens us up so we take our eye off the ball.'

'Or maybe they just want into the UK that badly?'

'Either way there's going to be catch somewhere along the line.'

'You've been in law way too bloody long Alan. You assume everything has an ulterior motive. Next you'll be telling me that you wouldn't trust Lee Trenchman as far as you could throw him.' That one managed a laugh all round.

'Well, talking of the Prince of Darkness here's one for you.' As Glenn reads from the envelope passed over with his keys. 'Tomorrow morning at nine o clock we're being collected for a day's golf at the Jupiter Hills Country Club. Nine holes, lunch then another nine then dinner to follow. Oh, go on Lee you've twisted our arms! Wherever Jupiter Hills happens to be that is?' Raised eyebrows in receptionist's direction.

'If I may interject sir it just so happens to be Florida's premier Golf and Country club.'

'Ahh, I see.' from Glenn. 'Hands up how many of us have not been practicing since the fax came through?'

'I've managed four rounds' from Alan.

'Bastard, I thought I was doing well with three' retorted Glenn. 'Well?' in direction of George.

'One…So, a sleepless night for me then! How many do you think Trenchman's had?'

'Probably never been off the fucking course George! Just try not to embarrass us too much.'

'Cheers Alan.'

Rachael agreed that this was the best way to go about it too with the proviso that her name be kept well and truly out of it. That much was a given. Now he'd had a taste of her it's unlikely he was going to pass up on her side of the bargain which was to give him another shag in a couple of days.

'So, who told you this Michael?'

'I know someone who's dad works for the council and it's his dad that was going out to America.'

'So, what's his dad's name?'

'I don't know.'

'You have a friend who's name you haven't told me and you don't know this persons father's name either! Dad's going to believe this less than I am.'

'Does it matter? I'm not lying! I swear to you I'm not making this up. It just sounds better if it comes from you as you have more clout. They'd never listen to me in a million years.'

'Yeh I get that! Sad but true!'

'Can you not just say you've heard a rumour! If I were to say that they'd laugh but you can say one of your University pals said it. They'll believe that.'

'You're getting good at this bro. Something's happened to you this past few weeks. I bloody know there's something you're not telling me.'

'Rubbish.'

'Don't rubbish me Mikey.'

'Michael!'

'Another clue! Your more confident and starting to think smart. Right I'll do it. It's actually a good idea to say one of my pal's friends from Uni as they'll easily believe I know some movers and shakers which is total crap but I'll do it in the morning.'

'You have to do it fast. Have they actually officially turned the offer down?'

'No idea. Joe would have been pushing for dad to do that as soon as.'

'Don't tell him whatever you do.'

'Well, I'm hardly likely to am I? When this is over, I want you to tell me what's happened in your life that you're not telling me?'

'Not a chance.'

Trenchman's opening tee shot simply reinforced the conversation that had begun at dinner and continued all the way through into breakfast. This morning's round would actually end up more a competition between the three of them than a match against a smarmy opponent who already had that seriously annoying habit of appearing humble when he was really anything but. Three hundred and twenty yards straight down the middle would be followed by two draws and a fade. More USA against the Keystone cops unless each was to get a grip on their nerves. A lack of appetite at breakfast for all three simply reinforced the apprehension of coming along to play probably Florida's finest. Only took the dizzy heights of four holes for Trenchman to ease back on the throttle lest his opponents capitulate completely. Dare I say it? Two of the visiting group had even ever so slightly warmed to him in the process because of it. The formality of meeting again on the first tee having long since dissipated by the time the beers were being shared in the visitors' bar.

'Cheers. I don't know how this course compares to what you're used to playing back home but I love playing here.'

'Completely different' said Glenn. 'We never had to use our waterproofs once which was a hell of a bonus for a start. Back home forget them at your peril.'

'The greens as well. I can't believe how fast they were. Half the time it felt like I was putting on ice.'

'Would that be the odd occasion when you were not taking five out the bunker George?' as if needed reminded by Alan.

'Ha bloody ha. A rare change for you playing a wide open course as you usually spend most of your time back home amongst the trees.'

Obvious for master manipulator Lee that beyond the camaraderie these three had a bond! They would all be looking out for each other and would have to be separated at some point if things were to go according to his plan.

'No complaints from me Lee over your level of hospitality' from Glenn. 'I'm just wondering how long it lasts before the bubble bursts and we have to justify to the tax payers back home why we're actually here in the first place.'

'Glenn the bad news is work starts in earnest in the morning after breakfast. Dons popping by so we'll meet you in the foyer at nine before heading off for some store visits. That will be our home store here in Florida then up to Georgia to see how we adapt our stores to a different audience and area.'

'Wow, that's going to be a hell of a drive' from ever observant Alan.

'Hell no! No driving involved apart from to the airport. Dons flying down in the morning by company jet so we're thinking of leaving here by noon. Get to the other store easy in a couple of hours all in.'

'One surprise after another Lee.'

'Glenn its no trouble at all! What we're out to do is show you we're serious about coming to the UK and making a success of it. This is our way of showing you some gratitude for considering us in the first place and heh, if we ever get round to building the place I sure hope we can take up where we left off here with some more golf. I don't mind admitting it's an addiction which sends my good lady crazy at times.'

'In which case I think we may have to drag things out to give the three of us time to work on our handicaps.' Laughs all round and maybe Trenchman had some humility after all.

'Now I said that was the bad news.'

'Yes.'

'So, the good news is tonight's dinner will be right here if your happy to be my guests. The food here is what I would describe as a bit more substantive than that of Park Lane.'

'Fish and chips time is it?' enquired Glenn.

'Ahh no that part has still to come. Don has never forgotten about that I can assure you. Now please let's talk some more golf and leave the business till tomorrow.'

'Drink to that.' from George.

So, why did Alan have his doubts about Trenchman when everything up to now had simply been plain sailing. Keen without being pushy and generous even if it was slightly over the top! Everything just seemed so contrived and polished but then again he was a cynical middle aged lawyer who had a wife that was forever telling him to lighten up. Was the disdain against the man based on a lack of trust or simply suppressed envy towards someone who chose a different route to that of public servant and appeared to be reaping much greater rewards for having done so! That he was a much slicker operator was beyond question. Alan never even came close to licking his boots in that arena but still the nagging doubt that somewhere along the line things were failing to add up without having anything beyond a hunch to prove it. George had been hooked by the time they got round to checking in. No great surprise there but he sensed that Glenn was now beginning to walk down a similar path to that of his more gregarious and easily swayed colleague.

Or perhaps something more fundamental! He simply didn't like the man.

Chapter 4

He should have had a spring in his step as he walked the early morning rounds but for the patriarch of the family notwithstanding matters resolved it felt really quite the opposite. He felt deflated. Just what the hell was he now going to do with himself? Nowhere near retirement all very well talking of multiple holidays but getting around to doing them, well that's another story. Then there's the small matter of Joe having complete control. The favoured one liked the thought of being charge but since being anointed increasingly nowhere to be seen. Now 8 am. In Jim's world the working day would have begun long before and increasingly played on his mind whether or not he'd made the right choice. The smarter of the two was the one that had chosen an altogether different career path and as coincidence would have it, also an early riser and heading right his way. She was about to make his day a whole load worse although it did begin with an olive branch.

'Dad let me buy you breakfast.'

'So, why would that be?'

'Because I'm your daughter and I care about you even if you do wind me up something rotten. That plus the fact I thought it best we talk alone.'

'In which case let's just talk where we are. Your mother will smell a rat if she sees us in the restaurant together and she's anxious enough as it is. What's on your mind?'

'Dad I have a friend at Uni called Alison. Her uncle works for the Council and he's gone to America to look at some garden centre operator who wants to open up down the road in Uxbridge.'

'Uxbridge?' He appeared visibly shaken when she mentioned where. Not exactly a million miles away. In fact right on his bloody doorstep.

'Their called B–Smart and apparently they are huge.'

'And you're just telling me this now?'

'Yes.'

'Why now? Why not when she'd told you?'

'Because I thought it a foregone conclusion you would both want to sell. What would be the point in telling you something that made no difference to you not knowing it? For the life of me I never thought you would pass up on an offer of two million pounds! That's not to say you can't change your minds.'

'We can't change our minds Carolyn. It's too late.'

'It's never too late dad! Just forget about Joe and hanging on for more. This is about getting out when the goings good.'

'No, you don't understand. It's too late because I have already turned them down.'

'You have?'

'I have. So, we just have to wait and see what happens.'

'You could always call them back! Not as if they're going to find a site as good as this one anywhere else?'

Good point. For the life of me I never expected this. OK just don't go saying anything to Joe or your mother. Even young Michael.'

'No, I won't I promise.'

Christ, at long last. Her father finally seeing sense! If he manages to pull this one off he would owe his youngest the biggest debt of gratitude to anything granted previous by his great aunt or bank manager. Not that dad was likely to believe the young one could ever be partial to obtaining such inside information in the first place and his sister equally flummoxed as to exactly quite how.

Difficult for a conversation in a garden centre to go unnoticed even for one beginning at eight o'clock in the morning! The favoured one had just arrived on site and by observing body language from afar it looked like his arch nemesis was not for letting this mutual bone of contention drop anytime soon. Like all the best schoolyard bullies his frustrations were now unlikely to be vented on those who gave as good as they got, rather on someone who'd come to expect nothing less.

'First impressions?'

'Looks like something resembling an airport terminal' from an unusually deadpan George which brought mild amusement to the faces of his colleagues but little to that of the hosts. Guess not the done thing to take the piss out of someone's new born baby thought Alan.

Now heading off the freeway and closing in, probably about five hundred yards left and for sure even from this distance it looked like one hell of a site. Five of them now having been joined by Walsh back at the hotel before quickly being whisked off in what was an infinitely more salubrious version of multi person transport to anything enjoyed back home. Walsh seemed different today, more focused which Glenn surmised easy to understand why. Today was the day he had to go about selling his vision so reticence thus far perfectly understandable. Trenchman likewise also a different beast from as little as twelve hours ago so obviously following his boss's lead. That they would relax as the morning progressed would follow as plans fell into place. The first stage of their underhand tactic was already underway of which their hosts were blissfully unaware. In fact they were suitably impressed.

'Good healthy flow of visitors considering its not yet ten in the morning' observed Alan.

'Well, if you look up to your right at the billboard there Alan it may explain some of the reasons why' replied Don.

'Wow! Twenty five per cent off today that's one hell of a bargain. Is this just with selected products?' enquired Glenn.

Given his economics background he was interested to see how they could possibly make any money from merchandising at such a massive discount.

'It sure brings people in as you can see Glenn. By noon I'd expect the car park to be overflowing as it always is.'

'But with that level of discount Don how can you possibly make a profit given the overheads of running a place this size?'

'Glad you asked me that one Glenn, I kind of knew it was coming and if you'll just bear with me for the time being things will become clearer by the time we're inside. On top of that remember what you asked me back in London about how could smaller operators possibly survive when we move into their very own back yard?'

'Yes, I remember it well and I'm even more intrigued now or do I already know the answer.'

'Well, just hold up there too. All will shortly be revealed I can assure you.'

So, far so good for Don! Needless to say, full of shit as always but the first stage of proceedings has gone without a hitch. Those heavily discounted meal vouchers distributed in every trailer park in and around Florida was obviously paying dividends as was the odd twenty bucks handed out here and there for people to simply show up by car before 11 am thus creating the illusion of incredible popularity. A few hundred yards left to go and here they were, already in a snail's pace queue of traffic lining up for the store car park. Driver under strict instructions to not use the visitor spaces and instead drive around the public lot at least twice before holing up! In Trenchman's mind this served to reinforce the illusion of just how busy B–Smart really was.

'Good work Lee' he said softly before turning to address his guests.

'Welcome to B-Smart my friends. Now you know what to expect when the show hits town your end.'

'Already giving me cause for concern Don. Think we'll have to revisit looking at our road network.'

'Hell, you're the economist Glenn! Nice problem to have though when the demand exceeds the supply. Sure you'll come up with something.'

'Already been noted.'

'Shall we head inside then? This is the fun part for me. I never tire of hearing the ker-ching at the checkouts.'

Now time for Alan to whisper something in Glenn's ear being the final two to leave the bus.

'Why would I not be surprised if Mickey fucking Mouse is not the other side of that door. The pair have the dollar sign stamped on their foreheads.'

Glenn's large grin at Alan's comment not going unnoticed by Lee! No doubt something snide and for sure his legal adversary definitely being the weakest link among the trio! The antipathy was fast becoming mutual.

The first shag had given him confidence but the second had made him complacent. This was the trouble with Michael having become smitten. A rose tinted mist had descended to cloud his judgement with yet another booby trap destined to lie in wait with his name on. No consolation other than yet further contributions made to his compendium of life's lessons to be learned the hard way. That the heinous act on the part of his brother was in any way planned would be a mistake as Joe was more the seriously impulsive type and today something was most definitely amiss. For his father to forfeit lunch it just had to be serious and why did Joe have this sneaking suspicion the younger siblings were in on the act. Mother Ann equally as reticent! If this proved to be anything close to what he thought he'd be screwed. For sure the decent wage but the family name also brought side benefits! The kudos of being one of Waltham's most eligible being one for a start and for every gorgeous girl promised the earth there was likely another being groomed in the wings as her replacement. Rachael would not be the only one now dipping her fingers in the till with many a garden design invoice regularly settled for cash without his parents being any the wiser. Include the flash company car and hours to suit and here were all the hallmarks of someone on a seriously cushy number. Along with everyone else working on site by five pm he'd learn his fate.

'Ok fair play Don, you're not exactly Disney but you sure know how to pack them in.'

'It's not that we drag people in off the sidewalk Glenn but we sure as hell incentivise them to come visit. This is now what's known as destination shopping.'

'Is that what you call it' spoken with a wry smile on his face.

The restaurant reminded him of a throwback to his student refectory days. A cross between that and the works canteen he experienced with his dad as a kid. Volume catering at its most productive and boy oh boy B-Smart sure knew how to drive the public through in their droves. With next to no time for indecision this morning's offering of five breakfast items for 99 cents before all the add ons quadrupled the price was a far cry from the silver service opulence back at the Breakers. Would he breakfast in a B-Smart cafeteria back home? Of course he would. Glenn was that stereotypical price-sensitive kind of guy. As for Claire and the kids he strongly suspected not.

Meanwhile George and Lee were in the thick of it outdoors.

'Heck of a size Lee. So, how big is this site exactly?'

'Not our biggest but certainly in the top ten! Twelve acres in total if you include the car parks.'

'And would that be lease or freehold?'

'Good God no! Never rent. We always buy. The business model depends on it.'

'How?'

'Increased asset prices over the years means improved borrowing and even better rates for expansion. Take this site alone. Multiplied in value sixfold if we were to bulldoze the place and sell it onto developers. It's always an option but so far retail generates enough in profit that we don't have to.' So, many clues that a sharper mind would have seized upon! He thanked his lucky stars that Alan was elsewhere.

'If you don't mind me asking. How much did you pay?'

'For this place? Six years ago you'd be looking at around eight hundred thousand US dollars. That would be in your currency sat five fifty, half a million at least.'

'Crickey! Not sure you'll get Uxbridge anywhere near that ridiculously cheap Lee. The site our end is smaller than this, say eight acres but prime land the council would be loathe to sell. Normally we're looking at negotiating on a ninety-nine-year lease.'

'Like I say George we never rent. Am sure we can come to some arrangement now we know you and you know us. Always room for negotiation!'

'We might struggle on this one. Glenn's an Economist by trade and knows the value of just about everything.'

'And you're a surveyor, right? No, we'll do a deal. Trust me I know we will.'

George Lee assumed it was already a fait accompli. The council and Glenn in particular would be looking for millions whereas B-Smart were obviously looking to pay peanuts. At some point Glenn and the team had to learn to play hard ball. This briefest of insights provided a glimpse of what was likely to follow. Sure Lee was confident but he could also be an arrogant bastard which George assumed went with the territory. He was also envious of Lee but slightly intimidated at the same time. In other words, Trenchman had him exactly where he wanted.

'Leave the number crunching for later George. Tell me are you a keen gardener?'

'Absolutely not! All I remember is what my dad told me after I had bought my first house and had a tiny patch of lawn out the back to lay with turf.'

'What was that?'

'Remember son. Always green side up.'

'Haha. You sound just like me. I enjoy looking at all the shrubs out on the course and the baskets back at the clubhouse but don't ask me what any of them are. Tell you what. Why don't I introduce you to a couple of our colleagues? I saw them working out here just a couple of minutes ago and they're real easy on the eye George.'

'Now you're talking. I'll have to try and come up with a decent gardening question then.'

Phase two now in operation. Discussing with Don the previous night that Alan was likely a dead loss two out of three would still be an excellent result in any crooks' books to aspire to. Female fixer and partner in crime Andrea incognito as always and shadowing nearby appeared to be in conversation with two young ladies circa early thirties, hair tied back pony style and each wearing a light jacket which was a touch out of context considering the heat. A nod of the head from Lee and off came the jackets to reveal B-Smart staff polo top and on with the company baseball cap. In the blink of an eye B-Smart Florida had just acquired two brand new female employees who happened to be pretty god damned attractive and even more adept as George was about to find out later when it came to putting on a show for the camera. Both buxom with staff top at least a size too small. Shallow and clichéd for sure but then again Andrea had realised back in London as George's eyes had followed her journey from table to exit door and back again that he was about as clichéd and predictable as they came.

'Ah here they are. Over here George! I want you to meet two of my favourite girls.'

It was the glare that gave the game away and young Michael as always the recipient of his venom. At his father's insistence a staff meeting had been hastily convened for five o clock in the coffee annex to put paid once and for all to the ever changing Armstrong staff canteen rumour mill. The eldest standing by his father's side was fizzing and as part of the assembled audience, for Rachael, not difficult understand why. Given her contribution to the proceedings, an unwitting Joe could easily have been forgiven for reaching out to grab each by the throat before the master of ceremonies got events underway. Not that many of the staff were really that concerned if truth be told. More an issue of envy than of job security! This place was a goldmine. They needed more staff not less but within the space of a few short minutes Jim would be quashing the idea that to work in Armstrong's was as safe as many in the town had assumed. Although he'd be putting across the best possible spin, a change of ownership does tend to have this nasty habit of making people feel less secure about meeting next month's mortgage payment.

'Ok folks. Thanks for staying back. I appreciate you all have homes to go to and dinners to cook so I won't keep you very long. There's a line somewhere that says the thing about rumours is that they usually end up being true. Well, I don't know what you've heard on the jungle drums up to now, but this is me giving it to you straight from the horse's mouth and where we all stand, every single one of us at this moment in time working here at Armstrong's. I want to tell you that the past three weeks have been the hardest of anything I've ever had to face in my entire thirty years of working here. Less than a month ago I was approached to sell the garden centre and after what can only be described as long and often very heated discussions with my family, I decided to forfeit the offer and remain. Got to be honest with you now! Having had time to think things over I now believe that was the wrong decision and have since had a change of heart. So, folks, after building this business up and giving it my life, I now have to accept there's only so much I can do in the world of horticulture so with a heavy heart I've decided its time me and my family moved on. Now the people that are coming here are a very large operation with deep pockets so I'd expect everyone's jobs to be safe, but they may have different plans to mine so you just never know. The way business is these days and the way things are looking it was always my plan to take on another two or three full timers so unless something dramatic happens its likely just business as usual but with a different team at the helm. That's basically it so any questions?'

It did cross Rachael's mind that there was one glaring omission from the little speech she could ask considering she was the catalyst behind her boss's change of heart in the first place but just think of the can of worms that opened. Carolyn brain box Armstrong may just put two and two together and come up with the source of her little brother's new found confidence.

'So, your just taking the money and running Jim' from the assembled audience.

'After thirty years of hard graft, thrift and sacrifice do you begrudge my father that much' interrupted his now increasingly reliable and supportive daughter.

'The trick my friend is to bow out when the going is good. I can think of many over the years in business that outstayed their welcome only to pay a heavy price years later with their health. I'm no spring chicken. I'm pushing sixty but I won't be heading off to live in a mansion in deepest Surrey if that's what you're thinking.'

'Why don't you just let Joe takeover then.' Obviously none of the golden one's fan club and no doubt about it, a curved ball that his father simply never saw coming.

'Because...this is best for everyone. This is a family decision and everything I do will always be for the betterment of my family.'

Joe had to chip in sooner or later. Considering the eyes of the room were pretty much focused in his direction he likely felt the pressure of at least having to pay lip service to his father's change of heart if nothing else.

'I support my dad's decision. It's his business at the end of the day.' Lip service indeed. Hardly the most resounding of approvals it had to be said. Nobody else was fooled either and boy did Carolyn struggle to bite her tongue.

'Everything is still at the preliminary stage' added Jim. 'Nothing is set in stone but we're all familiar with Chinese whispers. As things develop or not as the case may be, I'll keep you informed.'

'So, how much are you getting as a matter of interest' which raised a few laughs and lightened the mood.

'Let me leave that one to the rumour mill. All I'll say is its good enough to allow me to sleep soundly in my bed at night and surely you won't begrudge me that.' Good answer dad she thought to herself. Maybe she chose law because of him after all.

That he was now cold-shouldered by his guests was completely self-evident. Alan was more just making up the numbers with Walsh now following his sidekicks lead by focusing on the more suggestive of the group. George he could see from afar fawning over what looked like two attractive store girls and Glenn the last he saw appeared to be sharing coffee in an overcrowded industrial style garden centre canteen. No doubting their marketing acumen or the fact of their ability at generating income but at the end of the day was this kind of place what genteel East Sussex really needed? Try as hard as he may he just couldn't buy into this kind of thing. What exactly was it? More style in inverted commas over substance. If there was such a thing as a lifestyle store then this would be it. Everything to buy that you never knew you needed but somehow destined to enhance your wellbeing. Affordable tat would be the only decent description that sprang to his mind. Still, while he was here and with time on his hands, worth taking note of a few manufacturers' names of their big ticket items and trying to find out in the time that was left as to who supplied the greenery. He had an idea. Meanwhile in the cafeteria Glenn probed Don a little bit further.

'So, back to my earlier question then Don. Given your level of discounting do these sites actually make money?'

'See for yourself!'

'With respect that wasn't what I asked you. Businesses that perpetually have to discount might not still be around in ten or twenty year's time. From a Council's perspective we're looking for the kind of long term growth that comes from those with a bit of history.'

'You're a smart man Glenn and I'm not evading your question. I'm a businessman first and foremost and successful guys like me don't share their secrets too well in case some Joe Schmo comes along and takes their idea to put into practice someplace else, but I'm prepared to make you the exception. We do these promos once every now and again, Crazy Sales days because it gets folks talking and maybe instead of just husband or husband and wife coming they'll bring along their own parents too and maybe some will come after the schools close and have their main meal here on a night. Then after eating they start shopping. But we've gone to the suppliers beforehand and said 'look we're doing a big promotion and expect to sell this and this so what kind of discount are you now going to give us?' Don't get me wrong we still take a small hit on the margin but that's outweighed by the benefit of added cash in the tills. Retails is all about cash flow at the end of the day Glenn, you know that as much as anyone. So, we make small amounts off food, then drinks. More off the ice creams then cold drinks outside! Then we make even more from the plants and even more from furniture. We got the kids' play areas, small animals centre. We now got an aquarium Glenn and an indoor butterfly centre making good revenue and ask yourself how much it costs to produce a Goddam butterfly? All these small profits from lots of different areas multiplied by seven days a week times two hundred and twenty four stores. I started off with eight stores ten years ago and this is me now. Tell me what I'm doing wrong Glenn?'

'Very impressive! You're listed as well right?'

'Sure. A thousand bucks invested five years ago would now be worth six and a half thousand as of this morning.'

'Now you tell me! But what about all your smaller competitors? I asked you this earlier. What chance does a small guy have against a place this size and who's to say you come along to Uxbridge and then proceed to put a couple of dozen of the smaller operators out of business. You create sixty jobs but the county then loses eighty. In the UK we call that cutting off our noses to spite our face.'

'Time you were put out your misery then. Let's hop back aboard the bus and all will be revealed. No less than ten minutes back along the way we came so if a small guy was right on our doorstep you'd assume we'd then crush them right? Your about to see one of those blink and you miss them kind of joints but still does one hell of a trade.'

Sure enough the small car park of Jackson's Plant Emporium was indeed overflowing. Positioned at the far corner of what looked like a run down industrial estate this looked the kind of place that bore no logic to its exact location considering the nature of the business ultimately related to being seen alongside the need for passing trade. Maybe garden centre logic over here happened to be more convoluted than the simpler way of doing things back home thought George. A fraction of the size of B-Smart further up the freeway here was a scaled down version of its competitor that could be measured more in terms of yardage and fractions of an acre. If first appearances were anything to go by the place had a healthy looking trade with the odd handful of staff seemingly busy enough. A throwback perhaps to the Armstrong's of old but minus even a half decent backdrop behind.

'Heh there Don! It's been a while.'

'Jackson how are you.' Shaking hands and hugging like long lost friends. An obvious deduction of the man bearing the company name and in the minds eye exactly what you'd expect a small town seat of the pants operator to look like. Authentic or manufactured? Someone had his doubts. Probably mid sixties, dungarees, grey beard, the archetypal small business front man and as amateur Detective Alan acutely observed, remarkably clean hands for someone for whom you would have expected the complete opposite.

'By the looks of it Don you've brought along some folks to meet me. Something tells me you're looking to open up someplace which is why you're all here right?'

'You read me like a book every time Jackson.' All the while Alan's just that little bit further back from the rest of the group. Eyes never leaving his adversary of which his opponent was acutely aware. Talk about really having eyes in the back of your head.

'These are our guests from England. It's only a flying visit but if its OK with you could you take five minutes of your time to explain how you've been affected by us good or bad. You know me Jackson. Whatever you got to say I'll take it on the chin.'

'I don't mind doing that for you Don. Your company's always been fair with me so I'll just tell you guys how it is for me at least. I've been here how long? Say twenty odd years and I don't mind telling you that when B-Smart first came here six years ago I was a worried man. To begin with it all went according to plan. Trade just collapsed but then I figured why try and compete on price and by doing the same things they do but in a smaller way. It just tanked and never made sense. So, what we do here is give the kind of advice you'll never get any place else. We know what we're talking about here and with respect to Lee and Don a load more than our illustrious neighbour along the way. So, customers come here for the kind of advice they know they can trust and since I decided to be myself rather than a pale imitation of somebody else I've never looked back. When B-Smart are busy I'm busy and you know what? When we're quiet here and decide to close early and go home its usually the case the B-Smart car park's pretty Goddam quiet when I drive past there too. Am I glad I have them as a neighbour? Put it this way it sure beats having a TOYSRUS or candy store any day.'

'Does that answer your question Glenn?'

'Certainly helped.'

'Anyone hungry?' from Don who by now has patently hit his stride.

'Thought you'd never ask' from George.

'In which case let's eat. Lunch will now be served at twenty five thousand feet. The airports fifteen minutes away and the jets on standby! We should reach the Georgia store around two o'clock.'

'Are you guys for real?'

'Trust me it's not always been this way George' from Lee. 'Many a time in the early days it was one rental car after another driving from state to state to check up on stores. This way's more expensive but also a whole load more economical in more ways than you can imagine. Also means we can still get back home to our beds at a reasonable time.'

'Thanks Jackson, see you sometime soon. Back onboard the B-Smart bus folks' Don now loving every minute. Not even yet half the day gone and still not a foot wrong considering everything achieved thus far.

'George you got a minute' asked Lee.

'If we get back to Florida at a decent time tonight which we should do what do you think about hooking up with the two girls from the store later?'

'What, you mean the two blonds from before we left?'

'The very same two.'

'How do we do that?'

'Because I'm good friends with one of them if you know what I mean.'

'You dark horse.'

'I got to let my hair down same as everyone else. So, you up for some fun?'

'I'm always up for a bit of that.'

Andrea knew to expect a call.

Walking across the tarmac to the plane still enough time to grab Glenn's ear before the likelihood of being sidelined yet again.

'Glenn is it an act or are you actually falling for any of this?'

'What are you talking about Alan?'

'This! This vortex of crap the pair of you seem to be falling into.'

'Alan lighten up for fuck's sake. I'm actually enjoying this and it's about time you did too. What's your beef?'

'That bloody Jack what's his face back there.'

'Jackson.'

'Yes Jackson. Grandpa Walton lookalike! How long do you think it took them to come up with a name like that? Two minutes at most! Now why would a two bit plant shop owner on an industrial site be bosom buddies with the CEO of a multinational listed on the NASDAQ? It doesn't make sense.'

'So, CEOs only know other CEOs. Is that what you're saying?'

'Glenn how come you're not getting this? It's all fake. I'm telling you…'

'Alan your negativity is now beginning to grate. I'm being serious here. Lighten up and that's an order.'

'Michael can you hold these trolley's steady while I load them up with bedding plants for tomorrow. Ten minutes tops.'

'I'm finished for the day. Can you not find someone else?'

Just what he needed as he walked across the storage yard on his way home. Not from Joe, he was hiding inside but from one of his brother's trusted cohorts among the ground staff.

'Fair enough but don't blame me when Joe starts kicking off in the morning that the displays are still to be finished.'

'For fuck's sake ok.'

Successful subterfuge on the part of this particular store assistant who's card would be marked for future reference but in the meantime another ones of life's hair raising experiences for young Michael to live through.

The thick wooden door slamming behind would be the first alarm bell to ring but already too late. At the same time as his brain would be sending the signal to the legs to get the hell out an arm appeared from nowhere to twist one of his own arms up behind his back with another hand grabbing his neck to frog march forward to the awaiting half barrel of water several feet away. A knee to the back of Michaels legs, no time to draw breath and before he knew it he was under. Had the shock of it all allowed him to figure anything out other than staying alive then whoever had their knee on his back knew exactly what they were doing! That was the trouble with being the younger of the two. Yet what chance did this young lad have against the fully developed and stockier built rugby playing brother. With every part of his anatomy in lockdown the one free flailing arm was of little consequence try as hard as he may to rise up for much needed breath.

The head would be under for exactly ten seconds. Joe timing his siblings ongoing agony on his watch. His henchman stood guard outside to raise the alarm should anyone come calling. If only Rachael had known what was happening to her accomplice as she walked past the sentry guard on her way home with nothing other than a smile and a goodnight. For Michael some much needed air at long last.

'You know what you fucking little shit. This is all your fault. Off you had to go and open your big mouth about the Americans coming and now look what's happened. Pleased are you? Now I'm out a fucking job.'

To speak or to inhale and he chose the latter. Correct call as back down under he went. This time would be for longer, fifteen seconds. Even the sentry guard outside was beginning to feel a bit tetchy. The extra air in the lungs second time around had sure helped by the time Joe hauled his brothers head back up by the hair.

'That's what you get you little prick for costing me my job. You any idea what this place was for me?'

'Do it.'

'Do what?'

'Just do it Joe.'

'What are you talking about? Do fucking what?' Noses practically touching the contempt Joe felt for his brother was almost palpable.

'Finish me off. Do it again but this time do it for longer.'

'Is that what you want?'

'Yeh do it...but go all the way this time. What's up Joe? Lost your fucking bottle' as he proceeded to spit in his elder brother's face.

So, back under he went but not for long, the sentry guard coming to his rescue this time to drag Joe off.

'Come on Joe you've made your point' from a worried accomplice. 'Come on that's enough.'

'What's up Joe, lost your nerve' from a panting Michael. 'Thought you were going to go all the way?' For the first time in the inferior younger one's life, he actually saw fear.

'Joe leave him alone, you've made your point.'

'Not as tough as you think you are. Are you Joe? You don't need to worry I won't go saying anything.'

With the faintest of parting smiles Joe turned on his heels but for the trio in the shed that day and at that time the winner was clear. The youngest had made a point and would now be left well alone. That his father would pay a heavy price for his blatant favouritism would soon be made abundantly clear.

Back at the Breakers the trio, weary and still in their work clothes shared a cold beer.

'To give the Yanks some credit' said George. 'They do know how to pack a lot in to a single day. Back home that would have been dragged out to three days at the very least.'

'And still not over yet' from Glenn. 'Remember we're being picked up again in less than an hour.'

'Would you two mind if I gave this one a miss. I'm what's commonly known as pooped.'

'Plus the fact you're not really buying into any of this are you? Since day one you've always had some form of scepticism about the whole project Alan.'

'Don't deny it and to be fair to you I don't have anything concrete to go on either…yet! Just that somewhere along the line I smell a dirty big rat and I'm not just referring to Trenchman. I mean the whole damn thing. Something's not adding up and its annoying the shit out of me.'

'I'm nowhere near as negative as Alan, but I know we'll have to take a stance at some point when it comes to the land. I think they expect to pay buttons.'

'I'm ok with negotiating that part, notwithstanding I personally think it's about time our county was shaken up with some fresh ideas and to be fair Alan no one could ever accuse me of following the pack. With you I think it's just personal. You and Lee! Two cynical old lawyers with one trying to out point score the other.'

'Rubbish. More like I'm able to see through the charm whereas you two appear to be falling in love with the lifestyle being offered up.'

'I don't mind being schmoozed but trust me, I won't be taken for a fool either. So, George looks like it's a seafood platter for me and Don while you and your best new buddy go clubbing.'

'Don't be daft. Somewhere to eat and probably just a few drinks.'

'Let's just see how fresh you look over breakfast in the morning shall we?'

'Remind me. What's on in the morning?'

'Nothing till lunchtime then we start getting down to the negotiations. Times finally come to crunch some numbers. We can prepare after breakfast before we meet them here at one. I don't see me being too late so George just behave yourself and come back all in one piece. I need you fully compos mentis.'

'Of course I will and don't worry Alan I won't be giving away any trade secrets. Like you said Glenn it's us that hold all the cards and it'll be interesting to see once the shows over just how much it is that they're really prepared to offer. Listen you two I have my flaws but I know land values in every part of our county inside out. Lee can schmooz me as much as he likes because he'd confident and he's on his home turf but there's no way I'll be letting them snap that site up for a song.'

'Good to hear it. In which case here's hoping for a good night until another conglomerate follows B-Smart's lead and invites us over for a repeat performance. Sure I can't tempt you Alan?'

'Given that I don't like them and they clearly don't like me it's hardly worth it is it? You two youngsters go and enjoy yourselves. It's an early night for me.'

Not quite so early to bed as he had made out. There was still unfinished business. As the other two spruced themselves up before heading out Alan thanked his lucky stars that he still had one hell of a memory for numbers. Heading up to his room time was now of the essence.

'Dave…Hi its Alan…yes still here and the bad news Dave is that its still very warm and sunny…yeh I thought you'd like that one. Listen I'm phoning from the hotel and it's a five star joint so you can imagine how much I'll be paying for the call so I'll be brief. Tell me are you still on good terms with that friend of yours who works in the square mile?…You are? Thank God for that. Dave I need a favour and I need it like yesterday. Can you ask him to do some digging? I need the low down on a company called B-Smart in the States…Yes the very same ones that brought us over here and seem to be spending money like there's no tomorrow. All I'm asking is are they as profitable as they claim to be. I don't want us getting our fingers burnt with the adverse PR if they end up being a bunch of cowboys. Truth is I think we're being strung along but I seem to be on my own with this one…Thanks I appreciate that Dave and dinner's on me when I get back. Cheers.'

One down, two to go.

'Hi this is Alan Gill in Room 603. Could you organise me a car hire please, say 9 am tomorrow morning. I'll just need it for a few hours. Nothing grand in fact the smaller and more inconspicuous the better'.

The third phase would now have to wait till the morning. How to explain a brief disappearing act without arousing suspicion was the final issue that his mind could surely figure come daybreak. That his superior would have enough to contend with in wrestling with his own conscience would ensure no further explanation required.

For their final morning in the hotel Alan would most likely be eating alone.

He never probed any further but why would he? If the charade was that Andrea took care of the company PR then so be it. By looks alone she was already adding a touch of sparkle to this evening's proceedings as was obviously Don's intention but this was how he got things done. A combination of charm, charisma and blatant manipulation! For Glenn the trip had been a revelation and validation for him of the whole capitalist process. The trick was all about surrounding yourself with the right people, an area where, when he returned to the UK, he dramatically needed to raise his game. No doubt about it Don and Lee were a good team and this trip had simply brought it home that if his vision for the county were to be realised he badly needed a strong number two. With Alan something of a dinosaur and George a loose cannon the search would begin in earnest. For the time being just savour the moment. Window seat of a waterfront restaurant overlooking the Florida Quays and in the company of a multimillionaire and his glamorous mistress! Power and wealth does occasionally blur the vision of those of lesser means and safe to say by now Glenn had become truly intoxicated. As much by the experience as the eye contact from the most charming of dining companions.

'What do you think then Glenn? One thing the Quays are not short of is restaurants but I came here years ago and have never gone anywhere else since.'

'Excellent choice and given there's not a spare seat in the house I'd guess the food is just as good.'

'We love coming here' from Andrea. There appeared to be no attempt from either to disguise the fact she was Don's bit on the side. Hardly spoken of in terms of Chief Executive and subordinate!

'Great vibe to the place and you could be a CEO like Don, a teacher or a cab driver and no one would bat an eye.' This was Andrea giving it her we're all equal at the end of the day kind of thing although the menu prices were saying the complete opposite.

'I leave entertainment expenses to my accountants Glenn so let's all enjoy the finest food this place has to offer and trust me it really is that good. One small request if you'll allow me to be so bold. I've already pre ordered your main course.'

'Ahh, which is? As if I don't already know.'

'He's been looking forward to this for days' from Andrea. Just the sort of thing one would share with the company PR person.

'All I'll say, I hope it does justice to what you're used to back home.'

'You're always full of surprises Don.'

'I'll testify to that' from Andrea which brought a knowing smile from both her male companions.

Stinging George would be a much more straightforward affair and more up Trenchman's street. Just like George he liked them young.

Dinner at a run of the mill steakhouse with the two young fillies where one of the original girls had now been replaced by someone obviously a few years younger. With sufficient alcohol now swirling around in George's system what little inhibitions there were had now all but seeped away. Heading off downtown to a backstreet club Lee had already pre arranged to hook up with another one of Andrea's girls but this one for his consumption only so George therefore left alone in the company of two much younger girls who quite blatantly were leaving nothing to his imagination. By now delusional enough to believe that being handsome and English were sufficient enough ingredients to have their knickers practically placed at his feet.

Having been plied with enough alcohol the invitation back to their apartment was simply a given and the pair quickly set to task with porn experience precision. A quick undress for one then down on her knees she went leaving the other free to set the controls to record. Two cameras, one wide angle and the other zoom lens were to highlight their acting skills perfectly. Only on the flight home and with ample time to reflect would he remember that the sex did appear to be more adventurous than what he was used to paying for. Not only for the victims own gratification but for Don's. At a thousand bucks a piece each the girls had been under strict instruction from Andrea to perform or else.

For Glenn, at Andrea's insistence the process tonight would be one of slow seduction in contrast to the more primitive approach deployed several blocks across town. Who was her paymaster to deny her the odd indulgence if she saved him tens of millions with each gullible married landowner that came his way! She liked Glenn but then most available women did. What's not to be impressed by that rare species of male that somehow seem to improve with age! In London she thought he was handsome but by now a definite upgrade to distinguished. Not the only female in the restaurant who thought so either given the odd eye happening to stray. At least the odds were high that she'd ham him all to herself albeit with Don watching in on the action from the suite above. Here was yet another one of life's good guys at the pinnacle of his looks and profession about to have his conscience tested not once but twice in the space of twelve hours if you include the bargaining chip offered by tomorrow afternoon as his get out of jail card. The price Andrea now paid for an association that extended far beyond what was good for her own sense of self-worth was that her scruples were now as worthless as those of her boss.

Not that the fish and chips that had arrived as the main meal came as a complete surprise but served atop newspaper as is the old British way a nice touch.

'You're a smooth operator Don. Talk about attention to detail.'

'Just hope it does what you're used to eating back home justice.'

It did cross Glenn's mind to mention that his wife would be the first to hear of tonight's meal upon his return but chose instead to avoid. The mention of anyone's spouse this evening could prove to be a conversation killer.

'Oh, it's as good as but you wouldn't expect me to say its better. Not that many people would likely eat it with wine as nice or probably as expensive as this.'

As if on cue wine waiter appeared for replenishment. Under strict instruction to top up glasses when they dropped to around a quarter! Not that they wanted Glenn pissed, he was too self-disciplined to allow himself to be shown up but tonight's location, ambience and alcohol all lent themselves perfectly to creating a certain kind of mood. Just the type to allow even the most controlled of men to temporarily drop their guard. The night cap of twenty year old malts back at the Breakers would prove to be his tipping point. Patently obvious to all three that even the most influential of the group was now surplus to requirements, he made his excuse of an early night. He could either watch events unfold live on the monitor rigged up in the room or wait till the morning. He chose the former. A long time since Andrea had looked so eager to please.

'So, what does an Executive PR person do exactly?'

'You know I'm nothing to do with that Glenn so we can drop the pretense.'

'Ok. So, your what could diplomatically be described as a rich man's mistress.'

'You strike me as a man that's ever the diplomat on most occasions.'

'If it keeps the peace then yes but not afraid to step on toes or take risks when I think I can.'

Subtle hint number one for Andrea!

'I know Don likes you a lot. He said you'd be great for his business. Just the type to steer a steady ship were his exact words.'

'In preference to Lee?'

'I'm saying nothing.'

'When people say nothing it usually tells you everything you need to know.'

'You're smart Glenn. Smart, intelligent and kind! So, why is it guys like you are always taken?'

'Probably because women like you choose the wrong guys to begin with then end up having to play catch up.'

'Astute as always.'

Not so astute to notice Alan observing from afar in his own inimitable amateur sleuth kind of way. Guessing correctly his boss would likely return on time and have one for the road before bed he'd planned and looked forward to joining but in the present circumstance perhaps best not. She looked strangely familiar. Just where the hell from?

'Would you be embarrassed Glenn if I were to ask if you were available for lunch tomorrow?'

'No, not embarrassed but the reality is we have our parting meeting with Don, your semi other half at lunchtime after which its bags packed then home.'

'To your wife?'

'Yes that's quite correct. My wife and two daughters.'

'Ladies' man indeed. So, would you still be embarrassed then if I asked you instead to my room to join me for a final night cap?'

'Your room as in also Don's room?'

'God no! Believe it or not he always books me a separate room as sometimes I just like my own space.'

'Don't we all.'

'Indeed…so what's it to be?'

'…I think I could be tempted.'

Hunch number one had proven itself to be remarkably accurate. Within the space of a day, Jackson's Plant Emporium had reverted back to an empty shell on an industrial park ready for the next set of mugs to come along and be taken in by the butter wouldn't melt in the mouth approach of everyone's favourite grandpa. Whoever had cleared the place and he strongly suspected the outfit responsible, had done a great job with not a broken plant pot in sight. The stained outline of where the sign screwed in to the shop fascia still patently visible with the sign itself no doubt wrapped in a cupboard someplace till next time around. Glenn should have listened and a temporary flashback for Alan of the pair making their way across the airport tarmac and being told to lighten up. Hunch number two already bore all the hallmarks of predictability.

Needless to say visitors thin on the ground in the B-Smart car park this morning. The promotional sign now gone and no doubt probably now stored in the same cupboard as the plant emporium one marked fake merchandising. Given the timing of his visit was practically identical to the day before but no knock on effect from repeat trade it seemed. Just what was yesterday all about? Once inside staff thin on the ground to say the least given the scale of the place and it generally looked scruffy. Overall impression being that the place had just been left as it was from the day before. Into the restaurant where the appearance bore no resemblance to the highly efficient machine so evident from yesterday. What little business there may have been this morning resulted in tables still to be cleared and waiting staff spartan. Was there any real need to go check the welfare of the animals? He decided against as likely too depressing. The type of place it would appear that was likely losing money hand over fist irrespective of how they dressed things up. How they kept these places going told a story there was more to B-Smart than they were letting on.

Now a nasty feeling beginning to emerge when it came to the antics of his colleagues from last night! No sign of either at breakfast, not that he expected George but to be missing Glenn was definitely out of character. At least no awkward questions to answer over his temporary disappearing act! Time he headed back to the Breakers to make some calls and first up would be B-Smart HQ themselves. He could be equally duplicitous when he tried albeit with lousy fake American accent.

'Heh good morning. Could you put me through to Accounts Payable please?'

128

'You are?'

'East Coast Plants and Shrubs. It's about our overdue account.'

'One moment please.'

'Hi there, can I help you?'

'Yeh its Billy Foreman from East Coast Plants and Shrubs. I'm chasing up payment on my account.'

'Which depot?'

'Florida.'

'You got to be joking man what's the problem?'

'Problem is pal I got a wife and kids to support and I can't fucking survive on fresh air.'

'Well, you'll have to use your initiative then bud. You know the rules, you signed up to them.'

'Rules are I need the money.'

'Not for another ninety days pal. This is what you signed for and we got your signature in black and white.'

'No concessions?'

'I'll let you keep supplying us. That's the biggest concession your ever going to get.'

'You got a heart of gold.'

'Anything else I can help you with other than suggest that chasing up payment is never a good idea if you want to stay on our right side.'

'No, told me everything I need to know.'

'Take it easy pal.'

'I will thanks.'

All that was left now was friend Dave to fill in the missing blanks.'

The difference a few days can make. Without the weight of the world on his shoulders Jim now looked a visibly relieved man. By Carolyn changing his mind he'd resolved his three main issues in one fell swoop. That Ann should avoid some kind of breakdown, Joe revealing his true colours and having a discounter as a next door neighbour. A fourth issue also taken care of if you include remaining in the local Rotary Club with reputation intact being seen to sell up at exactly the right time. Play his cards right and he may very well go down in local folklore as one of the shrewdest to come out of the town if everything goes according to plan and there appeared no reason on paper at least as to why not.

The newly appointed twenty year old family legal advisor was now rewarded for her ingenuity and allegiance by being at her father's side for this morning's all important second meeting with mysterious middle men. Hopefully now shedding some more light on just who exactly was prepared to pay handsomely for having their name above the front door. For the sake of her sanity and her nerves Ann deployed a distinctly hands-off approach.

'All I want to see is the cheque. You two do the rest' would be her sum contribution over breakfast. Mood lightened by the absence of the prodigal one who was off likely licking his wounds in the arms of his latest bed partner. Not that either parent appeared particularly perturbed at this precise moment in time that their eldest was off in a sulk. More pressing engagements and deep breaths all round for father and daughter as word reached that invited guests had arrived.

'Good luck dad' from the youngest and increasingly confident of the clan.

'Thanks son. By the time you see me again I'll be a millionaire.'

'And I'll be the son of a millionaire.'

'And I'll be the millionaire's wife.'

'So, looks like I'm going to be the person that looks after it all for you to stop yourselves going off the rails' from the smartest of the clan.

'Michael go and ask Rachael for some bank paying in slips. I want to see the look on their faces when I pay in a cheque for two million pounds.'

'Mum I don't quite think this is how it works' chipped in Carolyn. 'There's a long way to go before it even gets remotely close to that stage.'

'Well, they better have some money on them' from Jim 'as I was proposing we all take the day off tomorrow and head off somewhere. Joe can look after things on his own for a change. Ok Carolyn are you ready?'

'Lead the way' and a knowing wink to her younger brother on leaving. This would be the first of many secrets between the pair.

As per last time the same duo. Two good looking professional guys who also liked to dress for the part with their polished suits, crisp white shirt and matching ties! Just the type that likely moved in the kind of business circles to which Carolyn aspired. This was her being given her first taste of negotiation and the art of making the deal. The kind of thing that normally happened upon qualifying and not two years before! The smile exchanged with the better looking of the two who now appeared ready to engage was one of equals. She already liked his style.

'Thanks for inviting us back Mr Armstrong. We were pleased to get the message when it came through that you'd had a change of heart.'

'I guess you must have planted a seed somewhere about knowing when to get the hell out.'

'No one as far as I know has ever looked back on their life and wished they had spent more time in the office. I think it was the right call.'

'Your right again! Obviously a wise man which is why they picked you for doing these deals. So, are you still looking to buy?'

'Yes, we are. Or should I say our client is.'

'Well, let's get started then. This is my daughter Carolyn who's standing in for her mother. Carolyn's studying law at university.'

'Are you really? In which case we'll have to make sure and be on top of our brief then.'

Predictable but at least it raised a smile. The type of guy that must have a line for just about every occasion and easy going with it. Used on this occasion to draw them in before landing the knockout blow.'

'So, where are we then?' from Jim. Eager to get the ball rolling.

'A slight change or seen from your perspective a more dramatic change on our client's proposition from last we met.'

'Which is?'

'Which is Mr Armstrong that our client is still keen but given their size have to take account of prevailing headwinds coming closer alongside the fact that the garden centre business is on the cusp of becoming seriously competitive therefore an erosion of margins is ever likely…'

'Ok, ok this is all very eloquently detailed but what your leading up to is the fact that we're about to be offered less.'

'Correct.'

'How much?'

'A million.'

'You are kidding?'

'Deadly serious I'm afraid Mr Armstrong. This highlights just how concerned our clients are for the future and they employ the best when it comes to economic forecasting.'

'But my business is booming.'

'For now that is' from the reliably more reticent of the two. 'A million pounds still leaves you in profit which might not be the case the longer you hang around.'

'So, you dangle the carrot of a generous offer to hook my parents in then start to play them once they return having changed their minds. The offer of two million was never there to start with was it? You should be ashamed of yourselves if this is how you do business' from Carolyn. Furious but still restrained.

'You have a vivid imagination young lady' from the smoother of the two who's stint atop the pedestal had proven to be short lived.

'Please don't try and wriggle out of this by being patronising. It won't wash.'

'I'm being nothing of the sort and there's nothing I can do if you happen to be thin-skinned but we are merely messengers acting on instruction. I actually take issue with your assertion that we're somehow behaving like a couple of secondhand car salesmen. Nothing could be further from the truth and to be fair it's not as if we're holding a gun to anyone's head is it?'

'So, I get a million pounds less and you expect us all to keep living here and be happy with the fact?'

'No, the offer is for the whole site Mr Armstrong of which the house is part. Means you can start a whole new chapter of your life elsewhere and start afresh.'

'I feel insulted. Let's just end it here.'

'I understand you're upset' from Mr Smooth 'but as things change in the economy perhaps you'll understand why our clients had to amend the figure. Remember it's still a generous offer.'

'No its not' from Carolyn, now feeling her father's pain. 'I like your analogy of secondhand car salesmen because that's exactly what I think the pair of you are.'

'As you wish. We won't take up any more of your time.'

Only one pressing concern left for Jim. Just how on earth would he face Ann!

That George would turn up looking like shit came as no great surprise when the team reconvened for the eleven o'clock debrief. That George's days were numbered upon his return now a forgone conclusion. Great company, a character and sharp as a tack when switched on, his natural charisma had got him thus far but now left clearly punching above his weight proving himself to be reckless and utterly unreliable.

That Alan appeared to be the only one with a clear head would be his colleagues saving grace as Glenn's mind at this crucial moment in time was also clearly elsewhere. No prizes to Alan for understanding why. An imposing man when he needed to be, this morning Glenn was coming across as distant and like many who had gone before falling victim to Andrea's charms, he carried all the hallmarks of a haunted man.

'Looks like I'm the only one who managed a full eight hours sleep judging by appearances. Half expected to see you at least at breakfast Glenn?'

'The meal from last night managed to sustain me through the morning and I think all the running around finally caught up with me if I'm being honest. It's not as if any of us could be described as spring chickens any longer is it?'

George may have bought into that line but Alan knew different and time to enlighten his superior before he commits himself to the greatest mistake of his career on top of that committed against his marriage.

'Ok so before we go in to see the gruesome twosome it's time I filled the pair of you in with some homework I've been doing since last night. Glenn you told me yesterday afternoon to lighten up, well see what you make of this! While you were likely still fast asleep this morning, I hired a car to go visit the very same B-Smart store we visited yesterday. On the way I stopped off at good old Jackson's Plant Emporium. You know the one, the store that feeds off its illustrious larger competitor. Well, all I saw this time around was an empty yard with a bloody big padlock on the gates. Completely stripped bare and that included the fucking sign as well. After that I went along to B-Smart which I can tell you bore very little resemblance to anything we saw yesterday morning. All they did was put on a show, nothing other than that.'

'They were always going to put on a show for us Alan. It's called marketing.'

'There's a world of difference George between marketing and deception. Get real. Hate to say it but it still gets even worse. So, I called an old friend of mine who has contacts in the city. Called him to give the run over B-Smart and see what he could come up with. Transpires there's been rumours about B-Smart for years as to just how exactly they keep producing the numbers and opening so many stores. The term smoke and mirrors was used. Retail makes them nothing. The big bucks comes with the land where sites are bulldozed and sold on to developers for housing making them a killing in the process.'

'Lee mentioned that to me before' said George.

'But did he tell you how they manage to buy these sites so cheaply?'

'Nope!'

'Thought not. They really do acquire them for practically nothing and we're talking serious prime sites. No one outside of B-Smart has figured that part out yet.'

'Well, it's not going to happen on my patch' from an increasingly jaded looking Glenn who's rose tinted specs had finally begun to lift. 'So, is that everything?'

'Afraid not!'

'Jesus Christ you have been busy. Talk about having the bit between your teeth.'

'I called their Head Office. Pretended to be a supplier chasing up payment where I was basically told to fuck off if I wanted to continue supplying the goods. Their payment terms are one hundred and twenty days. Four bloody months wait to get paid. It could bankrupt many of them which of course is what B-Smart want. Now I never had the opportunity to hire a jet and fly up to Georgia but somehow I think the situation there will be the exact same. 'So, its not looking so good now is it?'

'Not now it's not. I owe you an apology. You were right and I was wrong' from Glenn.

'One final point then as if you haven't heard enough and this is tricky for me.'

'Spit it out. After everything so far I can take it.'

'Last night Glenn I came down to the Bar expecting to find at least one of you for a late night drink. I saw you having a drink...'

'Yes that's right. I was having a drink with Don's PR Executive which is who I'd been having dinner with. Both Don and her! We all came back and he hit the sack early so we shared a couple of drinks.'

'I thought I had seen her before...and actually I have. We all have.'

'While here?'

'No, London.'

'London?'

'The very one! The Dorchester hotel to be precise.'

'I don't remember that.'

'Yeh I think I do now you come to mention it' from George.

'Enlighten me then?'

'She was at our adjoining table. I remember her strutting her stuff as she walked past and kept looking over. Was she blond then?'

'Likely a wig George but I'm sure it was her Glenn. I just knew she looked familiar.'

Not that Glenn was listening any more. The penny had dropped and he knew what was coming.

'Glenn are you ok?'

'Can someone get me a glass of water?'

'What's up? You've gone all white.'

The call came through for Lee in Don's room. Good timing with only minutes to spare till meeting up for a final time downstairs.

'Hi Lee, its Philip Bowman. How are you?'

'Am good Phil. Maybe better when I hear how it went?'

'It was father and daughter this time around. A bit of a firecracker with aspirations of becoming a lawyer.'

'Good for her. Pushed for time this end Phil so just tell me how it went?'

'We passed on the revised offer and not unsurprisingly it was rebuked.'

'That's ok. Things have gone according to plan over here. A few loose ends to be tied up then let's see how this Armstrong family react to us opening up on their doorstep. There's a lot of mileage left as far as this deal's concerned.'

'I hope your right.'

'I hope so too because your fee depends on it. Keep me posted Phil.'

'Will do.'

He knew that Glenn knew. Always in the eyes as his convicted fraudster of a father used to say, so for Don the name of the game now was to get the meeting over and done with as soon as to save further embarrassment and let the minions work on the finer detail. Both parties reconvening at dead on the allotted time in the small meeting room Lee had booked well out of sight and earshot considering the subject matter shortly to unfold. Tense to say the least, the Brits seated at one side of the rectangular table and the two Americans the other. As yet still no words spoken but Don now more brusque in tone would lead the way.

'I think you've seen enough of our operations and enjoyed our hospitality so, unless there are any objections, shall we start talking some numbers?'

'Actually I do have a couple of points which require clarification if you don't mind Don' from a now more highly motivated Alan.

'As you may. What would they be? Shoot.'

'Let's talk about our visit yesterday morning and Jackson's Plant Emporium where you seemed to have what could best be described as an affable relationship with its owner.'

'Yes.'

'Which in the space of less than twenty four hours now sits as an empty yard with padlocked gates.'

A clearly unsettled Don now looking in Lee's direction who's ability to think on his feet that much faster.

'Jackson served notice a while back that he would be moving to new premises. I guess he just decided to go sooner than we expected. Maybe you just missed him.'

'Maybe' from Alan. The two lawyers with blatant antipathy now ready to do battle.

'So, when I visited your B-Smart this morning it would be fair to say it appeared different from yesterday.'

'In what way Alan?'

'Most noticeably no customers for a start. Perhaps they had all deserted your store to go visit Jacksons new one' which brought a mild laugh from his colleagues much to Lee's annoyance.

'I think you'll find that in Florida a Thursday is our quietest day much as you want to make light of the matter. I think it would be fair to say Alan that you have never embraced our company or ideals so I guess your cynicism comes as no great surprise.'

'Oh, when it comes to B-Smart I am very cynical but it appears I'm not alone in that department. For example from what I gather several financial analysts of some note are questioning your liquidity and from what I saw this morning why am I not surprised. Then again, had I been able to book your expensively leased company jet and flown to Georgia no doubt I would have seen a repeat of yesterday's outstanding performance…or perhaps not. You make money from selling off sites that you buy for next to nothing on to developers. The only question that now needs answered is how you do it. You maintain your operations by holding suppliers to ransom taking an average of four months to pay which buys you time to sell off land that generates the income and keeps the whole charade ticking over.'

'Your use of the word charade is highly offensive considering your occupation.'

'Prove me wrong then Lee!'

Time for Don to reveal the opposite side to his more jovial personality.

'Listen friend I don't have to prove anything to anyone. Not you, your Goddam analysts, suppliers or fucking partners in crime sat next to you. You've been here, you've tasted the high life so it's time we cut the crap and just got down to business and did the fucking deal. I don't have time any longer to horse shit around with endless discussion. I'm a busy man, I got things on my plate so I'll tell you where I am right. On this piece of paper is an offer for the site in Uxbridge that we intend buying as you say in England lock, stock and fucking barrel. No ninety nine year leases or anything that comes attached with bells and whistles. Just straight outright ownership! This is the amount' as he slid the folded paper across the table in Glenn's direction to turn over.

'You are out of your mind' from Glenn. 'The local authority would never sanction this in a million years.'

'Well, you better work on them then because that's all you're getting.'

'In which case I'll thank you for your hospitality although considering your negotiating style it appears to have been a complete waste of our time coming here in the first place.'

'Sure - fine by us.'

'That's it then' from Glenn. 'No point in wasting any more of each other's time.'

'Oh, just one thing if you please.' Lee choosing his moment to turn the screw.

'I have here two envelopes. One for you, Glenn and the other for George. I suggest you study the contents and consider carefully what might happen should these photographs fall into the wrong hands. Someone's wife for example and then there's your local newspaper to consider. George you are aware that one of the girls you were with last night was under the age of eighteen? In this state sexual activity of the kind you were engaged in last night legally constitutes rape. This alongside the practices you engaged in were tantamount to buggery could well result in a seriously long incarceration. On your part Glenn, Don informs me that Andrea avoids all methods of contraception so who knows what may be the net result of last night's extra marital activity. By the way those are copies. We have the originals as well as tape recordings.'

'You pair of scheming cunts' and as Glenn stood the meeting room door opened for a couple of heavies to make their presence felt. A button had been pressed somewhere.

'I've been called worse than that trust me. There's transport waiting outside to take you to the airport and I'll get my legal team to start drafting contracts. These will be faxed through by the end of next week. The offer of one hundred thousand pounds is not up for revision so consider the matter closed.' With this Lee simply closed his briefcase and stood gesturing his visitors to leave.

From Don 'No hard feelings Glenn. By fair means or foul play. It's just business at the end of the day.'

'Or blackmail depending on how you look at it.'

It would be a long flight home.

Chapter 5

'Mr Armstrong's definitely not going to like this.'

Comment from one of the farm shop girls as they sorted out the morning's local papers before taking a handful through to the restaurant for customers to read for free with their breakfast. Joe's first policy decision since taking sole charge on all matters operational and his initial foray into the economic no brainer that was loss leader retailing. That father would actually have wanted any of his clientele to see this morning's front page headline was highly debatable.

'AMERICAN GARDEN CENTRE GIANT GIVEN GREEN LIGHT FOR UXBRIDGE'

'I see what you mean' from the more mature of the two shop assistants. 'Not as if it's going to do us any favours either is it?'

'What - you mean he'll cut back on staff?'

'Of course he will. It's the first thing business people do - cut back on the workers to save their own skin and now the locals will see this headline and hang back waiting to see if they can save some money when the new place opens. I heard on the grapevine that the deal for this place fell through because they wanted his house as well so he told them to go get stuffed.'

'Poor old bugger. He must be tearing his hair out what little he's got left.'

Still blissfully unaware of the breaking story Jim was about to find out the hard way. Talk about the perfect way to ruin someone's tea break.

'So, read this and tell me your still not concerned' as Ann virtually throws front page atop her husband's early morning sandwich.

'I can't believe this!'

'No, neither can I considering less than four months ago you turned down an offer for two million quid for us to get the hell out of here. Now you've left us all to die a slow painful death instead. How the hell did it come to this Jim? Like I'm living in the middle of a bloody nightmare.'

'Mum it's not our market so don't go getting all upset. We're all about quality here' from Joe.

'And we're expensive.'

'You get what you pay for in this life Michael.'

'So, when the new place down the road start selling bedding plants at half the price we sell them for who's garden centre are people then going to visit. Same plants different prices.'

'Nice to know we can count on your support then little brother.'

'You're missing the point.'

'Watch your mouth.'

'Oh, here we go again. What are you going to do this time? Break one of my arms?' Quizzical look from the parents as Joe simply shakes his head. The intimidation tactics of old no longer cutting it quite the way they used to.

'He's got a perfectly valid point Joe.' Supported by his sister.

'Not like you to perpetually take Mikey's side Carolyn.'

'Well, if you three continue to keep arguing then we really are up fucking shit street.'

'Mum!! Mind your language.'

'It's the way I'm feeling about this and it's not good. You three perpetually at each other's throats hardly helps either. Maybe the reduced offer meant those guys knew something at the time that we didn't.'

'Possibly but I doubt it' from Carolyn. 'I still think they were just chancing their arm because you called them back. You did the right thing Dad. What's to say they wouldn't keep changing their mind with reduced offers to wear you down?'

'Here's what we're going to do.' Jim now standing for effect as he always does when he's got things on his mind. The very act of being on his feet somehow brought clarity to the matter in hand and helped to impose authority.

'We keep doing what we're known for and play to our strengths. If we're seen to attempt to copy anyone it just sends out the wrong signals that we are panicking. I don't doubt there's going to be an initial blip but these things come and go. Just remember how long I've been here and I'm not about to give up yet.'

'Fighting talk Dad.'

'And I expect the same from you Joe. It's you that holds the reins now that I handed them over a while back so don't become complacent or take your foot off the pedal. I want to see things continually up to the highest of standards and that goes for everyone. Each member of staff out there's now going to be watching us all like hawks to see how we react so we put on a united front. Joe's right, we operate in a different market and that's the line we stick to. Everyone understand?'

A uniform 'yes' from everyone concerned but the faces were speaking a different story.

Ann was right though. From initial heresay in a garden magazine to the first JCB arriving on site all in the space of just over five months. How exactly an unknown multinational came from nowhere to landing such a prize spot in such a short space of time would be the hottest topic doing the rounds within the local business community. Seemed to be one rule for the big boys and another for everyone else considering the length of time it took the average householder to get planning permission for the most humble of extensions to their average three bedroomed semi. Certainly helped when the main man at the helm of the decision making process and one of his key lieutenants happened to be in hoc to the business intending to set up shop. Glenn had no option but to obey instruction. Hands tied firmly behind back. The fallout from flatly refusing could have been catastrophic and it was to his dinosaur number two Alan that he would turn to for guidance under the proviso that Glenn moved on to pastures new when this was over and recommend his legal deputy take the reins.

'If they want to play silly buggers with me Glenn then let them' from Alan. 'I'll just fight fire with fire and leave the rest to the analysts. You've been tainted by this and the longer you stay here the more you remain in their clutches.'

'I had you marked down as a wooly stick in the mud Alan. Truth be told I just took you over to run through any boring detail they may have thrown our way but your infinitely shrewder than I gave you credit for. So, fair play! You showed us both up and now I need you more than ever.'

'So, it's time for the pair of you to dig yourselves out of the enormous fucking hole you fell into by going all out with every trick in the book. I'll do my bit by helping you stay within the confines of local government planning legislation but the rests up to you Glenn. If we play our cards right you might actually come out of this with your reputation enhanced and dare I say it head held high.'

'What about George?'

'We save his skin and then he moves on just like you. You were going to get rid of him anyway right? You could always take him with you.'

'I'd sooner have my balls trapped in a mangle.'

If only it had been the blip as Jim predicted but instead the local headline proved to be the catalyst to the beginning of a painfully steep downward trajectory in trade. As if someone had waved the wrong kind of magic wand that made his faithful clientele bring about their very own disappearing act. Then things turned nasty for the Armstrong family. I mean really nasty. Bad enough the collapse in footfall, but now the full force of the vicious B-Smart PR machine to contend with and all the family could do was curl up like beaten dogs and take the kicking. Negative headlines selected for the East Sussex Gazette by none other than Don Walsh himself. The editor of the local rag, a man who knew his own mind now faced his own personal dilemma. Remain loyal to a local business and rebuke editorial interference or shake the hand of a new advertising client and bring a broad smile to that of his paymasters. He chose the latter. This was Thatcher's Britain where money talked and now all about survival of the fittest. Armstrong's were established enough to fight their own commercial battles no matter who came along their way and what about the old adage of no such thing as bad publicity. At least that's how he justified sticking the knife into a good employer and the kind of owner who had only ever played it straight. An act of treachery that would be remembered well by someone with a very long memory and thus bring about the paper's demise some several decades later. In the meantime the brickbats were coming thick and fast.

'B-SMART CLAIM ARMSTRONG'S RIP THEIR CUSTOMERS OFF'

'ARMSTRONG'S UNDER INVESTIGATION FOR OVERCHARGING'

'ARMSTRONG'S A TERRIBLE PLACE TO WORK CITES FORMER EMPLOYEE'

A family under siege, Ann has now become a prisoner in her own house.

'Why are they doing this to us? What have we ever done to them? We've never harmed anyone have we and now this B-Smart are making us out to be crooks or monsters to work for. Why are they doing this to us Jim? People are now crossing the street to avoid talking to me.'

'In which case I would question what kind of friends they really were in the first place. Times like these always let you know who you can really rely on in life which is why we stick together and stay strong. This is all just mischief-making and it will pass. Some bloody journalist's obviously out to make a name for themselves.'

'So, what do you make of this then?' as Ann takes a four page colour supplement from the paper. There's one of these inside the paper now every night comparing our prices to theirs and they claim to be half the price of us on just about everything. Its time you got on the phone Jim and called the agents back and tell them we'll take the million.'

'Mum don't be so foolish. Those guys were just at it.'

'Well, there's only one way to find out.'

'So, why not just put the place on the open market then and see what someone else offers instead?' 'Because we don't have time Carolyn do we? Your father's indecision has well and truly blown that avenue has it not? Do it Jim before it's too late. Tell them we'll take the million but nothing less. I can't bear living like this.'

'Ok I will.'

So, much for consistency and the reality was that this indecision was immediately being fed back to those out there working the shop floor. There was a traitor in the camp. The same person that realised their time was up on anything positive now likely to come out of this given their parents lack of cohesion on just about everything to do with what was fast becoming a financial debacle. Jim was now well and truly out his depth. Forget family unity. Self-preservation more like and much to the father's dismay and mother's disgust the most unexpected of opportunities would shortly fall on the golden child's lap.

'What's happening these days Mike?' from Rachael.

'Dad's soldiering on but they're prepared to take the smaller offer. He's got another meeting organised but that's just between you and me.'

'Hate to tell you but everyone on site already knows.'

'They know about Dad changing his mind?'

'Yep…Let's face it he's always changing his mind.'

'Yeh but that's because events keep changing all the time that's why. He thought he could cope with the new garden centre opening up but you've seen the headlines. The bastards want to put him out of business by spreading lies all over the place and now Joe's obviously going around opening his big mouth. No wonder my mum's a nervous wreck. If they don't sell they could end up going bust.

"So, why's Joe doing this?'

'So, some staff get pissed off and leave. The more that go the easier it is for Joe to keep drawing a good wage while there's still money coming in. He's only looking after number one. It's what Joe does.'

'You're getting smarter Mike. Maybe this and you helping me has made you into a stronger person. I really admire you now whereas before I just liked you. Well, kinda felt sorry for you actually. Now maybe this is not the time and I'll understand if you don't want to do it, but can you take me to a booking tonight. It just came in this afternoon and it's an all-nighter.'

'All bloody night?'

'Yeh but you just take me there and come back in the morning.'

'Don't see why not. How much are you getting for this?'

'Five hundred.'

'Shit Rachael that's good money. In fact that's a hundred more than I get each month.'

'That's why I want it. Some guy staying at the Commodore Hotel. Says he's here for the week and needs some entertainment. Truth be told I'm getting better clients all the time now and I couldn't have done it without your help. I've got enough saved up to put down a deposit on somewhere decent for me and the kids at long last.'

'Good for you. Who would ever think this is what we get up to in our spare time but the Commodore! This is the best place yet. Least it gives us the chance to drive past the site at Uxbridge and see what's happening.'

'He wants me for eight. Mum thinks you're taking me away for the night.'

'Tell her I'm taking you to the Commodore.'

'Somehow Mike I don't think even she'd believe that one.'

So, confident were the B-Smart crooks of getting what they wanted that building work had already begun by the time the East Sussex Three set to task. Some call it retrospective planning permission whereas others simply called it pushing your luck and B-Smart were in the higher echelons when it came to chancing their arm. No planning guidelines broken as such but to say the Council trio sailed close to the wind in speeding the process along would be an understatement. The right people charmed and cajoled where necessary. Especially when it came to selling the idea that by practically giving the land away so cheaply would somehow benefit the county in the longer term as more multinationals would be keen to follow in B-Smart's shoes. At least that was the theory and a magnified version of Joe giving away free products to entice spending elsewhere. Same principle but both ideas economically inept!

Crucial to the whole process was minimising objection. A task only made possible by keeping the public strictly at arm's length. Objection notices, a key component in keeping the layman informed were positioned in what could best be described as blink and you miss it locations for nowhere near as long as certain planning officials would afterwards claim them to have been. Those bureaucrats involved in the process acutely aware that something was most definitely amiss in this most rushed of rush jobs but for now made clear in no one's interests in terms of future career prospects to ask why. This was officialdom's very own need-to-know basis where there really were only three in the loop.

For the quaint little hamlet adjacent to the site, for those retired professionals enjoying their midsummer evening walks between the hedgerows, life was destined to never be the same again. Now under siege to an army of ground workers and heavy-duty machinery what little greenery remained after completion would be obscured by what George had described in Florida as an out of place glorified airport terminal. The scale of the project not lost on the two young adults driving slowly between the excavators and dumper trucks parked up and practically blocking all movement on the one and only road running alongside.

'Where have all the trees gone Mike? It's as if they've just flattened the place.'

'How to piss off the locals without trying! I'm surprised the rich bastards living here let them get away with it.'

'Maybe B-Smart are just even richer.'

'Good point. Dad's not going to like this that's for sure and look at the size of the place its fucking enormous.'

'Your dad's not been. Why not?'

'Too scared probably. Can't face reality. I never knew garden centres were that big in the States. It's all a bit scary but I'll have to tell him I've seen the place. What time is it?'

'Quarter to eight.'

'Time I took you to meet your personal cash machine.'

The line brought a smile to her face primarily due to the intelligence that lay behind the humour. As each week passed, he grew in confidence and now stature, a combination of the young girl's influence and having finally taken on and faced down his brothers constant intimidation. They were actually proving good for each other. Never in a million years the kind of bloke she would have chosen to ask for help but the act of desperation had unexpectedly come up trumps. That vital ingredient so missing in her life up to now had finally arrived, one of trust. She trusted him implicitly and her own self esteem enhanced in the process. At one time the mere thought of a booking at the Commodore would have caused sleepless nights on the back of an inferiority complex whereas now the opportunity proved to be relished. If Michael was intelligent Rachael was smart. Money made even from the outset being used to buy the kind of outfits a client would expect his expensive hooker to be dressed upon arrival. The very act of wearing simply enhanced the fact that tonight she was nothing short of stunning. Not quite the kind of car one would expect a drop dead gorgeous girl to arrive outside a five star manor hotel but being dropped off a hundred yards short and out of sight would do just fine.

'Give me a kiss.'

'What and smudge your lipstick.'

'Give me a kiss. You're good for me Michael. We make a bloody good team.'

'I know we do now go make some money.'

'Ok boss.'

At one time Michael would have been putty in her hands after a line like that but the young man's mind was now obviously elsewhere which simply endeared him further. The kind of established relationship that no matter the mood she could still count on him to be back at the allotted time in the morning and for that in her life no one else thus far had come remotely close. So, now down to business!

Hall porter on sentry duty outside complete with coat and top hat! The sort of uniform she expected to see in somewhere like Pall Mall rather than a rural part of East Sussex. This place was class. More the look of a squire's country retreat than a hotel the car park although sparse still carried enough clues as to its calibre of clientele. Not that she knew a great deal about anything with four wheels but there was Mike and his little Mini and there were others synonymous with much greater wealth. Rachael in such a short space of time was now selling her wares in the super league.

Tonight she'd just stick with her own name. Somehow Raquel just felt out of place and probably wouldn't work with a guy staying in a place like this. Another lesson learned. The more money they pay the more authenticity they prefer. Kind of puts them at ease and builds the all important rapport which for five hundred pounds for a night's work she could afford the odd concession. In the short walk along the drive an answer to every possible permutation had already been figured but by agreeing to meet in the bar the process should prove trouble free. A client who knew the ropes even more than she meant hardly a first timer.

Now the Commodore only had sixteen rooms, well suites actually and tonight only nine occupied of which only two of the suites had couples. Therefore this stunning specimen of femininity heading the hall porter's way might be someone's daughter, a long shot someone's niece or more than likely here to give one of the guests a good time. Who was he to pre judge, the happier the guests as he carried their bags to the car in the morning the more outrageous the tip. Far from feeling nervous she was actually in her element as the pair exchanged pleasantries and she asked for directions to the bar. When all they ask for is directions instead of a name then that's when hotel porters know they're definitely on the game!

Told to look for a guy late forties who'd be wearing a grey jacket and blue shirt and there he was. Good looking guy with chiseled features, full head of hair and rather athletic build. Obviously someone who kept in shape! The bar was deserted as one would expect and he sat at a stool enjoying his beer. Face lighting up immediately as if long lost friends he made his way across and took her hand.

'Hi, you must be Rachael. Really pleased to meet you!' The American accent more pronounced than on the phone.

'And you.'

'My name's Lee.'

Chapter 6

She'd told herself she'd make a great private detective but by the time the ass and legs had finally got themselves reestablished in the small passenger seat her future career had already been upgraded. Mike's little Mini parked up and waiting as always.

'You know what. After this in my next life if I'm not counting money or spreading them, I'm coming back as a spy.'

'You a spy! What makes you think you could do that?'

'Because of the things I can find out. Have a guess who's just had me for the night and I mean all night. The bugger never stopped. Like as If I've just gone twelve rounds. I should have charged him a grand instead of five hundred.'

'Ok so who?'

'The head guy of B-Smart.'

'Tell me you're kidding me.'

'Deadly serious. He said he's here to kick some ass with the building work and…this is where it gets interesting, says he's also got an offer in to buy another garden centre.'

'I don't understand, why would the guy tell you that?'

'Because this is what they do. They like to talk about themselves and all the amazing things they're doing. You know who he reminded me of? Joe. Totally up his own ass. So, I asked him why he was here and he said he was cracking the whip to get the place built on time as British builders were lazy and that he had other things to do. That's when he said he was also looking at buying a smaller garden centre. It's your dads place Mike it has to be.'

'I still don't get it. Why would they build one and buy another one. Why didn't you ask him?'

'What and let the cat out the bag. You can't really ask these guys questions because they'll twig. I just sit and nod my head and let them ramble. The less you ask the more they tell you. He just said he had an offer in. That's as much as I got.'

'If he's waiting to hear on an offer then your right, it is them. Kind of makes sense when you think about the fake headlines. So, those guys that Dad's meeting are actually just a front for the B-Smart guy to make him think it's someone else. Happy to pay you five hundred quid but wanting to pay my parents washers for thirty years of hard graft. I'll be telling Dad when I get back.

'You can't.'

'Why?'

'Because then he asks how you know and then you'll have to tell them about me. Carolyn won't believe you a second time around, she'll just trip you up somewhere and then you'll spill the beans. I can't let anyone find out about this. You don't understand what it's like being a woman and doing this line of work. You're the only person that knows and if anyone else figures it out I'm finished.'

'So, what do I do?'

'I don't know but you'll come up with something Mike. You're clever. You always do.

Therein lay the conundrum. Loyalty to his parents but absolutely to his increasingly dependent friend yet quite literally only days to play with before he'd have to decide either way. What did he get from Rachael yet what had he ever really had from his parents? Joe was the favoured one, Carolyn the smart one whereas he'd simply been left to his own devices. Father even overheard saying he wanted him out the place less than a few months back but still, this was family and blood always won over water any day of the week. Should he decide to tell his parents they then stay where they are but face being targeted by the yanks and potentially driven out of business with mother already proving close to breaking point as it was! This was before B-Smart had barely got underway with their smear campaign. How long was Rachael going to be in his life? With looks like that she's bound to be snapped up and then who's left at his side, but was it really that likely in the medium term? Where's she going to find someone as accommodating as he and let's face it, taking on and beating Joe would never have happened in a month of Sundays had she not given him some kind of backbone. To say nothing would be to leave it to his father to negotiate his own way out of this mess with some degree of dignity and so far that was looking anything but likely.

Caught between a rock and a hard place events would further conspire to confuse the issue for the young man but at least elevate his standing in the family hierarchy in one fell swoop.

Hot on her heels and driving out the entrance at speed literally minutes later she would have been rumbled were it not for Mike's tendency to escape scenes of crime as fast as the battered old Mini would allow. Not that Trenchman was following her. By the time the bedroom door had closed she'd already become an affordable irrelevance as there was a packed itinerary for his four day visit of which last night was simply an impulse decided upon arrival. A treat for the indignity of having to fly Business class over First! An excuse for the cashed five hundred pound company cheque could be drummed up on the flight home but as far as this morning was concerned it was time as Don had put it to 'start sticking some dynamite under a few asses' starting off with the main contractor appointed on site. Daft enough to sign up for a fixed price on completion but without a specific time scale, Lee needed to ruffle a few feathers which, given the abrasive personality tended to come quite naturally. Generally speaking Don was disparaging of the Brits whereas they made no odds to Lee. He came with a jaundiced rather black and white approach to people insofar as chances fell to everyone no matter what side of the fence they came from but there were winners and losers in life. If someone was dumb enough to allow themselves to be walked all over then they only had themselves to blame. Talking of which he expected Glenn to have read this morning's fax which he already had and to his cost. Both early birds but one now carrying a more haunted look than the other!

Fax

To: Glenn Daly

From: Lee Trenchman

Your obvious reticence and avoidance of further personal discussion is proving to be disappointing.

Meeting proposed for Thursday 8th May 8 pm at Commodore Hotel, Uxbridge. To fail to attand may prove detrimental considering documents discussed on last meet.

Regards.

Glenn was trapped. These guys were never going to let him go as the pictures were about as hot to the crooked pair as was his worth. So, valuable in fact that maybe B-Smart should think about opening more stores on the back of the victim's guilt and contacts' book. In the meantime, there was the small matter of using him to push through a planning application to demolish Armstrong's when the time was right and replace with an exclusive housing development. Probably just sit on the land in the medium term and watch its value appreciate while its past clientele makes their way to the B-Smart in Uxbridge for a more entertaining and less traditional English garden centre experience.

Since coming home Glenn had screwed up and knew it. He should just have confessed but he bottled it losing what little self respect was left in the process. He'd still have kept his job, an outside chance maybe even his wife notwithstanding the awkwardness that would follow mealtimes given daughters' allegiance to their mother. Several years of paying University fees to look forward to but little by way of dialogue as compensation!

Stay on the same path and risk going to jail at some point for misuse of public office or stand his ground and there's the possibility he could be searching for a batchelor pad alongside a smear campaign guaranteed to destroy twenty years of hard fought credibility. He'd already seen the local headlines and put two and two together as to who the real villains in the piece happened to be. From a family business he'd never heard of to now being portrayed as the county's very own public enemy number one he knew what this pair of bastards were capable of.

The pair did have this tremendous capacity to create problems for people which, only by drastic action would they ever seem possible to resolve. The Coroner's inquest concluded that it must have been a deer that caused Glenn Daly's car to swerve at speed and unfortunately lose control by ending up at seventy miles an hour headed straight towards and head on with an ageing sycamore. With the rush hour over and on that stretch of road at that time of night traffic sporadic it meant no available witnesses. He left behind a loving but grieving wife and two daughters whose lives in the short term at least were secured by their father's increased life assurance policy taken out several weeks prior. His medical history ensured it would simply be a rubber stamp job which it was. Advance planning or simply coincidence! The soon to be newly elected Chief Executive had his own thoughts on the matter which, for the sake of bereaved wife's finances would remain silent. Alan found the fax that was likely the tipping point behind his good friend's death. His personal insurance policy against future harassment and all the motivation needed to scupper any plans his nemeses had of making a killing off the Armstrong site. He'd have to wait a few decades for more fulfilling revenge but in the meantime this would suffice and he knew the gruesome twosome had likely read his mind.

Back at Armstrong's and trade now around a third lower than what would be the norm. Not the end of the world when taken into account that the site was freehold but after family salaries and running costs deducted the business now running firmly in the red.

All very well taking an axe to the wage bill but that simply meant customer's waiting longer at the checkouts and in search of someone to speak to when needing advice. Joe displayed a rather skewed power of negative press. Customers more picky than of late and prices regularly queried. Father and elder son's time now taken up by an increasingly demanding public who knew the business was on the ropes. How to kick a man when they're down as herd mentality had taken over and the knives were definitely out. The lucrative garden design side of things had simply fallen off a cliff with Joe's lucrative cash sideline all but a distant memory.

'Thank God it's only the local press that have it in for us' proclaimed Jim. 'If it was the national ones as well then we'd really be screwed.'

'Glad you can still find some humour from the situation' from Ann. Fast losing weight and becoming paler by the day.

Much as the family may have spent a greater part of each day holed up in the War Room that otherwise masqueraded as Ann's kitchen the bulk of the time consisted of rambling conversations by father that continually led nowhere and increasingly became plans of action which contradicted those agreed upon only days before. In many ways Jim had had it easy notwithstanding the hard physical graft as financially everything up to now had really been textbook business plain sailing. Not that there was a closed shop mentality operating among East Sussex garden centres but on the other hand no one ever went out of their way to upset the apple cart either. Nobody would dare trod on anyone else's toes by undercutting or aggressive marketing and if one operator appeared to be doing better than the rest it was simply down to them being better at what they did which in turn meant competitors in adjacent towns or counties simply had to raise their game by learning from each other which everyone appeared happy to do. This was still a semi genteel kind of business as English as cricket and with an etiquette to match. Therein lay the problem. When someone finally did come along who not only ignored the rules but made up their own as they went along the family were hopelessly out of their depth when it came to making even a half hearted attempt at response. Churchill one day then Anthony Eden the next, Jim had gone from resolutely standing fast by sticking to what they know best to then suggesting they take B-Smart on by suggesting all kinds of ridiculous promotions which, given they were a single outlet, bore all the hallmarks of financial insanity. True to form and in line with many a small business struggling to stay alive they did the only thing they knew how. They panicked.

Even Trenchman was taken aback. This evening's local paper hot off the press sat atop the reception desk as he checked in for his afternoon meeting with the editor of the Gazette. Threw him to such an extent that he would spend the next hour and a half in something of a quandary, mind well and truly elsewhere, consequence being that the latest minion on the books got off the hook lightly. Simply told to keep up the assault and to his surprise, work carried out thus far paid there and then. A huge relief as you just never knew when it came to a brand new but demanding client. Lee would take time to read the article in full in the car and sure enough Alan Gill had been appointed caretaker Council Chief Executive until a formal decision had been made on Daly's permanent successor but, cynic that Lee was could hazard a guess who this would be and the incriminating fax likely in his possession.

Someone taking their life had been a hell of a way to catch him out but that's just what had happened and as such there was no Plan B. Hardly a catastrophe, just annoying especially when everything seemed to be falling into place. To attempt the same with Gill would be a mistake and if anything he knew Alan was likely itching for a fight. As Don would frequently remind when business dealings were turning sour, always more than one way to skin a cat. The offer of eight hundred thousand had been rebuked which was only to be expected but the reality was that if Daly had still been on the go and put his weight behind the change of use Lee would likely have stumped up the million to be done with them. Now it looked like the only game plan available was one of attrition. Starve the Armstrong's of trade instead. As the only major competitor to B-Smart opening up, a slow agonising death for the family outfit could well mean the site still changing hands at an even better price than had originally intended. With the editor giving Lee the lowdown on the family hierarchy Don's oft used adage would shortly bear grasp of economics when it came to the current climate of adversity. Sacrifice was giving way to self preservation and the rot was not going unnoticed by those still hanging onto their jobs by a thread. Staff perks were instantly given the chop. No more discounted staff lunches and the mealtimes themselves reduced to what was statutory legal requirement. The working week would be shortened for the majority and closing times brought forward for the quieter days. Needless to say edge of a cliff stuff with staff morale yet all the while Joe kept hold of his leased company Range Rover at four hundred pounds a month with fuel allowance paid for the business under the guise of the car being used for work related matters only. Each trading day at best equal to the day before but the crucial weekend trade was proving particularly worrisome as this was big ticket item day as well as the two days when families splashed out on family meals rather than the midweek retired fraternity simply having two teas and sharing one of Ann's homemade cakes. The B-Smart newspaper inserts were also pointing out the meal deals soon to be coming the public's way and the savings were substantial by comparison.

'We can't even make it for what these guys are selling it for' A despairing Jim would frequently say.

'It's probably the same kind of thing that they feed us in the University refectory. The food will either be that bad or the portions so small that you might go there once but never again' from Carolyn who at least sounded as if she knew what she was talking about.

'Well, we better keep our fingers crossed on that one because if you're wrong our two cooks might be the next on the hit list and you'll be joining your mother back in the kitchen.'

'I sure as hell am not going back in there at my age dear so don't even go there.'

Unbeknownst to Jim his two cooks were already one step ahead in that sphere. With one of them travelling each day from Uxbridge and the other guessing the writing was on the wall they'd already stuck in their applications awaiting reply. Ann might not have any choice in the matter the way things were going.

One person still on the right side of redundancy was Rachael. As yet her days of work still the same under the guise that her flexibility in various sections marked her down as something of an asset whereas everyone else on site simply assumed it was likely because of her legs and they would be right. Not only customers who liked the look of pretty girls but bosses did too and Jim had as fertile an imagination as anyone. With the exception of Michael, these days it seemed to be nothing but older guys all the way. A combination of the younger ones assuming she was simply out of their league and in her professional capacity so to speak who the fuck else had the odd hundred pounds or so to throw in her direction without worrying about unpaid bills afterwards. Talking of which she'd just clocked a smartly dressed mature looking guy wearing shades who looked strangely familiar. Well, he should considering less than forty eight hours ago she was performing cart wheels for him in his hotel room. Giving the impression he's scanning the plants but likely anything but he seemed to be on the lookout and it can't be for Jim because the father of the business was easily within his line of sight. If only Armstrong senior had known the scumbag responsible for the fake stories was within eyeshot he may have been tempted to do more with the bagged manure available than simply have it on sale. Actually if anyone had to be discreet it was more like her. Walking over to collect this afternoon's paltry takings from the farm shop she'd managed to find herself out of sight behind the over ordered abundance of garden trellis. This visitor was trouble but not in her interest to spill the beans just yet.

'Shit Mike, where are you when I need you' she whispered to herself. Not even sure if he'd figure this one out.

Amateur sleuth that Rachael was - on the one hand shitting herself she'd be seen, but bizarrely getting her kicks as one of the increasingly central characters that was the unfolding drama. Far from his persona as being nothing short of dull the reality was that in Michael's company life had become increasingly eventful. Things just seemed to happen all around without him trying that particularly hard. So, putting her friend's head on was her client simply here as part of a recce or something more sinister. The Judas of the family would shortly provide all the answers.

'Anything for me?'

'Just this' as she handed her husband a solitary envelope.

172

Even though you could cut the atmosphere with a knife, being at home for Jim was still a better option than being out there on stage facing the public where a certain percentage were determined to drive him to the brink of insanity with the same banal questions he felt as if he'd already been asked a thousand times. All courtesy of a man he was only standing thirty yards or so away from barely minutes ago. At least at home there was a truce. With customers you don't get the option of selective questioning although his body language out there was trying its best to steer people clear. His slump into the chair spoke volumes.

'More bad news I take it?'

'Talk about sticking the knife in Ann. Listen and see what you make of this.

Dear Jim, given the recent adverse publicity concerning Armstrong's the committee feel that your attendance at this year's Rotary Club Christmas Awards may prove detrimental to both yourself and others engaged in similar business. With this in mind may we suggest you refrain from attending until matters are concluded! Yours…fucking sincerely.'

'So, after all this time you're being kicked out the Rotary Club.'

'Not immediately. That'll be the next letter. So, much for us all standing together through thick and thin not to mention I've probably been one of their biggest charitable donors for the past twenty years. It was the one event I genuinely looked forward to and now this. A good excuse to bring through some young blood but kick me in the nuts as a farewell.'

'You never deserved that but we'll come through this Jim and then you can tell them where to stick their awards ceremony when they come groveling back.'

Each daily knockback a blow to Jim's character as willpower, confidence and self belief had begun to slowly ebb away.

Looks like Lee had found who he was looking for and now engaged in conversation. The shaking of hands a clue that neither party was already known to the other and ensuing conversation firmly rooted to the spot. Surely if it had been anything to do with buying the place there would have been some sort of walkabout instead Rachael picking up on Joe's general unease, backing off as if wary of being seen. No way for Joe at least had any of this been planned and if what Lee had told her to be true then only tonight and tomorrow left for further dialogue between the pair which, given an exchange of business cards looked a distinct possibility. Spy that she was, Joe's car spotted in the Commodore car park the following evening when invited back as Lee's farewell treat. Not that she knew his modus operandi in practice but experienced enough to sniff a rat at fourteen paces and turn on her heels.

That Joe would tender his resignation several weeks later came as no surprise to one of the siblings and relief to the other. The golden one chosen to drive Armstrong's forward into the next millennia had instead fallen for the promise of more exciting things to come as newly appointed General Manager of B-Smart's first store in the

UK. One thing to be let down but quite another when the treachery is committed by your own flesh and blood. To betray then turn his back on those who needed him most would shock no one on site other than the parents responsible for creating this narcissist in the first place. Their paths would cross soon enough but never a word spoken between father and elder son ever again.

His son's desertion hit Jim hard. Mealtimes now a much more subdued affair compared to the norm and father increasingly finding solitude in the company of his own back garden rather than being out there advising customers on the upkeep of their own. On the plus side, free from the shackles of domineering older brother the two remaining offspring set to task attempting to right some of Joe's wrong's in a desperate attempt to stay afloat. Carolyn took to task taking care of all unnecessary expenses top of the list being the return of leased Range Rover and immediate cancellation of brother's fuel account. Five hundred pounds a month saved by lunchtime on her first day! The younger brother having a point to prove rose to the challenge by taking care of operations which began immediately with Joe's partner in crime from the waterboarding incident agreeing to leave by mutual accord. Store ordering got tightened up and a fresh look to all the displays. Staff less fearful of being creative than they had been under previous regime! No doubting takings were down but so too were the costs as many an excess continually came to light. For all their good work customer numbers were still heading south this but this time due to circumstance beyond the sibling's control. Interest rates nationally were going through the roof and in an increasingly home-owning enclave such as

East Sussex customers needed to stretch that pound in their pocket as far as they possibly could. B-Smart had arrived in the right place at just the right time and its doors were finally open.

It would never have entered Jim's head to turn up incognito. He was who he was. A simple straightforward man who played his life and business, best he could by the book. A visit borne more out of curiosity than envy! Always keen to pick up new tips he'd hoped he might actually come away having learned at least something and if this was the future of garden centres then surely they must be doing something so radically different to entice his eldest to immediately jump ship when the opportunity came calling. In the end all it seemed to be was bigger. Much bigger and without a doubt miles cheaper than anything he could get away with charging back home. It never felt like a garden centre, more like a place that just happened to sell plants along with dozens of other lines which as far as he could see had more in common with the interior of one's house than to be planted outside and left to face the elements. Then there were the queues of children waiting to be entertained by some machine or other that only functioned once the parents had handed over their hard earned cash. Maybe he should have listened to Joe after all and acted sooner. Was it a lack of support behind Joe's leaving or simply the extent of his ambition being far greater than anything the family business could offer! Now would be a good time to find out because there was the main man himself resplendent in company shirt and tie and as always enjoying the attention of the ladies, a few Jim recognised as not having seen for some time at his own place and now he knew why. Oblivious to the rather gaunt elderly gentleman who appeared to be rooted to the spot Joe was obviously in his element basking in the adulation of his female followers as well as presiding over a retail space that was to put it mildly, absolutely heaving with people. Unlike their more upmarket competitor half an hour along the dual carriageway the trolleys were laden and each checkout four or five deep but not through lack of staff. The sheer size of the place meant that they were now likely taking more in an hour than his own business took in a week. More than a handful of what were once Armstrong devotees spotted along the queues but choosing to look elsewhere than make eye contact with a man who'd spent so much of his time going out of his way to please them but as such now appeared frail and dejected. Call it a sixth sense but alerted to his father's presence a half hearted nod of acknowledgement would come Jim's way but destined to fall on deaf ears. He was only here to let his traitor of a son know that he'd been and Joe knew it.

'Your father just seems to have given up.'

It would be hard for Carolyn to disagree. The stockpile of empty bottles out the back told their own story. Kicked in the groin just that once too often the father had finally lost his sense of purpose and the fight was gone. From being disowned by the Rotary, abandoned by what he thought were faithful clientele to finally being deserted by his favourite son he'd reached the fateful conclusion that events had simply conspired against due to flaws of personal judgement.

Ann had her own demons to contend with, the majority of which centred around the family name and its fall from social grace. Try as hard as she may, she still lay the blame at husband's door. From a relatively humble upbringing herself it was his drive, acumen and not to mention inheritance rather than looks that became her pathway to prosperity and social positioning. Coming from the wrong side of the fence the options available for an unskilled woman in that part of county back then were scarce. Young Jim was the only likely escape route from the hardship experienced to that of her mother. Now reading more into how the family was perceived by the town's movers and shakers than she probably should she'd become convinced that not only had the pair of them been ostracised by the local business community but also the subject of some ridicule. Not only the Rotary where the invitations had been withdrawn but just about every other event on the town's social calendar too. As someone seriously affected by opinion those childhood feelings of inadequacy and inferiority resurfaced having lain dormant for so long during the golden years. As such the support to her husband which had bordered on nothing more than minimal now gave way to the increasing resentment of having once been the town's most prominent business couple they were destined to be remembered as a pair of incompetents. Not that this was as salient as issue as Joe's desertion but her frequent reminding on this particular evening would prove one step too far.

Dispatched to find their father with dinner fast approaching no sign of Jim from either sibling at any of the most likely stop offs until a light visible from one of the unused workshops at the far end of their storage yard. Both shouting from afar but as yet no answer! Michael making his way towards the window at exactly the same time as his sister would make way to open the door. No shouting, no screaming or crying. The pain was over and strangely at peace with himself albeit while hanging from a beam.

With the site being sold now a forgone conclusion the question would simply be one of how much and to whom. The bank, now twitchy about getting its loan repaid had decided to turn the screw and push for a quick sale. With Ann an emotional wreck it would be left to the budding lawyer of the family to rescue whatever she could that been her father's disastrous handling of the situation thus far. Far from relishing the prospect at least this time around there was a blank canvas and no interference from elder brother who simply dare not show his face though likely leaned on by his employer at some point thought Michael to do just that. The news being fed back of the demise of yet another one of the county's finest citizens would be of little consequence to the dodgy duo across the pond. Another example as far as Trenchman was concerned of British capitulation when the going became too tough.

For sure not a cat in hells chance of planning permission for change of use being granted while Alan Gill in the Council hot seat and no sight or sound of his sparring partner in Land and Estates George Davies who left the council upon Alan's promotion never to be heard of again. The only other option would be to buy the site under a different limited company and run as a going concern till Gill himself moved on himself or likely retired. He could be gone by the mid part of the next decade given Trenchman's opinion that those working in higher public office in the UK had a thing about retiring early to go live by the sea. The game plan would be to buy the place, strip back to the bare bone and just run alongside Uxbridge giving the land some time to appreciate along the way. Given the new breed of banker now taking hold in the square mile there was bound to be some young Turk or another he could convince to finance his master plan and so the agents were summoned and told to seal the deal forthwith. Closure now the old man was out the way should simply be plain sailing.

'I knew they'd be back now dad's gone. Hardly comes as a surprise does it? Have you not figured out who they are yet?'

'Tell me?'

'B-Smart.'

'Can't be They already have a place.'

'I know but they want ours as well. These agents are just a front Carolyn. It's been B-Smart all along.'

'It doesn't make sense.'

'I didn't get that bit either but trust me it's them. One of them was also here a few months back to poach Joe so it would further damage dad and make him want to sell.'

'How do you know all this Michael?'

'You can thank Rachael. It was her that put me onto telling you a while back about B-Smart wanting to open up in Uxbridge.'

'So, how come?'

'Because she's on the game that's how and she's now dealing with rich clients with big mouths of which the head guy at B-Smart when he's been staying at the Commodore is one of them. It's me that's been taking her all over the place to appointments.'

'Well, I never. So, that's where you keep disappearing to at nights. We all thought you'd finally got yourself a girlfriend. Not that any of us thought Rachael Compston right enough.'

'I told her I would never tell anyone but this is different. Just don't go saying anything not that it makes much difference now.'

'No, I won't but dad would turn in his grave if he thought the business had been sold to those bastards…and now they've got Joe on their side.'

'So, what do we do?'

'Well, I don't want this to go on forever and if we let mum put the place on the open market it could stop me from going back to Uni. There's someone I think might be interested but this is between you and me and you'll have to take me there. In fact we'll make it tomorrow.'

'Ok where?'

'Wait and see. I've got a lot of rehearsing to do.'

Made a pleasant change for Michael to be driving north of the town between the hedgerows and along quiet country lanes instead of heading south along the increasingly busy dual carriageway in search of the latest hotel and its next lonely male occupant ready to cross Rachael's palm to ease the pain of isolation!

To anyone out walking their dog along this particular woodland stretch the youngish couple in the slow moving Mini were likely here for no other reason than to pull up somewhere secluded until that is the little car pulled off the road and drove through the set of rather ornate wrought iron gates and along the manicured grounds for a mile and a half before reaching its destination. Not a soul to be seen but at this time of night even at a place like this television likely still took precedence over everything else. One thing was for sure though. Somebody somewhere would still have clocked them.

'Are you coming with me?' she asked.

'One of us better wait in the car.'

'Why?'

'In case they don't let you out. This way one of us is still able to open the place up in the morning.'

'Gee thanks.'

'You don't need me Carolyn. I'd just get all tongue tied and not know what to say. I'll go and park round the back then come back for you. How long do you think you'll be?'

'Worst case scenario five minutes. Anything longer and we're in with a shout.'

Not that she was oblivious to her surroundings. A traditional picture postcard English stately home complete with its very own lake and surrounded by the odd hundred thousand or so acres. All two hundred and fourteen rooms of it but little time tonight for nerves. Focus, focus just focus. With so little to lose, the single mindedness destined to be her trademark had told herself she just had to get this right tonight or at the very least try.

Surprisingly places like these did actually have doorbells even if they were of the porcelain push button variety and appeared to be silent. No doubt a small brass bell that rang in the servants' quarters down below! Another set of internal doors heard opening before the mother of all locks got underway with the front pair. Not quite the person young Carolyn expected to see.

'Good evening. How can I help?'

'Ehm…I'd like to speak to his Lordship please.'

'Looks like this is your lucky night then young lady. How can I be of service?

'You are actually the real Lord?'

'So, what were you expecting? A small elderly gentleman wearing black tie and tails who says please come this way m'lady. Times have changed Carolyn. We don't really go in for that sort of thing anymore'

'You know who I am.'

'Of course I do. I've been a frequent visitor to your garden centre over the years and I have a lot to be thankful to your father for. Goes without saying of course you have my condolences and I'll miss the man immensely.'

Sensing she might be losing composure he continued to speak allowing her time to get back on track.

'You can call me Peter and I assume you're here for a reason?

'It's to do with dad's business and especially the site itself. I wondered if we could talk.'

'I see. In which case you best come in then. Remember and wipe your feet.'

Sharing a smile she liked this guy already and felt it was mutual. Never acted like a Lord but the funny thing was even when these guys dress down they always manage to carry themselves differently! Unlike the agents who were also utterly charming at least his Lordship appeared authentic and as if she came here half expected. The first five minutes had now gone as Michael checked his watch. So, far so good! He'd be fast asleep by the time she finally reappeared.

Several days later and time for B-Smarts agents to resurface! A sense of urgency now injected into the proceedings now that the old man was gone that they expected the sale to be agreed in principle today lest the deal be put to rest.

'In other words, mum they're sticking a gun to your head.'

Meeting attended this time around by the smooth talking agent and his silent sidekick, Carolyn and now the family lawyer finally brought in by Ann to keep daughter on the straight and narrow. Hardly what one would describe as the most convivial of meetings but as far as the agents were concerned everything appeared to be finally going to plan. The daughter more reticent than of last and likely leaned on by family lawyer as to the kind of etiquette expected at this crucial stage of near conclusion. Here they suspected more for the experience than her contribution the father's demise had clearly knocked the stuffing from her sails and under orders from matriarch to keep schtum. The family lawyer coming across as more the journeyman type no doubt keen to conclude the deal and submit his own invoice as soon as. Time for the smooth one to wrap things up and finally look forward to being paid himself!

'Due diligence we expect to be a formality given Armstrong's trading record. More our client's accountants casting an eye over the business than going into any forensic detail! So, without further ado I have here the all important Agreement in Principle which if I can pass to you to approve then ask for your client as a named director of the business to sign. For the record once again can I offer our sincere condolences, I know at times the meetings have been fractious but I hope the money your mother receives provides some degree of comfort in retirement and I'm sure you'll go onto great things in whichever field of law you choose.'

'Corporate.' The first word spoken in about twenty minutes! Pen now in hand and signature imminent.

'Yes, corporate which I'm looking forward to immensely.'

'I can understand' as both agents fixated at document sheet placed in front.

'And would you like to know why?'

'Enlighten me?' from the smooth one.

He may appear relaxed but Carolyn guessed she now had the upper hand. Something was amiss and the pair of them knew it. The family lawyer knew it. As if there was a rabbit about to come out of the hat.

'So, that next time I come across guys like you I'll know what to expect...and I'll ask more questions...the right kind of questions and I'll also be doing my homework as to whether or not people are who they claim to be.'

'Would you be insinuating something Miss Armstrong?'

'Without being able to prove it I'll keep my thoughts on that matter to myself but that statement alone should be enough to tell you everything you need to know and that this document' as she placed the pen gently but rather confidently back on table 'is destined I am afraid for the rubbish bin.' Proceeding to lift and slowly tear in two then into smaller pieces. 'The business, indeed the site which is what your clients as you call them wanted all along is going to be sold and its new owner more keen for the business to continue in the same vein as before. Before a certain conglomerate came along and started to carry out dirty tricks if you get my insinuation. The new owner has much deeper pockets than my father ever had and I suspect he's much smarter than my father ever was too but my dad's legacy will live on and it will live on much longer than some new upstart on the scene offering cheap gimmicks. I'm not sorry I wasted your time because people like you waste people's lives. See yourself out.'

Not quite what anyone had expected least of all the family lawyer who'd sat there for ten minutes being upstaged by a third year student! Two young girls destined to play an even bigger part of young Michaels life in the years to come and each sharing the principles of thinking on their feet and keeping one's cards close to one's chest. Remembering what her dad had told her about his Lordship's family being outsmarted by her great aunt when the site first came on the scene she'd figured he'd like to make amends should the opportunity ever present itself which now it had. Obviously exaggerating the price somewhat the family still left with a generous six figure profit and as important to the town and her father's legacy he agreed the business would continue with name intact. For someone still so young the beginning of mastering the art of doing the deal.

Chapter 7

2015

Ann lasted longer than anyone had anticipated when you consider just how close she'd been to the cliff edge in the run up to the sale. The deal with his Lordship involved selling the site lock, stock and barrel but given first refusal should the family home adjacent ever become vacant and at a price fair and consistent with market value. A classic case of one good turn deserving another!

In the end he only had to wait a couple of years as mother succumbed to the olive branch held out by her eldest and gave up the ghost on memories past by downsizing to a much smaller two bedroom bungalow a stone's throw from Uxbridge. Near enough to act as nanny and doting grandmother to the favoured one's first child and should the mood take her, visit son's local B-Smart for cheap bedding plants.

'Mum, you have to let bygones be bygones' as Joe now seeing himself as some kind of elder statesman frequently reminded her.

The irony of it all not lost on her two youngest, the same two responsible for saving the family business in the first place. Uxbridge is where Ann would stay for just short of the next twenty years ostensibly providing Joe with a safe bolt hole to return to every time his latest relationship hit the skids. The odd visit from Michael and even more fleeting from daughter who had since grown wings to further her career by moving abroad!

Not as good an inheritance as two of the family had predicted but why in the end should they be surprised. Joe's predilections for high living over a twenty year period would erode much of mother's savings and current account but at least there was always the bungalow even if it had been refinanced to help pay her eldest's expensive divorce. Cordial would be as good as it got at the funeral. Cordial as in at least Joe was acknowledged by the pair but little else.

With both parents now been and gone simply left to Carolyn and Michael to carry on with what was left of the bare bones of family unity. What had once been regular contact now more sporadic as Carolyn forged ahead in the international arena light years away from the more practical but less lucrative occupation now enjoyed by younger brother! He'd been given the opportunity by his Lordship to stay on and run the place which in itself made perfect financial and practical sense but in the end his demons won the day. An opportunity Lord Peter had thought for the young man to step out of the shadows of the past and try to put his own stamp on the place which would also have meant going head to head with Joe down the road. Anyone else would have relished the opportunity but try as hard as he may, with mother's allegiance resolutely in eldest brothers camp and Carolyn back at University there was little Rachael or the new owner could do to shift the inferiority complex Michael held at the hands of the man he'd always considered the more talented one. All very well physically standing up to a bully but competing directly in business with the kind of brass neck his brother had was the kind of stuff to induce sleepless nights.

Needless to say Rachael never agreed and brought about what was once a friendship destined to last to an abrupt halt. Michael wanted a fresh start which ultimately meant a complete change of career whereas Rachael thought everything he needed was actually right here in front of and more importantly she and her two kids potentially being part of it. Rather than face his demons head on she accused the career change as an excuse to just run away. Who's to say this most unlikely of companion was just the same as every other man in her life who'd held out such great promise to begin with only to leave later on. Rather than wait to find out Michael had just passed up on a relationship many in the village, especially Joe would have thought incredulous. Rachael Compston living with who? What a way to get one over on his brother. Maybe father staying around and that vital arm around son's shoulder could have made all the difference but for now starting afresh was the only way it would be. To think Rachael would ever return would be the stuff of fantasy but by the time she came back some twenty years later it was because he'd become a different beast altogether and she had to see for herself if it was one and the same man.

Michael had probably come into plumbing at the tail end of the good times. Just as his father he went it alone upon qualifying and for the next decade and a half reaped the rewards. No doubting he put in the hours but with a national shortage in the UK of this particular trade the money was there for the taking. Now married having met Alison on the job so to speak the time was right financially to start a family and the flexibility of self employment made it able to work around her shifts as a nurse when it came to childcare. Then, some years later, same as his father circumstances dramatically changed. The British government under Blair had relaxed its own immigration policy with several new EU member states and what had been expected to be a trickle of migrants taking advantage of burgeoning British prosperity quickly became a stampede. Those arriving from Poland took up the lion's share of newcomers with wages in the UK for identical jobs at least four times higher than was on the table back home.

The downside for Mike was that many of those arriving happened to be highly skilled especially when it came to the trades. Net result what had once been a national shortage was fast becoming an over supply as others in the UK got in on the action alongside their East European counterparts. Not quite as devastating as the damage inflicted on his dad but still a blow to Mike and Alison Armstrong's standard of living. Bad enough the collapse in margins but now everything in the new millennium just seemed to have become so damned difficult with an explosion in red tape and financial outlay all for the privilege of doing something off one's own bat. His latest bug bear being his bank! One of the country's biggest declaring yet another set of sterling results which pleased the city and its shareholders but enough to drive Alison and the kids demented during dinner as Mike offloaded yet again with another one of his elongated rants.

'This is the trouble with the bloody banks. They don't employ managers any more. Just spotty kids with a

University degree in Natural Sciences who haven't got a clue what it's like out there in the real world.'

'Mum can I be excused?' asked Andrew.

'And me if you don't mind' from his sister.

The kids Andrew and Stephanie. Twelve and fourteen respectively and a mirror image of parents! Andrew the more thoughtful and Stephanie taking after her mother as the more outgoing of the two!

Not that Rachael in his previous life could ever have been classed as a partner but up to now when you include Carolyn into the mix Mike did appear to be drawn to the more outgoing assertive type. Two would have been a coincidence but three of the same meant definitely a pattern.

'So, what's so important that the pair of you need to be excused?' from mum.

'Because dad's about to go off on one about the banks just for a change.'

'No, I'm not.'

'Yes you are dad' from Andrew. 'Mum says you're like a broken record at times.'

'Did she really?'

'Nice to know you can keep a secret Andrew.'

'I'm just saying.'

'And what do you think Steph? These two are ganging up on me.'

'Well, you do go on about it a bit. It's as if when we sit down to dinner I always know what's coming.'

'Hmmm that is bad.'

'So, it's not just me then darling is it. So, why don't you do something about it?'

'Oh, yeh like what?'

'I don't know. Start a protest or something. How's anything ever going to change unless you make a stand.'

'Ok, seeing as you suggested it. I've had this idea for a while now so I'll shut up and promise never ever to mention the banks again but you have to help me out doing just one thing. Won't take up much more than a few hours of your time.'

'And you promise dad to never ever, ever mention the banks ever again' from a beaming Stephanie.

'I said I won't! Don't you want to know what it is then?'

'No, none of us care' from Alison. 'Whatever it is it has to be worth it.'

He never anticipated making the early evening news but the seeds of an idea recalled from the impact the local rag had had on his father's business a couple of decades earlier. Newspapers love a good David & Goliath story he thought. If he could only win around a handful of other people to his plight then their collective voice through word of mouth may just be enough for his bank to show a modicum of compassion when it came to overdraft charges and annual fees. Little acorns and all that! Not that this sort of thing came easy to him. The kind of man who preferred the background to his brother's love of being centre stage there remained an innate desire to right some of life's wrongs that obviously had its origins in his father's demise. If nothing else there was no way on God's earth that this was what Alison or the kids had been expecting. Be nice to spring a surprise and show a different aspect to his personality as well as inspiring the kids to stand up and be counted when the mood took them. He now had the rest of the week left spending each evening after work in the garage honing his most primitive of sign making skills and they'd be ready to go. Everyone was actually quite excited about what lay ahead. The thrill of the unknown was about to come back and bite them on the bum.

In the meantime he had a more pressing concern to deal with before heading off to ruin an existing client's day with the installation quote for their new gas boiler. With his local garage having decided to hang up their boots Mike had decided to give the nationwide Fast Fit chain a try out for a new exhaust for the van. Having had one fitted only three weeks prior it was in obvious need of attention given the looks received from passersby. With the van up on the ramp Mike gets the bad news from the depot manager dressed up as an explanation.

'I can see what it is straight away. Must have happened when you went over a pothole or driven over something and its come up and cracked the manifold.'

'But it can be fixed right?'

'Sure but it's going to mean a completely new exhaust.'

'Fine by me I've still got the receipt.'

'Yeh but that makes no difference in this case.'

'Why?'

'Because it was you that damaged it. It's not a faulty part.'

'But how do I know I damaged it? If it's happened so soon after fitting then surely the parts substandard to begin with!'

'Makes no odds. No can do. Company policy, not covered am afraid.'

'So, that's it?'

'Unless you buy a new one yes.'

Back home little by way of sympathy from Alison either.

'So, why did you go there in the first place. Nobody I know uses Fast fit.'

'Because they had an offer on.'

'Ahhh and you fell for it. At least you'll know better next time.'

'But that's not the point. They had an offer on but does that then make it ok for them to rip me off?'

'No, but what else do you want?'

'Ehhh my money back for a start. This is the trouble nowadays. The big boys out there have run all the smaller operators out of business and now they're just pleasing themselves because there's no place left for the rest of us to go.'

'Well, whatever you've got planned for us for this Saturday with the bank just do the same with Fast Fit. Just don't start ruining our dinners all over again by moaning about them too.'

Not quite what the kids had expected. Standing outside a high street bank on a Saturday morning in the pouring rain carrying a placard each as mother, father and Mike's best friend Malcolm hand out leaflets complaining of unjust charges and boardroom excess. Strategically positioned at the entrance passersby appeared to enter into the spirit of things with words of agreement although Malcolm did note the majority appeared to cast a spurious glance at the leaflet then simply throw in the bin when they thought no one was looking.

'Dad this is embarrassing. If any of my mates see me I'm finished' from young Andrew. His street cred collapsing by the millisecond!

'So, how long do we have to stand here for to stop you moaning at the dinner table' chipped in Stephanie.

'Till lunchtime.'

'You have got to be joking dad. It's only just gone ten.'

'Yeh and I've got the football at three remember' from Malcolm.

'God strewth give me a break you lot. It's only a morning out your life. Not like I'm asking for anyone's kidney.'

The rebels in the camp would not be here that much longer if the assistant branch manager had anything to do with it. Rather than enter into a slanging match outside with the middle aged bloke and his mid life crisis a simple phone call to the local constabulary would suffice but by the looks of it a member of the cavalry had already beaten her to it.

'Good morning sir.'

'Morning officer.'

'Not a very nice morning for a protest is it?'

'You could say that.'

'So, can I see you permit please?'

'Permit? Why do I need a permit?'

'All public demonstrations of any kind require approval from the local authority which then issues a permit to the organisation or person in charge of the event.'

'Ok, no. I never knew that.'

'If that weren't the case then there are days when things could get a bit chaotic don't you think?'

'So, does that mean we can now go home then dad?'

'I think that would be best sir unless you want a fine on top of the excess bank charges.' He was pleased with that one.

'Very droll officer. I take the hint.'

'Never mind dear. You'll know better next time.

Alison meant well. He was being consoled even if her comment did have a slightly patronising feel to it. So, much for making a stand he thought to himself on the silent drive home. The system thus far appeared to lend itself in favour of those already having it all their own way and if the palaver of getting a permit involved standing in a queue at city hall for hours on end why would anyone bother. At least Fast Fit was well away from the town centre.

This time around it's only the two of them having managed to cajole Malcolm for a second time. Needless to say Fast Fit's thirty three and a third off promotion still intact! Standing by the depot entrance and flagging down potential customers their antics quickly coming under the watchful eye of site manager recognising Mike from several days prior. Four mechanics two of whom would not look that out of place in the wrestling arena being dispatched accordingly!

'Fuck me Mike what have you got us into' from a clearly nervous Malcolm at the sight of the hit squad fast heading their way.

'We're not standing on Fast Fit property are we? We're both on the right side of the line so therefore not trespassing.'

'Good luck with that one. The big fucker in the middle really looks like the shy, retiring conciliatory type. Shaven head, tattoos and a neck like Mike fucking Tyson. What was there to be nervous about?'

'Heh you, smart arse' from the scary one himself. His mouth clearly in proportion to his size.

'You were here last fucking week causing trouble right?'

'No, I wasn't.'

'Shut it prick. I'm going you two options! You either fuck off right now or I use this steel toecap to stick it where the sun don't shine. What's it to be?'

'We're not on your property. I've got nothing against you. All I'm doing is warning people against your company's blatantly false promotion.'

'Did you hear what I said' as the big one drew so close his nose was now touching. I'm giving you ten seconds pal or you suffer the consequences.'

'Come on Mike lets go' from a clearly petrified Malcolm who preferred to keep a hold of his kneecaps.

Shades of Joe all over again and not that Mike was intimidated but by appearances alone the thug was at least twice the size and likely enjoyed nothing more than giving someone a good hiding. Not that any of the cars given leaflets thus far had displayed any sign of solidarity by turning on their heels and going elsewhere. The quartet retreated to the workshop confident their services would not be required second time around.

'Listen Mike, you mean well and your heart's in the right place and all that but I've got a living to make too. You've made your point and you tried your best so now just leave it be and concentrate on Alison and the kids. Ask yourself is being threatened like that really worth it? I said I'd help you out and I have but that's it mate. I'm out.'

Mike's dejection that evening only to be expected but she'd listened to just about as much as she was prepared to take with the tales of woe.

'So, there we have it. Now you know why the little guy ain't got a hope in hell when it comes to getting a fair crack of the whip. You either come up against beaurocracy or face getting your head kicked in when they send out their very own A-team.'

'So, you just give up after two attempts?'

'Show me an alternative then Alison. I do have experience in this department remember. You know...dad and everything he had to contend with. Well, how's this any different and I don't want to end up being driven to despair like him.'

'A, you could have applied for a permit from the council and B, you could put your thinking cap on and figure out a different way of getting your own back with Fast Fit and C, your dad was inexperienced and from a different era but you're not. But then again this is not your style is it Mike?'

'Meaning what exactly?'

'Meaning you just walk around with a massive bloody chip on your shoulder moaning about all the injustices of life instead of actually getting off your backside and doing anything about it.'

'Don't give me that. I tried and look what happened.'

'You never tried! You gave up, that's what you did. You gave up after only two fucking attempts. You call that fighting? I call it a token gesture. Why don't you start by having some self respect for a change and giving it your best! This is your trouble Mike, you're stuck in the past and you can't shake it off. Don't say you're doing this to prove something to me or the kids or even your dad. Do it for yourself Mike. Whatever it is you want to prove just do it and be happy for once in your own skin.'

Distinctly out of character how bad must he have been to cause his wife to vent her spleen quite to that extent. But by God it hit the mark.

Coming up with his own Plan B involved a double delivery of ink cartridges for the printer which would be on overdrive printing leaflets for distribution across suburbia in the wee small hours before work. For no other reason than the thug threatening to beat him to a pulp Fast Fit was chosen as public enemy number one with anyone sharing similar experience to reply and then join his local boycott. Setting himself a target of a thousand leaflets each morning for a month he'd set off at four am and still be back in time for breakfast with the kids. Both of whom now thought he was going a bit nuts as did Alison but underneath quite pleased she'd actually touched a nerve.

No feedback from the first week but then again only to be expected. Week two and Mike's now making straight for the answer machine on an evening only to end up coming away disappointed! The digital display finally springing into action by the beginning of week three and the excitement akin to winning his first client when he ventured self employed.

'Come on then' from Alison. 'I'm dying to hear what someone else has to say about them.'

'Hello, this is a message for a Mr Mike Armstrong who put a flyer through my door in the early hours of the morning. Can't you read? There's a not on the door that clearly states no cold callers. Next time I suggest you wear glasses. Goodbye.'

'Hmmm good start' from Mike.

'Don't worry handsome, at least that's the bitter and twisted one out the way.'

'I sure hope so.'

Next night no messages continuing this way for the rest of the week! Deciding against saying anything at the risk of it coming out all contrived she simply let him be.

Still no uptake other than a lady from the free local Gazette wondering if he'd like to pay for an advert voicing his concerns. This before the grand finale some ten days later! Mike himself picking up the phone only to be berated by an angry grandmother castigating Mike for obviously holding out some kind of agenda against her Grandson's employer and would be better off targeting politicians than a business creating jobs. Unable to get a word in edgeways he simply hung up.

With Alison's approval and a heavy heart the time had finally come to call it a day.

Chapter 8

'It's for you.'

Eye's half asleep having eaten more than he should he lay stretched flat out on the living room settee. Result of a wife's good food and an honest days' toil. Whoever it was had chosen their wrong moment to call.

'Who's phoning at this time of night for god's sake?'

With her hand still over mouthpiece 'It sounds like somebody old. I think you're in for yet another ear bashing.'

'Shit not again. Alison please, just this once?

'No chance. It was your idea dear so you take the flack'

'Thanks a bunch'

Eyes barely open remaining stretched out he takes the phone.

'Hello.'

'Ah hello. Is this Mr Armstrong?' comes this surprisingly polite and gentlemanly tone of voice as Mike goes straight onto the defensive.

'OK listen. To save your time and mine I'm really sorry for the inconvenience caused. It was just an idea I had after I was ripped off at the Fast Fit garage. Putting leaflets through doors I know it's kind of annoyed some people so for that I truly apologise and all I can...'

'Good heavens no, I thought it was a great idea. I'm the one that should be apologising to you.'

'Ehh?' Eyes spring open and raising eyebrows in Alison's direction.

'Yes I'm sorry for taking so long to respond. Really struck a cord not only with me but many of my friends down the bowling club who've also been fleeced by this motley crew.'

Now completely upright an element of disbelief at what he's hearing.

'I was wondering if you would like to pop round on an evening and see how we can put an idea into practice. If you don't mind I was also going to ask a few others along too. Knock a few heads together kind of thing and just see what we come up with. The names Harry by the way! Harry Wright.'

'Great...I mean excellent. Any evening's fine with me Harry and thanks for getting back. You've made my night, you really have.'

'My pleasure Mike and I look forward to it.'

So, within the confines of Harry Wright's sitting room some three nights later the seeds of a protest movement began which comprised Mike, Harry and half a dozen of his elderly friends two thirds of which share a common purpose and the remainder because nothing better happened to be on the telly. The kind that wives are always glad to be rid of from under their feet! Needless to say no shortage of Fast Fit horror stories shared and just about all to do with serious overcharging or the fitting of parts simply not required. The mechanically naïve or the elderly in particular falling prey to a Fast Fit free inspection but always coming away several hundred pounds lighter in the process. Unaware that their perfectly running car was actually a 'death trap' or in 'urgent' need of a complete set of new tyres.

Putting Mike's unfortunate experience from first time around to good use it was decided that if they were ever to win the day and dent Fast Fits trade it would be more through guile than effort. They needed to mix things up a bit. Still working in pairs but now standing some fifty yards back at the beginning of the slip road and just about out of sight of the workshop there was a discreet word in the ear to potential customers warning of likely plight! No hard sell, just a few minutes of their time to share experience. The depot's busiest times of day recorded with more elderly men than normal just happening to be out walking the dog as traffic picked up. Leaflet distribution continuing but since modified and with access to an old print press in someone's garage production could be cranked up saving Mike a small fortune on ink cartridges. One of the group had a son working in IT and was sure he could knock up a website in no time which made it quicker to refer people to than stand and explain their plight. The name of the game was speed and with several retired professionals looking to become involved the limbs may have been weary but minds still very much intact.

'When do we find out if we're having an impact' asked one of the group.

'Just our success rate at turning cars around I guess' replied Mike.

'I used to work for a multinational in Sales' chipped in another. 'These depot managers get big fat bonuses every month for hitting targets which is why he likely refused your refund in the first place. If he had already hit the mark then there'd be no problem but he obviously had a way to go. It won't take us that many cars before we start making a difference. In a months' time just keep an eye on promotions and advertising. If there's a big jump then it's likely because of us.'

Not just for Mike but a new lease of life for everyone concerned. A win-win all round apart from if you happen to be in the firing line that is. At long last something for the retirees to get their teeth into over and above wandering around DIY stores on a weekend and generally speaking getting on shop assistants' nerves! Thus far everything seemed to be going according to plan. Mike occasionally joining in the subterfuge when his own work allowed but otherwise Harry enjoying being group coordinator. Best of all for Mike no sign of anyone caving in and with most having seen much tougher times in their lives already why should they. Fast Fit fire the first salvo with an earlier than expected local marketing blitz which is met full on with the group simply continuing with more of the same and it's the independent local garages who see the benefit from an increase in trade. Further good news when a friend of Harry's asks permission to form his own club in a neighbouring town to boycott Fast Fit with copycat tactics! A segment of society's elderly fraternity clearly showing that they're not quite over the hill yet!

It would be a retired journalist that would provide Mike with his first real breakthrough given the momentum already underway. A man who knew the Armstrong story of old had put two and two together and figured out the likely motive behind this middle aged man's antipathy towards the major concerns. Given that he also had been chucked on the scrap heap prematurely to make way for young blood a certain degree of empathy in showing the business whizz kids what some people classed as past it were capable of. Still with his contacts in Fleet Street he was welcomed into Mike's inner sanctum of the movement almost immediately.

Not that being disenchanted with Fast Fit was the exclusive preserve of the elderly as social media had now come alongside local press to win newcomers from much further afield. A spoof video doing the rounds on the internet showed Hitler at a meeting with his Generals and becoming apoplectic when informed that one of the SS had taken his car to Fast Fit for a new exhaust instead of a local garage in Berlin. In a single week it would be 'liked' by three million people in the UK alone. Hardly the type of positive spin the company was looking for.

For Fast Fit's publicity seeking CEO it was time to take note considering the double digit drop in sales. With the expanding boycott of his stores having now made it onto the business pages its major shareholders had taken note although yet to pick up the phone.

Steve Graves was one of the country's more colourful multi-millionaire entrepreneurs. A few years younger than Mike this ex city trader had taken a loss making outfit of two hundred depots and mainly through acquisition built it into Britain's biggest replacement exhaust and tyre specialist with a network of eight hundred sites in every corner of the UK. Known for aggressive marketing with its 'we'll beat any price' philosophy turnover had now passed the billion pound mark with analysts having penciled in profits of eighty million for the current financial year. With a twenty five per cent personal shareholding Graves featured regularly in the super league of Britain's wealthiest aged under fifty.

His PR team may have gone into overdrive but word of mouth was proving itself to be infinitely more persuasive with trade along the South coast having virtually ground to a stand still and now gaining momentum heading north. With little being seen of Alison or the kids, Mike's days were spent at work, a bite to eat then back on the road for his next meeting to gee up the troops. Not that public speaking came easy but confidence still growing in line with each engagement coming his way. Not just antipathy towards Fast Fit specifically but the general flavour of the boycott had caught the mood of the public towards the behavior of multinationals in general. Not unsurprisingly the analogy of David and Goliath being milked to death by most fresh-faced journalists picking up on their first major story.

A public statement from Fast Fit to the extent that they are aware there have been some customer service issues of late which have since been resolved and relish the opportunity to show disaffected customers their appreciation by holding a one day special of twenty five percent off.

'A step in the right direction' from Harry.

'Oh, come on, they'll be back up to their old tricks in no time if we take this kind of lousy bait' replied Mike.

'You think they're underestimating us?'

'Of course they are. They're not taking us that seriously but then again neither are the media. It's as if we're a source of amusement. Some of the country's OAPs having a valiant last stand before they kick the bucket but at the moment it's us that have the upper hand or else why bother running a national promo in the first place.'

'So, what is it we say we're after?'

'Every customer that's ever been there and been ripped off to be reimbursed completely. If Mr Graves is that rich then surely he can afford to pay us all back instead of fleecing us so he can keep running his hundred million pound yacht in the Mediterranean. These guys can pay for the best advice going but it's us that carry public opinion so if we stick to our guns what's the worst he can do? Who's the one with most to lose Harry.'

'I never expected things to get this far Mike, I thought at a local level would be as far as it would ever go. But I'm seventy three and on my own and life gets a bit lonely now and again if you don't fill your time somehow. You've given me a reason to get out my bed at a decent time instead of simply getting up and going through the motions. There's only so many games of golf you can play or rounds of bowls before it all becomes a bit tedious. I'll join you for the ride and I'll give my opinion when it's needed but you're a passionate man with a point to prove so the big decisions are all yours.'

'I'm happy with that.'

'In which case I think it's high time we sat down and decided on our best team and came up with a name. Mike Armstrong's retired army! No disrespect but it's not exactly twenty first century is it?

It would take a seasoned hack quite literally five seconds to come up with the kind of name that had been staring the pair in the face all along.

The real breakthrough came when the retired journalist in Mike's team was rewarded for his perseverance as Britain's biggest middle market tabloid ran a feature on the protest albeit on page five. A decent sized story and accompanying photograph of Mike centre stage with his inner sanctum of elderly advisors. The double whammy they'd been waiting for of free national coverage and a half decent name plagiarised from the original article.

'PEOPLE POWER WINNING THE DAY IN FIGHT AGAINST FAST FIT'

For Paul Anderson travelling on the 6.42 Guildford to Waterloo the same morning his early commute religiously stayed the same. Times crossword to kick start the brain to be completed by Wimbledon at the absolute latest then depending on gridlock into the capital time remaining given over to the country's most popular newspaper primarily its football coverage before being disposed of in the bin at the station. The one item of reading material for the sake of his gravitas within the organisation kept hidden from peers. His twenty minutes of pure escapism in an otherwise mentally taxing and occasionally arduous regular fourteen hour day.

A product of the Scottish state school system a young Paul managed the grades which propelled him onwards towards Glasgow University graduating four years later with a First Class Honours degree in Mathematics. A guiding hand from the Principal about serving Queen and Country and Paul was steered in the direction of a thus far very successful but not quite as lucrative as his contemporaries career at Thames House, the official HQ of Britain's internal security service otherwise known as MI5.

Not that he paid a large amount of attention to the papers content beyond a leaning towards one particular Scottish sports journalist but the very act of his reading the rag but one facet of being able to blend into the crowd. Ask anyone alighting from the train to remember ten fellow passengers and it's unlikely that this most unassuming and indistinguishable of men would be one of them. Desk officers liked to dissolve into the background just as much as their cohorts out there in the field.

Nothing to hook his interest which given his occupation was only to be expected until the feature at the top of page five answered the question that had proven itself to be something of a puzzle for him over the past month. With his skill set why pay a financial advisor two per cent annually for the privilege of building a stock portfolio when he was more than capable of going it alone. The Times business pages were kept for the return leg but at least the Daily News coverage was finally shedding some light on something that had defied logic notwithstanding the fact that the stockmarket was always a law unto itself anyway. Fast Fit had been an excellent investment until four weeks ago, the star performer in his modest portfolio but now down a third and the root cause a bunch of bloody disgruntled pensioners with nothing better to do all day than form a protest movement. Hardly the most subversive organisation in the world judging by the photo but as for its ringleader, depending on how things developed and chances are they would not, for the time being the name taken note of but little else.

'Remember why we're here. Don't go getting too carried away.'

A gentle reminder as to why Mike and the team were there in the first place. Invited up to Fast Fit's purpose built HQ in Basildon for a meeting with the great man himself. The paid for train journey and unexpected but lavish buffet seemed at odds with what this lot were doing to screw up his company's credentials. Not so much a boardroom more a shrine to someone hardly averse to a bit of self promotion. The standard mix of glass, brass and mahogany overwhelmed by canvas prints of Graves postulating with an eclectic mix of business elite, politician and the odd celebrity or two. Shrinking violet most definitely he was not.

'His exhaust's might be crap but he sure knows how to put on a spread' from one of the group.

'It's called buttering us up' from Harry. 'Anyone noticed he's already half an hour late.'

'You know why that is don't you' from Mike.' 'So, you all fall asleep after having stuffed your faces leaving me to fend for myself.'

'You're a cynical bastard, I'll give you that much.'

'Granted but don't forget who we're dealing with here Harry. This guys no slouch.'

'And you're his equal if not smarter and now's your chance to show it. You have the passion in spades Michael and you have the drive. Now all you have to do is learn to play it smart. Just let him do all the talking to begin with. Always helps when your opponent underestimates you. It lets you catch them unawares.'

Try as hard as he may and much as he had everyone's support still difficult not to feel intimidated by someone likely to come in all guns blazing. Shades of another Joe, just this one happened to be wearing a more expensive suit. Of all the times for an inferiority complex to kick in! The sudden realisation of where he was and who he was about to meet. Water off a duck's back to a man of Graves' pedigree and the photograph of him shaking the PM's hand did little to dissuade that right at this moment in time having his head stuck under someone's leaking sink still a much more preferable option to taking on a seasoned City pro. Graves' tactic was to keep them waiting and Harry had just about had enough.

'Tell me my dear' to one of the office staff posted as sentry by the door.

'Is Mr Graves going to be much longer?'

'I'm not sure.'

'Well, we are. The meeting was for 1 pm and it's now gone well beyond. Could you inform him he has ten minutes or we'll be gone.'

'Thanks Harry. It should have been me that said that.'

'You're ok! He's just playing silly buggers and the longer we stand around the more we play into his hands. Just let him keep talking as long as you like till you find your composure then go for the jugular when he least expects it.'

As if on cue and by an amazing coincidence the star of the show appears and makes a B line straight for Mike, greeting as if long lost friends. Handshake with the right hand using his left to rub Mikes shoulder as if intent on forming an immediate bond instead of being the deliberate intimidation tactic it clearly was. Graves appeared as confident in private as his public persona and it was already obvious after less than a minute who'd won the opening round. Firm enough handshake from Mike but deadpan delivery had Graves PR sidekick thinking they may not be needing quite as many gift vouchers as originally intended. The whole group bar Harry appeared in awe of this commanding presence.

'We appear to be outnumbered so please be gentle with us' started Graves. Seven on one side of the boardroom table facing just Graves and his two henchmen on the other.

'OK so first off apologies for being so late. We were asked this morning if we'd like to be the sole provider of replacement tyres and exhausts to Thames Valley Police force in the capital which is great news for jobs and I've just been asked to do the same with one of the world's biggest car hire companies. Hectic to say the least but you're here so let's get down to business and sort this out.'

Harry was right. Just sit back and let him talk.

'Michael can I just start by congratulating you on your efforts so far. No doubt about it what you've done has definitely given us a kick up the backside with the impact on sales and given I know a thing or two about selling that's no mean feat. I'm now holding out an olive branch and hope that I can appease your obvious gripes on customer service and assure you it's an issue that's the closest to my heart. Rest assured by the time you leave here today my PR Director Steve has a whole stack of tokens which should more than make up for mistakes made in the past.'

No sign of guilt whatsoever from Graves. His pre rehearsed speech delivered smooth as silk. Was he so arrogant as to assume a half decent buffet and gift vouchers meant fait accompli because as his sidekick lifted his briefcase onto the table only to bring out what appeared to be shiny bundles of glorified bribes the answer to the question appeared to be a resounding yes. A tapping of Mike's heel from Harry to the left.

'Ehhh right......so is that it? Gift vouchers to you all then be on your merry way?'

'Unless there's anything else Michael! I'm acknowledging that the issues you raised are being dealt with and this afternoon's lunch was just a token of my appreciation.'

'With respect we came here for slightly more than being entertained by your expensive outside caterers and a twenty per cent off gift voucher.'

'Which is?'

'Complete reimbursement to anyone who's visited your stores in the past three years and been grossly overcharged for either shoddy workmanship or more than likely slick marketing.'

'Two things. First off marketing is marketing. One man's slick is another man's successful and as for customers being reimbursed'...taking a deep breath as if to compose himself...'our company solicitor sitting to my left am sure will be more than delighted to enlighten you.'

Harry senses Graves has been rattled and prays to God Mike's also picked up on it. Probably passes over to his lawyer every time he senses implosion.

'Fast Fit offer a full guarantee on work carried out deemed as below company standard. We've always gone above and beyond our legal obligations in this area and where customers are still not satisfied a full refund is always offered in exchange.'

'But it's not a refund is it? It's simply a credit note that states the work will be made good provided it's in another branch of Fast Fit. Hardly fair in my books at all' chipped in Harry.

'I think sir with due respect our policy is very fair considering our competitive pricing and that customers should at least be prepared to give us a second chance.'

'Then when you screw up that chance you rely on your customers simply walking away?'

'I'm not aware of this happening myself.'

'Well, tens of thousands are judging by how empty your forecourts are in the south' from Mike sensing they were completely unprepared for any of this. The very fact he was now being addressed as Mister meant the gloves were finally coming off.

'There are some out there Mr Armstrong who may have fallen for your propaganda but many have not and our forecourts are still ticking along nicely thank you very much although granted not as they were. Like I said, I extend an olive branch to show you that we've listened and intend making good errors from poor customer service in the past.'

'You keep banging on about customer service but that's just you attempting to continually divert us all away from the fact that what you're really doing is blatantly ripping your customers off.'

'I'd be very careful with the language deployed Mr Armstrong' as the pin striped lawyer Mike could tell was dying to flex his muscles. Graves was clearly annoyed with no attempt being made to disguise the fact either. The charm offensive had fallen flat and criticism did not come easily.

'We can either agree to kiss and make up or if you want to drag out your fifteen minutes of fame Mr Armstrong then don't expect us to sit back as we've done so far' as Graves returned once more to his favourite tactic of intimidation.

'All we're doing is alerting others to the way we personally have been treated and it's up to others to make up their own minds. It's called democracy Mr Graves, seeing as we're now ignoring the pleasantries. We're doing nothing wrong and the man sitting on your right knows this and there ain't a damn thing you can do about it.'

'You're a smug bastard Armstrong aren't you?'

'Beg your pardon.'

Graves' two advisors either side clearly taken aback as much as everyone else. The lawyer attempts to reconvene but gets slapped down as Graves lets rip with one person in particular in his sights.

'You any idea whatsoever what it's like running a business this size? Any fucking idea at all? Be great if we could please everyone out there in life but things don't work that way apart from obviously in your rose tinted little fucking world. To reimburse everyone out there who thinks they've had a bum deal would bankrupt us overnight…'

'But you can still find the money for your lavish bonuses and yacht in Monte Carlo' chipped in Fred, the retired accountant in Mike's team.

'Yeh and I've got outgoings just like everyone else and mouths to feed and I also happen to work seven days a week unlike you lot of old fucking twats who've got bugger all to do all day but stand outside our exhaust centres and wave your fucking placards.'

'If I can just interject here…' from Graves PR man attempting to stem the unfolding eruption.

'No, back off Steve, I've barely started. You're a plumber Armstrong right? One man band kind of same age as me! One an achiever who did something with his life and the other one jealous because he never had the guts to go for it and give it his best shot. So, here you are trying to make a name for yourself targeting me because of my success and the fact I don't mind shouting about it.'

Mike thinking Harry had this guy weighed up from the start. Sure does like to talk. His way or the highway on just about everything.

So, here's what I'll offer you. The chance to walk away now when the going's good or else I'll come after each and every fucking one of you for defamation of my business. I'm known as a maverick in the city. You know why?

Because I don't play by the rules. Up to know I've been nothing other than fair but the gloves are now coming off old boys. You guys better have had a half decent lump sum as your pension pot because your legal fees are going to gobble it all up. I can well afford a fight in court but something tells me you fuckers can't'

The return train leg home subdued to say the least. Wind well and truly blown from sails Mike knew he'd been pushing it but not to say there was ever any room for negotiation. For Graves to show even a shred of humility might be considered a bonus instead of the stage managed affair it had always been intended to be. Be a good twenty minutes before anyone broke silence and dealt with the elephant in the room.

'I'll tell you where I am Mike' from Harold. A retired lecturer who up to now was absolutely brilliant at organisation and coordinating the troops.

'I've gone as far as I can with this. At my age the last thing I need is bloody lawyers' letters. This guy's trouble and could quite easily make all our lives a misery. I want to be able to at least have a decent night's sleep than worry about someone looking to sue.'

'I get that Harold but it's all bluff designed to scare and because we're all getting on a bit he knows none of us will want the hassle but scaring people off is what these guys do.'

'Mike's right' from Harry. 'First off I don't think this guys got as much money as he likes people to think and if he did go ahead and do anything daft I think between us we could come up with a plan to twist and use to our advantage.'

'Good thinking' from Mike who continued.

'The way I see it is we can either cave in or do the opposite of what he's expecting which is just to keep going as we are. He'll be sitting back in that office of his wondering what the hell to do next and it sure as hell won't involve building a court case. His lawyer will be earning his keep buying time with their creditors now that we've knackered his cashflow. So, come on Harold what's it to be. Leave just because a bully with a big mouth has made some threats or stay with us for the ride. Remember what our headline was in the paper, power to the people, strength in numbers or something like that.'

'Congratulations Mike' from Frank the retired marketing man.

'For what?'

'You've just given us the perfect bloody name.'

Crucially the boycott began to kick in within and around London and no sign of the Thames Valley Police force visiting the tyre centre's en masse indeed if at all. Just more Graves' bullshit in order to impress! The protest website rebranded by Frank as Power to the People gained two million followers in its first week hundreds of whom were happy to share their experiences at the hands of the Fast Fit crew.

An infuriated Graves phoned through to the newspaper's editor to voice his disgust with the story they ran considering how much he spent on advertising each year only to be reminded that he was hardly the fastest payer in the world at the best of times and a couple of hundred grand per annum was chicken feed compared to the bulk of their clients.

'With a daily newspaper circulation of two million I hate to say it pal but you need us more than we need you and at this rate those old codgers are running rings round you. Worse still the way things are going Power to the People may well end up being front page as it has a whiff of populism about it'

'Cheers mate. Thanks for all your fucking support.'

'Anytime.'

Abbreviated to PTTP the organisation was fast becoming fashionable. Never one to miss a trick a retired retailer still with a vested interest in making a fast buck or two had the brainwave of introducing some merchandise as a form of badge of membership. The revamped website did the promotion and a small workshop on London's docks produced the rest. Power to the People was on the periphery of becoming the UK's fastest growing brand.

Tee-shirts, badges, sportswear, car stickers and stationary! The fact that collectively people could hold companies to account by orchestrated boycotting en masse had caught the public's imagination and just about brought Fast Fit to its knees.

One last roll with fingers crossed tightly behind back and Graves invites Mike up to London for a private meal at one of the Capital's finer hotels. They agreed to have dinner at 6.30 pm leaving Mike ample time to catch the last train home at ten. This time around there just had to be concessions. As Chief Executive of a major PLC under fire he had no other option.

Mike would be the first to be taken to his seat at the five star Gainsborough Hotel's main restaurant. No sign yet of his dining companion and the table had also been set for three. Likely Grave's legal sidekick, Giles whatshisface which meant some kind of inducement would be on the cards. Paranoia or just very difficult not to be suspicious when dealing with a certain kind of person! His formative years had plainly left their mark.

As it stood he was wrong as Grave's companion for the evening was nothing short of stunning. To be his wife was unlikely, his mistress more probable or a paid companion just about evens. She looked at ease as they made their way towards. The kind that somehow seem to flow effortlessly through crowded spaces as if being here was simply a home from home. For someone of her calibre it quite probably was. Mike stood to greet the pair as they arrived, Steve confident and assured as always although this time around a single handshake dispensing with all the touchy feely tactic of last. A gentle handshake with his companion.

'Hi, nice to meet you I'm Antonia. Do you prefer Mike or Michael?'

For a minute there he thought she'd share a private joke and suggest Mikey.

'Mike's fine.'

The hard part for the rest of the night would be trying to avoid calling his old friend by her real name of Rachael.

'Thank God for that I thought he was never going to go for a piss. Well, well Rachael or should I say Antonia . Nice to see you at long last.'

'And you Mr fucking champion of the consumer but he's not gone to the toilets. Just watch where he goes as he's likely gone through to the cocktail bar to make sure everything's in place where you'll be invited to shake hands on a deal and have one for the road which is going to be heavily spiked. It's a relaxant, doesn't make you feel drunk, just loosens inhibitions.'

'Then what?'

'We all go up to his suite. He then disappears leaving me to work my charms, do what I do best while the hidden camera records the action. It's all the rage in the corporate world these days Mike. Someone started it in America and brought the tactic over here. You'd be surprised how many takeovers go through all on the back of a CEO shitting themselves that the wife's going to find out the hard way.'

'I see. Here was me simply expecting a padded envelope passed under the table.'

'Am glad you do because tonight was going to be the end of you but I volunteered when the agency told me the client's name because if nothing else I figured I could find stuff out and pass it on. I never expected this and I only found out an hour or so ago. I've been following your progress with your little protest movement and now you're making the pages I think back to all the times we used to drive all over the place in your battered old Mini. I keep all the newspaper cuttings in a little scrapbook and I'm even a PTTP member online. This is my redemption for all your help and keeping your mouth shut.'

'We'll need to hook up again.'

'Let's do that but back to the here and now. Somewhere in the restaurant and I really don't know where there's a photographer taking pictures of us. It's all just part and parcel of the stitch up. He told me to get the seduction process underway as soon as he left which explains why he's taking so long supposedly at the loo. The story he's going to sell is that I'm your mistress and this was us having dinner before we got down and dirty upstairs.'

'Good job I came prepared then isn't it.'

'How come?'

Because you don't think for one minute I came alone do you? Cast a glance over my left shoulder and a bit further to the right. Two, shall we say rather mature gentlemen and their lady friends who also happen to be their wives.'

The fact that everyone's eyes caught at the same time reassured Rachael that Mike knew exactly what he was doing.

'You old dog Mike. To think when we first met you were completely wet behind the ears. Now look at you.'

'So, whatever pictures have been taken so far, my side have also got some of their own in case he tries to frame this as some kind of tryst. Think how much the papers would like my version of events more than his.'

'He's come back into the restaurant now with a big fat fucking smile on his face thinking he's just about there. Time for me to slip back to being Antonia once more. Good luck and for what it's worth am really proud of you.'

'Thanks.'

'Well, you two seem to be getting on well enough' as Graves returned to his seat and a kiss on the cheek for his companion.

'Transpires Steve that we actually used to live in the same county' from Mike.

'Really, well how about as we've sorted everything else out we head through to the bar and discuss this aspect further. Agreed?'

'Sounds good to me Steve seeing as your buying. If you'll just excuse me then my turn to head to the loo.'

She'd saved his skin and just earned herself one hell of a thumping later on by way of compensation.

Chapter 9

In the end she knew the agency would simply wash their hands of the affair. They only ever did what they had to do which was find the clients, take their cut and pass on the remainder which in Rachael's case would leave her just shy of twelve hundred quid for the night's work.

A black eye and three bruised ribs all because one Stephen Anthony Linden Graves refused to believe she'd played no part whatsoever in Armstrong's sleight of hand by disappearing out the hotel side door and into the masse of Green Lane just as his drink was being spiked at the bar. Her client had a reputation for having a short temper at the best of times but positively apoplectic when he finally got her back upstairs. Considering there'd been another set of eyes on the man over and above the ones Rachael was already aware of what had possessed the man to leave so quickly unless he'd been tipped off. Unbeknownst to Mike's old friend a retired CID Inspector and PTTP devotee living in the capital had visited the hotel the two evenings prior on the group's behalf and given the lowdown on the smartest way to leave the building should he need a quick escape. Universally agreed with party members the night before that Graves was a desperate man and highly likely to have some dirty trick or another up his sleeve.

This was the price the highest of high-class hookers paid for being in the company of those making a fortune but sailing close to the wind in the process. Were she to make a song and dance or woe betide a statement to the police she'd be dropped by the agency like a brick never to frequent the hotels of Knightsbridge ever again. London was full of drop-dead gorgeous Russian, Latvian or Lithuanian girls simply waiting to step into her shoes and she knew it.

At least the consolation of seeing her old trusted friend! For someone so attractive even to this day she still found herself with no one to fall back on, her luck with relationships continuing in much the same vein as twenty years before. An inability from preventing herself from being drawn to the same type! Not that with Mike there'd ever been anything going on other than association but at least he'd broken the mould of every other scheming charlatan who appeared to continually cross her path and time was fast running out to find someone similar. Now in her mid forties and definitely at her peak the body was no longer recovering from these bruising all night sessions as quickly as once before and at some point she'd have to hang up her boots and then what? As was always the case with Rachael, just one decent client did have this nasty habit of making her hang on in there just that wee while longer.

In the meantime her reward for taking the blows would come just two weeks later when a beaming Mike surrounded by several of his elderly colleagues finally made the front pages of several of Fleet Streets finest. Not to mention a two minute interview on the national evening news. Power to the People had won the day and someone's brother watching on from the comfort of their half million pound townhouse could only shake his head in disbelief. How had this scrawniest of fellow sibling ever ended up being portrayed as the country's latest hero? For

Joe a deep sense of foreboding that younger brother was on the warpath and likely his own name was on the list.

Under pressure from the banks Graves had no option but to shut up shop losing his own shirt and that of his shareholders in the process. For one desk officer in particular at Thames House the news was particularly galling but as yet no alarm bells ringing from on high. The general consensus from those in office appeared to be here was someone enjoying their fifteen minutes of fame and the victim had by all accounts had been on a sticky wicket for years. Protest movements always tend to catch the public imagination early on then peter out as its leaders look for more lucrative ways to pay the mortgage.

Operating completely under the radar and with confidentiality arrangements put in place almost immediately wherever they go Doha Investments Inc were first on the scene with Fast Fits bankers in an attempt to take over and rebrand the redundant concern once the Fast Fit name had successfully been erased from public memory. This is what Doha Investments Inc did best. Buy well known but near defunct billion pound turnover businesses for next to a song, stick in a decent management team then flog on several years later usually making themselves a killing in the process. Virtually nothing was known of the outfit other than the name being a clue as to operating from overseas. Those in the know would remain tight lipped lest falling foul of their extremely litigious nature and to be in their employ meant being considered nothing short of being exceptional in your field.

For the banks to be approached in the first place sent a clear signal that that Doha had done their homework and if there was a deal in the making its completion would be swift. Needless to say they demanded a substantial discount from the bank's valuation but at least their immediate intervention which caught just about everyone by surprise drew a line under the sorry episode and went some way towards investors recouping at least some of their money. With little to no time to organise his own one off special dividend or a sizeable director's loan Graves would find himself being pursued to the hilt for liabilities already owed to the company and by one particular female lawyer a damn site more tenacious than his own. Dodgy ex directors would never escape Scot free once Doha arrived on the scene and almost always they aimed to settle. The only way Graves would be sunning himself at sea now would be atop a cheap cruise liner. His hundred million pound yacht already impounded in the bay of Monte Carlo courtesy of Doha's private security team.

As the public rejoiced in at last finding a home grown hero the media and financial district were now abuzz with rumour about who might be next on the PTTP hit list. Mike's next masterstroke was to put that one out to public consensus with the website tweaked so members could cast their vote making it a people's decision this time around rather than his own.

'It's the public that call the shots not me' he would profess but he was becoming more streetwise by the day. In no small part due to encouragement behind the scenes from group stalwart Harry and wife Alison who enjoyed her husband's success but happy to stay in the background!

With more experienced retirees stepping forward to offer their services it was the internet and marketing sector Mike knew were of greatest value. Tap into their knowledge then hit the ground running when it came to the next target and the protest group would always remain a step ahead. The harsh lessons of old were now ingrained. Just as B-Smart had perpetually outsmarted his father lesson number one was continuously to be on the offensive. Taking the foot off the pedal at any point signaled being doomed to fail.

It was actually his daughter Steph's idea that the PTTP website have the facility to offer members their choice of three top targets to be boycotted from which cyberspace and the websites internal calculator did the rest. With a third of the UK now officially registered as members the vote was cast over seven days and the winner conclusive. Even making the national news, next in Power to the People's firing line would be the Highway Bus Company!

Starting in the 1980s another beneficiary of Thatcher's attempts to deregulate and free up the market the Highway Bus Company set about taking care of bus routes that had once been the sole responsibility of local authorities. Understandably in order to turn a buck the business model was dependent on more streamlined operations which was a euphemism for shedding staff by the bucket load. As per the script aggressive expansion was to follow with smaller rivals driven out of town by deliberate undercutting until eventually all went bust. Left with the bulk of the UK public transport network Highway was now viewed as treating its customers with contempt by slashing services and thrice yearly well above inflation price increases. Along the way directors regularly awarded themselves huge bonuses while continuing to rake in Government subsidies in the process. The fact that they were so far ahead in the PTTP poll of likely targets came as no great surprise to anyone.

This time around Rachael would wake up to seeing her old friend on the front page of not one but every national newspaper in the land. For Paul Anderson on the 6:42 from Guildford he simply thanked his lucky stars Highway had not been part of his portfolio with its share price tanking forty per cent literally minutes after PTTP announced the unlucky winner of its nationwide poll.

At first the response appeared fairly muted. Commuters needed to commute after all and when there was no viable alternative one could hardly have expected commuters to walk through the night to be at their desks for daybreak. So, in this instance the company decided to come across as being quite nonchalant about the protests impact. A public relations disaster of epic proportions! Adding fuel to the flames the Chief Executive's rather dismissive and smug interview on national TV simply wound the public up even further. Shareholders could have been forgiven for crying into their handkerchieves as this extremely well paid man's arrogance provided all the motivation the public needed to prove him wrong. The following days headline in the Daily News said it all:

THE PUBLIC TELL HIGHWAY THE GLOVES ARE OFF!

The evening news bulletins convey the rare right of Highway buses pulling into crowded bus stops only for no one to get on. Tailbacks of crowded cars following on in the bus lanes behind offering to take commuters to onward destinations but this time for free!

Sensing the change in public mood but making a better job of PR spin many local authorities announce they will not be extending lucrative school run contracts to Highway when the current ones expire and putting them back out to tender instead. Local bus operators seize the mettle and start winning back lost passengers without having to worry about being undercut by Highway who themselves rush to reduce fares a la Fast Fit tactics in a valiant attempt to prevent a collapse in trade. Taxi firms suddenly see an up lift in early morning trade across the UK at times usually seen as quiet. More people cycling than ever before which please the green lobby and those who purely out of principle begin to leave the house earlier to try and walk to their place of work than hand their hard earned cash to the arrogant fat cat at Highway. The odd billboard or two across the capital now emblazed with the letters PTTP and the wearing of baseball caps and jogging tops bearing the protest logo now de rigeur for the pretty girls out on their early morning jog. Everyone seems to want in on the act and in boardrooms the length and breadth of the country executives work flat out to spruce up their public relations.

The jittery Fund Managers with reputations to maintain now began to offload their sizeable Highway shareholdings onto the open market. Having watched from afar with Fast Fit there was no way they were going to make the same mistakes and hang on for too long. These were the same highflyers whose colleagues had already been dispensed for calling it wrong and for those still in well paid employment self preservation was firmly the order of the day. With so many Highway shares being dropped faster than a hot potato the value of the company itself had all but crashed. From safe bet to scrap heap all in the space of less than six months! Its demise inevitable and just as before the public rejoiced in the fall from grace of another large concern that took them as mugs. All the while the nation blissfully unaware that behind the scenes a highly secretive Middle Eastern investment fund had already drawn up contingency plans for another billion pound acquisition on the cheap.

Hardly on the same scale as the group's first two targets but the next scalp would be personal and Mike was making no attempt to disguise the fact. Payback time for the editor of the East Sussex Gazette who unfortunately for him had returned to the paper for something of an easier life having failed to make a name for him himself with the broadsheets. Talk about bad timing.

Mike made it perfectly clear why he held such antipathy towards the paper and its role in his father's demise. Unable to spin his way out of this one the collapse in sales and small advertising revenue meant the paper's collapse was as brutal as the fake headlines that killed off Jim Armstrong's lifetime of hard work.

Unemployed and dejected as if to rub salt in the wound the now ex editor getting out his bed around midday opened the solitary had written envelope from this morning's mail. A nondescript view on the cover but carrying a more salient message inside.

'He who laughs last!'

Impossible for those in power not to be aware of the protests increasing significance given their popularity in the press and one hundred per cent success rate thus far against too big for their own boots multinationals. Downing Street publicly playing it coy by applauding the efforts and determination of a segment of the UK's senior society but behind closed doors increasingly concerned that unless kept in check who's to say their own jobs may end up being at stake should the movement suddenly become political. No indication yet that Armstrong's ego was out of control but if history was anything to go by only a matter of time.

Then there was the loss to the Exchequer. All very well thousands of small operators popping up to fill the shoes of the now defunct business scalps but these outfits tended to be one man bands and not so good with declaring all their income. Much easier for the Treasury when a large chunk of tax receipts are received regularly and on time from a sole provider than having to pay tax inspectors to go look over a small businesses books. The Home Secretary had a meeting over at Thames House later on that afternoon. The name of Mike Armstrong was quite near the top of his agenda.

For Joe the silver tongue and capacity to schmooze had served him well. His younger brother may never have set foot in a B-Smart but there were plenty others the length and breadth of the country who did with the company twenty years down the line now enjoying pole position as the UK's leading garden centre operator and Joe Armstrong was now the main man at the helm.

Used in the interim stages to open up new stores in and around the South coast as store numbers grew he was given overall responsibility with monthly trips to Florida for trading updates and nights on the tiles with his new best buddy and drinking partner, B-Smart global CEO the one and only slippery Lee Trenchman. His predecessor the ebullient Don Walsh having cashed in his chips a while back! Being promoted to UK Managing Director Joe continued the tried and tested B-Smart way of expansion through a combination of bribery and acquiring smaller rivals with attractive offers only to renege on the money once they'd taken the bait. Once contracts were signed the smaller rival usually accepted a smaller amount than face a costly court action and the inevitable family stress to follow. It mattered little to Joe that his devoted father had lost his lust for life and passion for his business the very same way. Joe had the kind of morality and lifestyle completely alien to previous generation of Armstrong. If his father refrained from turning in his grave then grandfather Frank would never have thought twice.

His latest twenty eight year old Ukranian girlfriend even if seriously high maintenance at least was a constant at home while the rest of the time was spent visiting sites and handing out his contact number to the more impressionable of the younger ladies working in the stores.

'Always take on the pretty young divorcees' he'd actively tell the store managers.

'They need the money.'

The store managers naïvely assuming his rationale was therefore based on the girls being more reliable but Joe had other ideas and the older women in the stores read him like a book.

Meanwhile for no other reason than to tease and with any luck induce some anxiety in his elder sibling's direction Mike did an interview in the national press where he came clean on father's demise and the circumstances leading up to it. No mention made of the culprit and their dirty tricks campaign, but one had to be fairly blinkered not to know exactly who he was talking about. For a certain retired Council Executive of some significance who'd only recently hung up his boots the chance to finally make amends! Believing that the day would never come Mike may personally have wanted Joe's head on a plate but for Alan Gill on behalf of his dearly departed old friend Glenn Daly at last the opportunity to settle a score once and for all. Already a PTTP member he set to task with some information he reckoned guaranteed reply.

'So, what do you guys have on him?'

'Nothing.'

'What do you mean nothing?'

'I mean exactly that Home Secretary! Not as if he's a threat to national security is it and if you'd stop taking a knife to our fucking budgets then we might have the manpower to plant a mole some place and see what they come up with.'

'Point taken but this is coming straight from number ten. The Prime Minister reads the papers same as everyone else and he'd rather see his own face and reaction to government policies making the front pages than a plumber with his old friends apparently running absolute rings around everyone they come across. Bear in mind there's an election in less than eighteen month's time. The last thing we want is this messiah showing his allegiance to the other side while his merry band of half the country's population fall for his every word.'

'He's a very clever and shrewd operator I'll give him that. Whether it's him or all those retired brains behind the scenes I don't know. I like his touch with publicly turning down endorsements and advertising. Simply endears himself to the public even more.'

'Dear boy it sounds like you're a fan. Just see what you can come up with and I'll call in some favours from Fleet Street as its time we brought this lot back down to earth.'

'Leave it with me. One of our desk officers down below has a vested interest in digging up some dirt on this Armstrong fellow. Lost his shirt with Fast Fit shares although he thinks we're none the wiser. Likely chomping at the bit for revenge so there won't be much of a pep talk.'

Good. Set him loose. This Michael Armstrong fellow is on the fringes of becoming seriously bloody annoying.'

Mike had arrived home via the back door and into the kitchen where Alison was in the process of making the family's dinner.

'You've got a visitor.'

'I already guessed that much.'

'Because of the car?'

'Not so much the Merc more the number plate. JA 1 was a bit of a giveaway.'

'Well, he's through the sitting room. He still looks the same from all the old photos. He's very charming.' A wry smile coming over her husband's face.

'That's Joe for you. Best see what he wants then as if I don't know already.'

'What are you going to say?'

'Absolutely nothing. After a hiatus of twenty years I just want to savour every fucking moment.'

This time around not even the smallest trait of hesitation before making his way across the hallway. The difference a couple of decade's life experience and no small amount of nationwide success had made to a one-time understudy's self esteem. The sitting room door was open giving the pair at the very least a fraction of a second to weigh each other up upon sight before the annoying familiarities which Mike so hated but his brother had off to a 'T.' Although still in the chair Joe looked trim, grey hair in abundance as one would expect for a man not far short of the big five 0. Not that little brother would ever acknowledge but Joe still looked bloody good with the clothes fitting around the shoulders as perfectly as ever but with his kind of budget nowadays how could it be any other way.

He never stood to greet his brother like a long lost friend but at least there was a smile, fake as they come for Mike on the receiving end but with anyone else quite possibly plausible. Joe was first to extend the hand of friendship.

'Mike been a while. Good to see you.'

'Don't lie Joe. Pretty obvious why you're here.'

Neither wanting to show their hand but already the first battle of wills underway as to who gripped tightest. Joe plainly determined to score an early point but completely underestimating the strength of a man several years his junior and used to demanding physical labour. First round pendulum swinging Mike's way but the night was still young.

'I won't deny it Mike but my conscience is clear when I say that I'd wanted to come and see you long before events kind of forced my hand. It really was eating away at me to think it's been this long and I'd never gotten round to meeting Alison or your kids.' No response which meant Joe had little option but to just keep on plugging away.

'You've done well. Really well! Dad would be proud of you.'

'And would he have been proud of you Joe?'

Time for another wry smile but this time on the part of the guest.

'The way things turned out for me I sincerely hope he would.'

'If you say so Joe but let's just cut to the chase. What is it you're after?'

'You already know that part. It's obvious to just about every man and his dog you're going to tell the public to stop shopping at B-Smart. We're not even a fraction of the size of the first two you destroyed so if the public stay away in their droves the lack of cash could finish us in a week.'

'Which is a lot less painful than the experience dad suffered don't you think?'

'Dad went on for too long Mike, the signs were there long before B-Smart ever came on the scene, Christ I remember you telling him as much over the kitchen table. Don't go blaming my business for everything that happened because it's just not true and you know it.'

Joe now with the bit between his teeth and doing what older brothers do best, they know what strings to pull and seem to know just that little bit more. No Carolyn around to kick her older brother's claims back over the net. Mike was being given time to think and to his cost. All he could do was nod giving Joe time to hatch his plan.

'Doesn't have to be this way Mike. There's also a way where we both walk out with our head held high and you a much richer man in the process. Think of the difference it could make to your life, not just your own but Alison's and the kids'.'

'And how does that work exactly?'

'The group CEO's coming over next week and has a proposition. I'm just the messenger but he actually really likes what you're doing by shaking things up. At least hear him out before you go pulling us under. Look at all the jobs lost not to mention quite a few of dad's old employees who went to work at the site in Uxbridge when his Lordship brought his own people along and got shot of the good ones who'd never let us down. So, much for Lord Peter and loyalty! Would you really want to see people like Rachael Compston lose her job given everything she did when she worked for us?'

'Rachael Compston? She's working for you?'

'So, you remember her after all. Most men do and not difficult to see why. You want to see her now, still pretty fucking hot.'

'So, how did she end up working in your bloody B-Smart store?' aware that he might be coming across slightly more interested than he should be.

'Don't ask me. Just happened! She was only one of a handful kept on when Lord Peter took over but they had a bit of a fall out over something. Rumour was it was his wife that thought there was something going on behind her back so it was her that came to me asking if there was anything going. What was I going to say to a girl like that? Anyway she now works in our Head Office in Merryhill. She's a bit of a kept woman in more ways than one.'

'I see.'

He had to get out of this and fast. From completely composed to head all over the place all in a matter of seconds and Joe was just the type to pounce on his instability.

'OK Joe bad news is this is the time I always go for my evening run before dinner.'

'Fine, don't want to hold you back' but he knew his younger brother was rattled and Rachael Compston was the bloody reason why, no doubt about that. Definitely something had been going on and he wondered if Alison was any the wiser.

'Broken Window on the move wearing blue tee-shirt with Nike logo and red shorts. Evening jog by looks of. Heading east, repeat east along Rochester Place. Charlie seven one confirm eyeball.'

Why would Mike pay too much attention to the Ford Transit parked up thirty yards along the road emblazoned in the marketing of Sky Sports TV. Inside one of the operations' team masqueraded as a service engineer in Sky company uniform filling out his timesheets while the team leader sat through the back with his headphones on eyes glued to the bank of monitors in front.

'Charlie seven two confirm in place.'

'Roger.'

'Charlie seven one sitrep.'

'Dirty Window running in direction of public park four hundred yards ahead from current location. Unable to pursue in vehicle.'

'Charlie seven three you've got two minutes to get changed and follow on foot. He looks fit so try and keep up.'

'Charlie seven three, cheers for that.'

'Team leader don't mention it.'

This was Paul Anderson in his element. A desk officer's job could be arduous at the best of times even if it did guarantee eventual promotion but being out there on operations was much more exciting. The adrenaline rush of anticipating targets next move and being proven correct. In other words the right guess. In his eyes no different to playing the stock market. All about having a hunch. This was why 'C' selected him for this particular job over and above his vested interest in getting even with someone who'd made a significant dent in his savings plan. A meticulous attention to detail and ability to cover the options. The best spooks were always several moves ahead and being born without a silver spoon tended to make a certain percentage of them more streetwise than others. Noticing that targets house was not a million miles away from a municipal park there was always the possibility of an evening stroll with the dog or the odd run to keep in shape which Paul had noticed with a degree of envy he decidedly was. No harm in having 'Mary' and 'Mark' from Charlie seven three, both good looking and in late twenties having running gear packed and ready to go if needed.

The Sky TV van was also on the move. If spotted which it undoubtedly would be given its multicolour wrapping it could be any one of dozens spotted on a regular basis given the company's propensity for offering once in a lifetime deals to all and sundry. A quick change of jacket and cap for its driver and nothing out the ordinary about yet another service engineer enjoying a brief skive off route in a public park with a cup of tea and a sandwich.

'Charlie seven three Dirty Windows veered off track now running across parkland north, north west. Unable to follow without making it obvious. Anyone else got an eyeball?'

'Charlie seven two in visual. Dirty Window now backtracking and retracing his route. This guy's been trained someplace.'

'Charlie seven three agreed. No option but to keep running ahead and take us out the equation.'

'Copy that' from Paul. 'Charlie seven two sitrep.'

'Got a visual. Dirty Window now making towards a single oak south west your direction. Now seated at base of tree and retrieving mobile telephone from shorts.'

'Team leader crafty so and so. Never saw that one coming.'

With the Sky van now parked up in its new location Team leader Paul set to task in his state of the art Tardis like control room using the radar to pin point Broken Window's exact grid reference before activating spectacularly expensive and sophisticated communication tracking to hone in on his call but all to no avail. Just as he'd wanted and got to the final stage of eavesdropping the message on the screen flagged 'call encrypted.' Whoever it was he was speaking to did not want to be heard.

'Ok team leader Charlie's seven one, two and three return to base. We're done for the night.'

Nothing unusual to go for an early evening run but to veer off course then backtrack your route before finding a secluded spot from which you could retrieve and then make a call on your encrypted phone was a different matter altogether. Anderson was consumed by the man. There was a hell of a lot more to Mike Armstrong than his halo would have everyone believe.

Entertaining the editor of the Daily News at his official London residence, dinner was proving to be less fruitful for the Home Secretary than had originally been planned.

'The problem you have Tim is this guy's a national hero because he's mobilised half the country into collectively doing the things you said your Government would do but never actually got round to doing. Teaching the conglomerates a lesson, tick. fat cat pay, tick. no faith in the political classes to do anything for the working man, tick.'

'It's not as straightforward as that Jim and you bloody well know it. Why can't you point that fact out in the press.'

'We're both in the selling game. You're selling a message whereas we try and sell good stories and that's exactly what this guy Armstrong is, a damn good story. He's selling something as well. A vision that everyone's buying into and we're just reporting it. He's done wonders for our advertising revenue I can tell you that.'

'We go back a long way. Saints always have a skeleton in their cupboard somewhere. Surely that would make just as good a story.'

'You think we haven't already tried? Half of Fleet Street's been traipsing over this guy's past trying to find some dirt but so far two speeding tickets and a father that topped himself is as much as anyone's got and even that seems to have just endeared him to the masses even further',

'Just be creative then, you do it with our lot often enough.'

'Quite but this guy's a smarter operator than half your bloody cabinet put together. Who's to say he won't accuse us of running a smear campaign and tell thirty five million people to stop buying our paper and then where does that leave me. You rely on reelection and we rely on advertisers to pay the wages and they don't hang around very long when sales drop trust me.'

'Flash in the pan or not?'

'Hate to tell you Home Secretary I think he's barely started. Everything up to now I think has just been the warm up act and God help you if he takes up with the Opposition.'

Two of the most influential men in the UK at the moment and each wrestling with their own personal dilemma! What to do of someone outside of the mainstream holding the balance of public opinion in the cusp of his hand and for that very same person just what the hell is Rachael Compston up to. If the press were to find out about his early days shenanigans as a glorified pimp he's a finished man.

Chapter 10

We're all creatures of habit and that still includes the high and mighty. For the head of B-Smart Lee Trenchman now that the feedback from Joe was favourable it would be a case of the same tactics that had proven themselves so effective in the past. Make an offer that's simply too good to refuse before reneging at the last minute by which time the other party had become so emotionally hooked they would eventually settle.

The only difference this time around was that his greatest adversary to date had nothing to sell so if Trenchman were to double cross with the bait of three million then what had Mike to lose? He'd simply tell his merry band of thirty five million followers to boycott his stores and overnight Trenchman's business would be kaput. The problem he had was that B-Smart was a different beast to the one presided over by the ebullient Don Walsh. For the garden centre chain the writing had been on the wall for some time now which likely explained Walsh's not so unexpected decision to retire. With so many analysts voicing their concern over his company's viability the only logical way forward was to remove B-Smart from the stockmarket altogether and raise the funds to take back into private ownership. Such was his dubious reputation however most of the inward investment therefore came courtesy of the burgeoning Florida drugs trade where B-Smart had since become the primary vehicle in the States and the UK for laundering their cash. Probably for the first time in his seriously slippery career Trenchman was under the cosh and he had to get this one right lest fall foul of the kind of investor one dare not upset. Bad enough the business going under but for unethical investors to see their ill-gotten gains go down the tubes the odd selective knee capping may be called upon and Lee had already been given a gentle hint that those in hiding were watching events closely. The plan was that for Armstrong to be even filmed discussing a payoff could likely prove sufficient to make the public question his authenticity. No smoke without fire and all that.

First off Mike needed to be softened up a bit and boxed in so that the only means of escape involved taking the bait, or at the very least being seen in discussion about it. The source of this deceit none other than economical with the truth friend of old Rachael Compston!

Knowing he'd be less than impressed she omitted to tell Mike that B-Smart and its head honcho were the insurance policy she hedged against having a nonexistent week in the more lucrative field of what had euphemistically been rebranded in the nineties as escorting. When what was left of the Armstrong family departed Rachael was one of the few kept on by his Lordship but his wife had other ideas about her suitability given her husband's roving eye and propensity for enjoying the company of the new girls on site deemed by her Ladyship as being distinctly downstairs. Not necessarily fired but by mutual consent Rachael found herself out of work and now with no driver either to ferry her around and two young mouths still to feed she was left with little option but to take up Joe's offer and relocate to Uxbridge to work for a business that on the one hand she loathed but at least provided the income to keep a roof over her family's head in the short term.

Trenchman's periodic visits were the additional bonus that supplemented her paltry wage, the double life of which Joe was only too well aware but at least she had the safety net of a sugar daddy being her boss's boss so he followed orders and remained at arm's length. Determined to have some degree of autonomy over her life once able to drive the alter ego was resurrected and she took up where she left off but now operating within the higher echelons of the capital a couple of days a week and still the safety net of an administration job within the company's Head Office as much for her sanity as the income. The field of escorting now experienced the same issues as most other service businesses in the UK in that the market had fast becoming saturated.

Joe thought Rachael perfect for the snare because in this instance at least there was history and as far as he could surmise some unfinished business between the pair. She duly made contact and to coincide with Trenchman's visit for the first time in almost two decades the good news was that Mike had agreed to head down memory lane with his invited visit to the Commodore Hotel only this time parking out front as someone of note as opposed to two hundred yards along the leafy road and out of sight. Was there finally a flaw in being so brazen considering such a risk? Sure he knew who'd be paying for all this but if Rachael had it all under control with the timing and no one the wiser then why pass up on a long overdue indulgence. The sting was on!

'You're not the only one Paul who now has his suspicions' said 'C' as the pair sat in the Deputy Director General's office overlooking the river on the fourth floor of Thames House.

'I was keen to find out about the whole family over and above what this fellow Armstrong's been saying in the press. Deceased parents, three siblings two of which very much alive and kicking but one simply disappearing off the face of the earth and that would be the solitary sister! First class honour's degree in law from Sussex University then heads off to work in the City where the feedback tells us she was something of a flyer before going off to work in the Middle East exact location unknown. Passport logins are telling us she spends her time flitting between Abu Dhabi, Qatar and the UK. All stations have now been made aware that the minute her passport flags up to notify and we'll have a team waiting this end to follow, if this is where she's coming and my gut tells me she is. I don't know what it is but there's a link we're missing out on.'

'It was plain as daylight 'C' that Armstrong had been taken aside. It's one thing trying to avoid the Press but this was the kind of stuff we're all put through at basic training. As for the encrypted call and its length we're talking thirty seconds tops and that was it.'

'Then all we do then is wait, join the dots and hopefully see the connection.'

'And if not?'

'Well, Paul, maybe he is the saviour of the masses after all and if the rumours are true buy some cheap summer bedding plants from my local B-Smart store before he buries them too.'

As Rachael duly made contact details of the date forwarded to Joe to take care of booking one of the

Commodore's finest suites for its illustrious visitor and figuring out best place to conceal the camera. Times had moved on since Trenchman's early days of staging a sex sting. All that was needed now was the most basic of digital camera on a timer or even Rachael just using her mobile to take care of the awkward part. Not wanting to feel excluded Joe opted for the digital camera option then made his escape to collect Lee from the airport before returning later on for the meeting around eight. Now up to Rachael to do the fun part which the duplicitous brother simply couldn't wait to see.

Looking as good as she possibly could they met up in the bar, resistance proving futile as they duly headed upstairs. The performance not quite what the duo on their way there would be expecting. As the call came through to the room exactly ninety minutes after arrival an invitation for Rachael and guest to join Lee and Joe downstairs in the bar. With phase one complete phase two should for all intents and purposes have been a fait accompli. How could this happily married man who as far as the British public were concerned walked on water possibly turn down such a generous offer and therefore back off from proposing a mass boycott of B-Smart stores. With the pair photographed both entering the hotel then the suite upstairs denial would prove impossible. Joe was practically salivating at the thought of retrieving his camera from the room. Trenchman checked his phone.

'Leaving room now.'

'I'm looking forward to this Joe' eyebrows raised from Lee in response to Joe's Cheshire cat like grin.

That sense of anticipation would be as good as it got as the past had just walked into the bar to haunt him. In the time it took Rachael and invited guest to set foot inside and walk the thirty feet or so to his table Trenchman had literally seconds to compute just how his old arch nemesis Alan Gill of the East Sussex Three had managed to ingratiate himself into being filmed upstairs having sex with a hooker when he'd passed up on such debauchery practically two decades earlier.

'Lee it's been a while.'

Remembering the face from somewhere although right at this minute with so much going on in his chaotic life not quite sure where from.

'I'm sorry but would you like to remind me who you are?'

'Of course. My name's Alan Gill and we met more or less twenty years ago when I was part of a trip that came out to Florida at your invitation under the auspices of seeing how well your business was doing in the States. We were to help you pull the necessary strings but in the end you simply pulled ours with one man losing his job and the other his life in the process. Remember me now?'

'Yes I sure do although obviously I would question your interpretation of events.' Lee doing his level best to remain composed but underneath dying to grab Joe's throat with both hands.

Joe himself the innocent bystander not having a clue as to what was going on other than somehow or another he'd been hoodwinked by the person in receipt of the full force of his glare although Rachael appeared anything but intimidated. Always nice to know when a very streetwise even if retired lawyer with an axe to grind has your back.

'Well, my ex-wife always accused of never being able to let my hair down so when the opportunity presented itself even at my ripe old age who was I to refuse. I'm assuming you have the performance captured on tape somewhere so feel free to report back on how I did. Did it work out for you Rachael?'

'No complaints from me dear.'

'Sorry a certain person couldn't make your feeble attempt at bribery but he'd rather be at home with his lovely wife Alison and his two teenagers.'

'No idea what you're talking about' from Joe.

'Oh, I think you do and your ever so reticent boss certainly does.'

'Congratulations Alan. So, does that mean we're even?'

'Yes it probably does. Twenty years in the waiting Lee but it sure tastes sweet and I have to thank someone much cleverer than the pair of us for giving me the opportunity to come back and screw your plans. If I may say so Joe you took your brother as a mug. How could you possibly think he'd fall for something as blatantly obvious as this? The pair of you nothing other than a couple of one trick ponies now literally days away from being put out of business. Somewhere up there I hope my old friend Glenn's looking down and having a damn good laugh at your expense Lee.' Turning to his glamorous companion. 'Shall we go?'

'You've just made the biggest mistake of your life Rachael' from Lee unable to resist a final swipe!

'Looks like that makes three of us then doesn't it.'

The recording afterwards revealed nothing more exciting than the pair sat drinking tea.

A text from Alan to Mike who wasted no time in texting Harry who then called through to the elderly IT lieutenant in charge of the PTTP website input. Within minutes the faithful following blissfully unaware of the shenanigans going on behind the scenes would read the latest statement about the group's next target and their assistance required in bringing around its downfall. Not that after all the speculation the public were not already aware but at least it was now official. The time had come for swathes of the population to make their own breakfasts on a weekend because a boycott of the stores and its restaurants was now on and its impact within days plain for all to see. From the car parks being full on a weekend to practically deserted but for a handful resolute to do as they please rather than follow the lead of the UK's very own home grown messiah.

To compound matters unlike Fast Fit or Highway this was a company with a significant presence Stateside where thanks to the global spread of social media there were no shortage of takers across the pond resonating with the UK group's ethos and decided to do their own bit against this goliath of the garden world and follow suit.

What events did was make it extremely difficult therefore to launder drugs' cash. How to put money through the books disguised as turnover was impossible when customers were practically nonexistent on the ground. Now that the business was on the skids the narcotics kingpins would want their money back so at the very least make some kind of return rather than it being used to simply keep someone afloat. Trenchman was in the shit and there would be a queue of vengeful small operators the length and breadth of the country loving every minute of it.

Joe just fled the scene. Complicit in dubious money transfers disguised as sales he quickly upped sticks and left knowing full well that Trenchman would have no hesitation in hanging him out to dry if it meant saving his own ass. The leased Mercedes was deposited in the dealership car park at 6 am when no one was around and the keys to the rented townhouse placed in an envelope and shoved through the agent's letterbox leaving his buxom Ukranian girlfriend to arrive back from the airport only to find a 'To Let' sign at the front door. More hacked off at finding somewhere decent to stay than losing a partner who'd seen better years.

Over at Thames House the message had just flagged up on Paul's screen.

'CA Bkd. Doha – H/Row. Arr T/DY 14.10, BA Flt 3497'

'C's hunch proving correct, the elusive Carolyn Armstrong was on her way here.

He checked his watch, just gone eleven. By operating standards the debrief was the easy part, just a pain in the ass having to drive out to Heathrow on a midweek lunchtime. One attachment was added which would be her photo from checking in at Doha and for the first in a long time for the ops team a target that was real easy on the eye. Likely at her peak, age forty five, brunette shoulder length hair, tan obviously helping and just the type to stand out in the crowd even for one as congregated as airport arrivals. With any other flight she likely would but this one was coming in from Qatar, tax haven of rich British expats where likely not the only glamour puss disembarking from First Class. Still, would perk everyone up at debrief where there was a spare ops team on permanent standby to deal with the unexpected.

Unlike the brother having been under surveillance in the leafy suburbs this time the second target was to be tracked in one of the most congested spaces on the planet, Heathrow Arrivals Terminal Two. Given her professional status Paul reckoned a high probability of either her being collected or failing that a taxi into the capital. The Piccadilly line also an option and in this instance the preferred one due to ease of tracking. The debrief straightforward enough with indicators pointing to a possible financial collusion between brother and sister, the service just needed something more concrete over and above a hunch that would help bring the pieces together.

No need for the team to suffer the indignity of having to mingle with the rest of the waiting public the wrong side of the arrivals' screen. Their security clearance was such that Carolyn, target name Lazy Sunday, was being tracked practically as soon as she'd stepped off the plane. Charlie seven one finding the jacket a bit on the stale sweaty side but still managing to pass himself off as part of airport security.

A taxi it would be, noted that not at any single point did she resort to using her mobile, not even to check texts. Most unusual for someone who had just alighted and in her professional capacity likely to be in constant demand! At no point did any of the four car ops team well versed in the art of trailing suspects on the nose to tail congested A4 lose a visual which simply validated the assumption that this one hell of an attractive lady knew she was under surveillance and Paul suspected given her demeanour enjoying every minute of it. Whoever she worked for had trained her well. Arriving in Westminster and deposited at the Waldorf it was inevitable one of the team wouldn't pass up on this golden opportunity for a touch of sarcasm.

'Charlie seven two. All this way and back again for a hotel that's only two minute's around the fucking corner. Don't suppose anyone thought of sticking her name into the Booking dot com network?'

'Charlie seven zero, well seeing as your so fucking smart while we all go back to the canteen you can stay back and do some digging. It's a posh place so don't let the side down.' Howls of laugher all round from the other two cars parked up close by.

'Are you sure that's a good idea' from Harry. 'I'm old enough Mike to know that the most important part of anything is knowing when to get out.'

Mike was also under surveillance tracked for only as far as it took him to reach Harry Wright's three bedroom bungalow less than a fifteen minute car journey from his house. This time around just the two of them, a throwback to days of old when a man on a mission got a helping hand up from someone adjusting to his latter years alone!

'You've made your point, we all have but there's only so far you can go before the tide will turn and you'll finally come up against an adversary much smarter than you are. It hasn't happened yet but it will.'

'Yeh I get that but so far all we've done is scratch the surface. These were business's that had been sailing close to the wind for years anyway and all we did was come along and give them that final nudge over the edge.'

'So, what is it you actually want out of this Mike?'

'Contrived as it may sound I actually want to make a difference.'

'You already have. It was you that brought us all together in the first place and galvanised the movement. Your passion shone through. Companies out there are a lot more wary of using slick marketing techniques than they used to be living in fear that Power to the People may just return and kick them where it hurts.'

'I want another scalp, in fact a couple then I'll gladly give all this up a happy man. I'm doing this in memory of my father Harry. His legacy is that never again will those people at the top of large corporations get away with walking all over the little guy and treating their customers like dirt. There are still a few out there, yes much bigger and smarter than we've taken on before but we can do it. Everyone's on our side! Why give up when the goings good.'

'In which case Michael I wish you well. I thought after this latest success we may just draw things to a close and I really have enjoyed the ride. You came along and gave me a new lease of life when I needed it most but the time's come I'm afraid to bow out. Not just me but I think you'll find there's a few on the committee now finding it all a bit much.

'I get that. None of us are getting any younger.'

'Therein lies the problem. It's all become a bit too time consuming Mike. There are times when I'd rather be tending to my greenhouse than dealing with journalists knocking on my door. You'll have to speak to everyone else but I think you'll find those in my age bracket feel the same. It's time some of us finally stepped off the bus.'

'Sure I can't tempt you to stay for one last protest'

'No, my mind's made up but you won't be short of people wanting to be part of your inner team. Just choose wisely and follow my lead about knowing when to pack it all in.'

With that the tone of the conversation changed in an instant. The connection had gone and the atmosphere became stifled, somehow awkward. As if Harry had more to say but opted to hold back. Mike could only surmise that ultimately Harry disapproved of his desire to keep going and he'd be right because for Harry it almost felt like his companion had fallen into the trap of believing his own publicity. After a few minutes of pleasantries and not wishing to be rude Mike would bid his final farewell, the last he would see of his former trusted number two and the one responsible for providing the self belief in the first place.

For the surveillance op listening in to the bug that had been planted on the underside of Harry's wall cabinet nothing to pin anything on either of them other than one man's determination to cost the business world dear appeared resolute.

He was not your everyday run of the mill Waldorf type of visitor. Late twenties with a kind of backpacking around Europe look about him minus the rucksack. Not unsurprisingly he caught the attention of the eighteen stone but well suited and booted head doorman as he sauntered up the front steps towards the revolving door.

'Can I help you' the doorman asked. With his experience the young bloke was either coming inside to take photos for posterity or to use the toilet. In London with the closure of so many public conveniences in recent years most probably the latter.

'No, I'm fine thanks' the visitor replied making direct eye contact with a confident smile on his face. The sheepish washroom users are normally the ones that avoid eye contact at all costs as if the guilty look on their faces suffices to give the game away in advance. No response from the doorman but he would follow the cocky young shit of a visitor through the door nonetheless and keep an eye from a distance as the hotels latest visitor headed straight towards reception.

'Good afternoon sir. Can I help?' from the incredibly courteous and well groomed male receptionist likely the same age.

'Yes I'd like to speak to the manager please.'

'I see and do you have an appointment?'

'Nope, no I don't but I'd still like to speak to him in person if he's on duty.'

The receptionist now looking over in the direction of the doorman who is yet to move further forward!

'I'm afraid it's not quite as straightforward as that sir. Unless you have an appointment it really won't be possible.'

'In which case to make both our lives easier could you ring through and tell him or her that there's someone here to speak to them as a matter of urgency and he's using the code Kaleidoscope two five seven four three.' His face now commanding a degree of authority!

'If I were you, I would do this right now.'

'If you just bear with me sir, I'll only be a minute.'

Standard practice for Charlie seven two or any of the other ops when visiting what one would only describe as the more discernible of London's hotels. They got off on looking completely out of character for the context but the capacity to exert power and control with a solitary snap of the finger. As the atmosphere changed Charlie watched as the receptionist engaged in hushed dialogue with someone he assumed of higher rank. The heavily built doorman had now come forward several feet not wanting to miss out on the unfolding action as the cocky young upstart held his eye.

'The hotel manager is on his way now sir. I've been asked to see if you would like tea or coffee.'

'Thank you no that's fine, I'll just wait here. Spoken while still holding doorman's gaze and who had now taken the hint and gone into retreat. No sooner had normality returned to the front desk than the manager himself appeared. Tall and good looking with the kind of accent and handshake that had fee paying school background written all over it. The type that if you ever imagined what a five-star Waldorf hotel manager would look like then he would be it.

'Pleased to meet you. I am Simon James, hotel manager. Do you have the second part of the code?'

'Hairspray.'

'Thank you so how can I help?'

'You have a guest just checked in that we're particularly interested in. Just need to have a look through booking details.'

'Follow me.'

The Waldorf was one of a half dozen illustrious hotels within the Westminster post code on 'friendly' terms with the Security Service. Their history and prestige such that even some of the world's wealthiest undesirables were still drawn to savouring the finest of the capital's hospitality.

No great surprise that she paid for the booking herself but at least they now had the card details where the issuer would be obliged by her Majesty to pass on transaction details that at some point was bound to lead back to who the hell she worked for. Being booked in for three nights she'd surely lead them to something or someone and at fifteen hundred quid a night the suite big enough for at least two or three strategically placed listening devices going undetected.

The doorman on Charlie's exit holding the side door adjacent to the swing doors open for his influential visitor. When one has a job on the side for cash over and above his salaried income it pays to keep on the better side of some of the government's more arrogant public servants!

'Fuck me! I never saw that one coming Paul did you?'

'No, this woman's already full of surprises' he replied.

From trailing Carolyn as she left the hotel by taxi the following morning the assumption was a two mile but half hour's drive through congested traffic into the City's financial heartland. Correct guess in that this was where she'd eventually end up but a rabbit out the hat to start off. No more than an eight minute journey across the Thames and on into Lambeth. Heading along into Citadel Place and parking up outside the headquarters of the

NCA, otherwise known as the UK's National Crime Agency.

'Any ideas then?' from Charlie seven one, Paul's preferred driving companion. Entered the Service the hard way via the Army and just like Paul not a silver spoon in sight when it came to the pair's formative years! Something of a kindred spirit and coming from Manchester's notorious Moss side as street wise and savvy as they come.

'Not in the fucking slightest. I just haven't a clue. I don't get any of this and to make matters worse these NCA bastards are the world's best for keeping the juicy stuff all to themselves so they can avoid cutbacks with the best headlines.'

'But if they're made to hand stuff over…'

'Depends whose case it is. I'll just have to pass this bit up and see if there's any dialogue at the top. I won't be holding my breath for a quick reply.'

If only Paul had been party to the conversation about to take place upstairs in the higher echelons of the headquarters asset recovery team. Common knowledge among the international movers and shakers of the finance world where the global players in the narcotics' trade deposit their cash and B-Smart were already on everyone's radar including the NCA. Now that the garden centre chain was nothing other than the business equivalent of a dead man walking only a matter of time before the drugs' lords sought to recoup some cash by selling a few of their prime sites, proceeds of which the NCA would rather keep all to themselves.

Forever the master strategist, times had moved on from cutting her teeth negotiating with his Lordship to now negotiating with some of the most powerful institutions in the land. Her skill set honed over the years learning to second guess the motives of those sitting opposite and always managing to find the kind of deal up front that bypassed future protracted negotiation. Helped in no short measure because she had the Doha group's unreserved support with her favourite line:

'Trust me. By the time the inks dry the funds will be on their way.'

Her suggestion to the NCA even if it were several years down the line before anything came to fruition was that should there be a legal sequestration of B-Smart assets then rather than the very expensive and time-consuming process of putting these assets, primarily land up for sale, the Doha group were putting forward a proposal to buy the whole lot including a substantial deposit up front as long as being given the green light for preferred bidder status. This alongside a substantial discount required in acceptance of their offer, somewhere in the region of forty per cent she considered fair in the circumstance considering risk and timescale. The fact of the matter was that Carolyn was playing B-Smart at their own game from an idea that she'd remembered from her earlier encounters with them as a student at her dad's side decades back. Buying prime sites on the cheap to ultimately convert into more lucrative housing, just that Doha would actually finish off this part which Trenchman never quite seemed to get round to achieving. Having gotten used to juggling so many goddam balls in the air it simply became a practical issue that the poor bugger never had time.

The NCA would of course do their financial checks in the City from those in the know and find out for themselves if Doha was always as good as its word. Carolyn reckoning that the thought of a few extra million in the NCA's coffers up front likely sufficient to entice speeding proceedings against B-Smart along a whole load faster now that the fattest of carrots was dangling in front. Not to mention the headlines of yet another unmitigated success for the agency. As she set about seducing the agency's bean counters her trump card was to underplay this idea as being her own and instead allow those few in attendance to take the public credit in a you scratch my back I'll scratch yours kind of way.

Checking her watch she couldn't help but wonder how little brother was getting on the other side of the capital with the first of several TV interviews to tell the nation his enthusiasm and passion for the cause were undimmed and those of stained reputation would pay the price. Articulate as always, the personification of fairness and integrity, barring a few notable exceptions he came across well. No doubt adding a few more hundred thousand followers to the protest group's website in the process such is the power of TV.

For Harry watching at home the man on the screen was becoming a different beast to the one behind the first and most memorable success in the boardroom of the exhaust and tyre tycoon. Had events conspired to finally get him to this position of power or is this where he'd always wanted to be. For this elderly man who was the catalyst behind getting him up and running in the first place the jury was most certainly out.

Chapter 11

For one of the UK's most prominent retail tycoons he'd just about had enough. What was planned to be a relaxing morning in the comfort of his penthouse apartment following an eventful night with his latest female paid companion was being ruined by the sight of 'that bloody Michael Armstrong' pontificating yet again on breakfast TV. Not often one of Britain's leading retail billionaires volunteers to cook a Full English breakfast but that was this morning's pre meditated attempt at humility. That underneath the bling he really was just the same as everyone else, but Mike's face had put the brakes on that plan. Fixated to the screen and with a stomach likely in knots it was left to Rachael to improvise in a kitchen infinitely superior to that of the quality of the food about to be cooked within it. Extremely rich men she noted did have this propensity for watching their pennies a whole load more than your average Joe when it came to spending their hard earned cash on life's essentials. Fine when it came to dining out to impress but when it came to cooking at home they were just as frugal as everyone else.

Within a cooking space that had probably set him back at least six figures, wall to ceiling glass paneled view over Regents Park and his Bentley down below in the underground car park here she was about to start frying sausages from a packet marked everyday essentials. Even the coffee was supermarket own label. Her latest client was not alone, Trenchman was just the same. In fact they all were. This whole concept of demanding your pound of flesh was indicative of this kind of self made but populist tycoon, surmising that at twelve hundred quid a night for her time the economies to pay for it all had to come from somewhere, usually the household budget as it at least gave some kind of peace of mind.

'Who the fuck does this guy really think he is? He's making us all out to be some kind of parasite on the economy. Take a risk, work like a dog, put your house on the line and create a few thousand jobs or so then simply sit back and wait for this fucker to come along and try to put you out of business. So, much for wealth creating and entrepreneurial Britain!' The best she could do was purse her lips and raise the expensively manicured eyebrows. Good old Mike. There just seemed no escaping the guy these days, as if he'd become a de facto part of her life. Now here he was looking in on the same room albeit from Grey's fifty five inch plasma TV.

The only time Rachael reckoned she'd ever see Trenchman again would be on the inside page of the papers wearing an orange boiler suit and draped in shackles so she could do with a new reliable sugar daddy but perhaps the escort agency knew something she didn't. Just about all her wealthiest clients now seemed to have some direct or impending connection to Mike Armstrong and not exactly on the friendliest of terms either. After everything that had happened thus far had events just made her paranoid or was there more to her meeting up with certain clients than was being let on? No and yes! Mike was only in a television studio after all so sense of perspective required but for the small paunchy man sitting opposite still in his bathrobe and hooked on Viagra a feeling of inevitability that these two men were going to lock horns at some point.

Her latest high-end paymaster was Charles Grey, one of Britain's most well known and flamboyant retailers and like many a self made man not known for taking prisoners. The man who eschewed further education to start his working life as a market trader selling denim jeans from a stall on the Old Kent Road had by sheer guile and absolute hard graft risen to become king pin of the UK's high streets owning a raft of the country's best known fashion labels all in the space of a little over three decades. A colourful character, his reputation somewhat tarnished in recent times by questionable accounting practices painted in the press as nothing other than decidedly shady. But he was smart, streetwise, smart and somehow or another no matter how much crap thrown his way always managed to end up smelling of roses although no doubt about it Armstrong was now seriously beginning to annoy. Reason being he saw himself as the likely kingpin in PTTP's firing line and he'd be right, to a point. Not so much on Mike's immediate agenda as he was spoiled for choice with suitable candidates but certainly on Carolyn's.

Up to now Power to the People's targets had more or less been based out of town being either industrial estates or retail parks with the major high street retailers as yet left well alone. As if they did not have enough on their plates as it was with internet shopping coming along to help customers vacate the high street in their droves. Not to say though that city centres in the UK were finished. Change was coming and for Doha transformation spelt financial opportunity. A certain someone in the retail world owned some of London's most prestigious sites as well as others in similar prime positions spread across most other major cities. Given how much he was already on the ropes and what with being pilloried in the national press a public blockade of his stores could just about seal Charles Grey's fate. Carolyn's formative experience with the two charlatans attempting to buy her father's business for peanuts had left its lasting legacy. She was now as scheming and manipulative as the best of them. With each target now becoming more profitable than the last this was the second reason behind her highly productive but flying visit. Her piecing together the final stages of an investment strategy likely to make her backers literally billions in profits and a gargantuan bonus for herself along the way! Younger brother had proven himself to be the kind of money spinner no one in the family could ever have imagined.

Her highly inventive proposal to the forensic accountants of the NCA had also been particularly well received. So, much so that by an amazing coincidence B-Smart's headquarters in Faversham were raided as part of the agency's ongoing investigation into money laundering in the UK as little as one week later. Not that there was anyone of note left to interview. The rats had left the sinking ship a while back but at least it meant the UK's National Crime Agency were on her side and likely to speed bureaucracy along while two miles along the Thames and with their noses distinctly out of joint the country's Homeland security service could only scratch their heads in disbelief trying to figure out just what the hell she was playing at.

'I don't want this to go on forever Mike. We see more of you on the TV these days than we do at home' from a somewhat deflated Alison.

'Yeh and what about the fact that you were the one who told me to just go for it in the first place?'

'Which you did and I'm really proud of you. You persevered when it was looking like things were never going to get off the ground and you've given more than a few ego's a bloody nose but the whole Power to the People thing has taken over our lives and for what? When all this ends things will go back to the way they were and you'll be history.'

'Thanks for your support Alison. That makes me feel so much better.'

'I'm just trying to give a sense of perspective. Don't feel it's your duty to help everyone out because most people out there have very short memories when it comes to gratitude. Are you doing this because you've still got a point to prove or just relishing the attention.'

'What do you think? You should know me well enough by this time. We've been married twenty odd years.'

'I think you're doing it for all the right reasons but liable to get your fingers burnt if you're not careful and I'll tell you another. I don't know what part Carolyn's playing in this but now's as good a time as any to tell you I don't trust her. She's smart, polished and always got an answer but you know how you just know.'

'Don't know what you're on about.'

'Oh, really? Well, when someone has to go to a public park to call their sister in the Middle East on a secure phone, there's definitely more to it than meets the eye and I know it's from her end not yours so whatever it has she's got planned just remember you were warned.'

'The phone's all about security.'

'Yes, hers not yours! Get real. You're a smart guy so start waking up to the fact there's something going on here that none of us know much about so do something about it Mike and soon. Have you never asked yourself why Harry and the gang suddenly quit? Forget everything he told you about tending to his roses, he loved working with you but he smelled a rat and got out while he could.'

That's half the problem with blood family, trust just gets taken for granted. Albeit not to include the Joes of this world who make their positions in life so glaringly obvious one would be dumb not to walk away but here there were one or two worrying signals that he'd either deliberately or subconsciously chosen to ignore.

'I'll speak to her on her own when she comes down to visit the kids tomorrow.'

'Why do you ask Rachael?'

'I'm just curious that's all. Seems to be the case I'm getting a certain kind of client at the moment and that's not to say I don't want them. Just wondered if there was any particular reason why?'

Neither was on the friendliest of terms as such. More a mutual understanding and extremely rare for someone on her books to request a meeting and as such bring attention to an enclave in one of South Kensington's more discreet yet ridiculously affluent locations.

She'd only ever known her Madame as Maxine but under no illusion that the neighbours likely knew her as someone who's first name was a tad more conventional. Times had moved on and for sure Maxine had utilised the internet as a marketing tool just as Mike had milked it to death with PTTP. Yet still her client base was such that for the very top end they still wanted the personal touch and for the super wealthy lengthy discussion in often forensic detail on a particular girl's attributes and suitability. She knew that these kinds of men got off on talking about girls as much as meeting them.

Rachael was old school when it came to escorting. Perfectly capable of finding clients of her own accord but at least through an established agency this way she was guaranteed a 'type' rather than the lottery of whatever awaited the other side of the front door. Maxine operated from the shadows but in this case a better class of shadow in a mews lane on the periphery of where Kensington encroaches onto its more well-heeled Knightsbridge neighbour. This was where Prestige Escorts marketed themselves as supplying suitable ladies for only the most discerning of clientele. Rachael was one of Maxine's longest serving ladies and each had served the other well. No camaraderie as such, more an understanding.

'You're one of the few that gave up being classed as an escort a while back. You're more a paid companion Rachael and there's a world of difference as you know. You know how to stroke a successful man's ego and these things only come with age and experience and the feedbacks always the same. Just look at how much these men are able to relax in your company. If you're referring to Charles Grey who's a very strong character you were the first person that sprang to mind when he came calling. Very few girls can handle men like that which then makes them feel uncomfortable which then defeats the whole object of the exercise.

'I see.'

'You don't sound convinced. All I'm doing is occasionally fitting pegs in holes Rachael but fifty per cent of the time it's just random so not exactly the well-oiled machine I like my girls to think it is. Whatever it is that's really on your mind I take it you're not going to tell me.'

'Correct.'

'Fine but if there's something you want to get off your chest you only need to ask. The door's always open.'

'I'll bear it in mind Maxine and just for the record no issues seeing Charles Grey again. He's a pussycat.'

'I'll tell him that. He'll love it.'

With that it was obligatory middle-age women small talk which did little to disguise the fact that neither believed the other was being completely open and up front on the matter in hand. There would be at least one curtain twitching upon Rachael's leaving. In a micro community like this rumours are always aplenty and there'd been enough about Geraldine Parker Jones aka Maxine Lafitte for years. The sight of an attractive middle-aged brunette with great legs leaving after such a short visit would be enough to keep tongues wagging for some time to come yet.

She gave it a few minutes before retrieving the smallest of notepads from the bottom drawer which sat alongside two pay as you go mobiles each with a different colour strip on top. There were certain clients it paid to deny all association with should the shit hit the fan. Primitive as they were by today's standards the pay as you gos were still highly effective.

'Hi it's Geraldine. Just to let you know I've had Rachael Compston here asking some probing questions. She's onto something as she requested a visit at short notice so she's twigged more than she's letting on. Just thought I'd keep you posted.'

The Armstrong Sunday lunch could at best be described as cordial. As two women both of strong character but polar opposite interests the dynamic that joins people together as friends had simply never been there. A relationship as an in law but very little else!

As always the kids were spoiled. True to form Carolyn came out the taxi laden with gifts for her beloved niece and nephew and got idolised in return. Having a very rich aunt who worked as a corporate financier in the Middle East was the stuff of serious bragging rights at school. For once having such a well-known father and rumours of an illustrious aunt meant that it was no longer just his good looking sister getting all the attention the other side of the school gates. For son Andrew, a kid just about as reticent as his father was at that age the novelty of being on many a pretty schoolgirl's most wanted list but as yet too scared to do anything about it.

With lunch over, a return train leg to London beckoning and daylight hours on the wane just about enough time left for the more senior of the two siblings present to enjoy a catch-up stroll around the local park. It did cross Alison's mind whether or not she'd been unduly harsh in her assessment of sister-in-law as Carolyn had been nothing other than modesty personified over lunch but then again those at the pinnacle of their profession with years of experience did have this ability to schmooze through self-deprecating charm. For Alison she was prepared to give benefit of doubt out until husband's return.

The Sky TV van was back. Parked up at its same spot in the local park, not that Mike was paying much attention to its driver in the distance eating a sandwich and seemingly enjoying his hot brew although Carolyn certainly was. Her personal life may have been far removed from mundane English suburbia but still able to feel when things seem out of place. Just how many people would want to have their satellite dishes realigned on a late autumnal Sunday afternoon?

A different team leader this time around as Paul's weekend off, his stand in giving less thought to the suitability of certain vehicles for surveillance than Paul ever would. With a fair selection of communication vans from which to choose this particular leader went for comfort over camouflage.

Her antennae alerted to the likelihood of surveillance she'd make sure the pair kept their distance. Her training reminded her that an external listening device of the kind likely atop the van could pick up conversation in open spaces within no more than a hundred yards. Anything over that and it was practically impossible but likely others were in on the act as well and the park did appear to have its fair share of joggers alongside a couple mid thirties walking arm and arm who simply appeared to be going through the motions than enjoying each other's company.

Thinking on her feet was Carolyn's stock in trade. To share her suspicions with brother meant passing on this snippet to Alison and he likely had enough on his plate at home as it was without the added hassle of a wife's paranoia over being watched to contend with.

'It might sound daft but when you live in Abu Dhabi you don't get to see a great deal of grass. The ground here looks dry enough, would you mind if we walk across the park Mike. I want to feel something soft under my feet for a change.'

'Whatever you say sis.'

Unlikely the four members of Blue Team deployed in various roles in the park that late afternoon would have bought into that being her reason for deciding to drift off piste. Out of ear shot meant being out of danger but at least the team finally had some photographs of a discussion taking place quite blatantly for their ears only.

'Now's as good a time as any to say I'm out Carolyn.'

'You are?'

'Yep, I've done my bit. Ruffled a few feathers, had my fifteen minutes of fame and all that but it's taking its toll and I want to be spending more time at home than going up and down to London every other day for a TV interview.'

'I thought you'd been a bit quiet over lunch but it's not going to be so easy to walk away as you might think. We're both in a lot deeper than you appreciate.'

'So, given that it was my idea I don't see what the problem is.'

'The problem is Mike your naïve when it comes to business. All these companies, these very large companies that you've helped destroy. Who do you think it is that's been buying them for next to nothing, turning them around then selling them on! The firm I work for that's who. When you think back to what dad went through this is us now turning the tables at long last and we're both going to end up very rich because of it. It was B-Smart that wanted dad's site so they could bulldoze the place and stick up a few hundred houses. Well, look who's laughing now?'

'I don't strictly follow. You just said you were happy to do the rounds and encourage other businesses with better reputations to take these duds on.'

'And that's what I do only it's my employer that buys them in the first place before working their own magic stripping out costs to make them more presentable before it even gets round to sticking up a For Sale sign. At least that's what we've been doing so far but with the garden centres we'll maybe keep a handful and sell off the rest for development. It was B-Smart that gave us the idea in the first place, they just never had the nous to finish it off but what do you expect with Joe at the helm and his own boss spending so much time having his wicked way with your old friend Rachael. She just diverted him from the job in hand.'

'You know about Rachael?' from Mike who made himself out to be more surprised than he actually was.

'Course I do. It was you that told me about her in the first place twenty years ago and when I saw her with one of her clients at a corporate do a few years back I just did some digging to find out who her agent was to keep tabs. She's come in handy so far has she not? Who do you think it was that keeps having a word with her pimp when it comes to what clients she sees? It's the one thing most of your targets have in common Mike, they all like a bit of danger and if we can use Rachael to get us some inside information then why not.'

'Yeh but does that not make you just as bad as the guys that put dad out of work? In my rose-tinted world I wanted to make companies change the way they operate, not go ahead and lay thousands off just so my sister can make a fast buck.'

'Its business and the way the world operates. It just boils down to what side of the fence you want to be on. You can do things by the book like dad did and look where that got him or you can keep doing things your way working fourteen hour days as a one man band but that won't get you within a sniff of the kind of money I'm talking about. Whether you like it or not you're already implicated by mere association and the wheels started rolling a while back. Jumping off the bandwagon right now might raise more questions than answers.'

'What's happened to you? What made you become so callous? I'm doing something for a cause, something I genuinely believe in and all the while you've been giving me advice you've just been plotting to make millions behind my back. What's your problem? Do you not make enough as it is?'

For the team leader watching proceedings from afar the sight of brother and sister facing each other off in the kind of discussion that appeared anything but convivial.

'It's the environment I work in. People change and I'd rather be looking at the world through this pair of glasses than the ones I had on as we sat around the kitchen table as kids. Now before you give me another lecture here's the name of Power to the People's next target' as she handed Mike a small, folded piece of paper which he opened immediately.

'No way Carolyn!'

'So, I take it you know who it is and I'll leave it to you how you present the case to your faithful followers. Everything else is in place and the ball starts rolling Monday morning. Rachael's already spent the night with the guy so at least we already have a mole in his camp. After this you can consider hanging up your protest boots Mike because he's sitting on property assets worth billions. Only trouble is he's smarter than all the rest put together so be careful and tread very, very carefully. Things will work out fine just trust me.'

With Alison's words ringing in his ears how does he explain this one away when he gets home without being reminded 'how she'd told him so.' To come clean now or try and wriggle out of one hell of a precarious situation and only minutes to decide before arriving home at that. With so much on his mind and Carolyn temporarily distracted by calling for her taxi he committed the schoolboy error of throwing the folded piece of paper in the public bin as they came back through the park gates. Not that Mike gave it any thought but someone watching from a van with a zoom lens certainly did.

'Forgive me for being naïve but I was led to believe if what the Home Secretary had to say to the Parliamentary Select Committee is true that we had entered a new era of cooperation between intelligence gathering agencies then as such you would therefore be willing to share the reason that lay behind Carolyn Armstrong's visit to these headquarters last Friday?'

This was Paul Anderson having come straight to the NCA from Waterloo first thing Monday morning unaware as yet of the little gem retrieved from the public waste bin a few hundred yards from Armstrong's house. Having been fobbed off the day of Carolyn' s visit eventually given access to speak to one of the case officers working at the higher levels of the organisation.

As the country's newest and so far highly successful kid on the block when it came to fighting organised crime, the NCA looked upon its more established neighbour along the river with a degree of disdain! More old school than cutting edge! Never mind that Paul was one of a new breed of desk officer recruited in MI5's attempt to rid itself of its old boy public school image once and for all. Not that that cut much slack with those NCA operatives who'd spent their formative years patrolling the beat cutting their teeth with the proverbial aggressive Friday night drunk unlike their silver spooned university educated counterpart.

This particular case officer was one of the got there the hard way brigade and anything but intimidated by a spook poking his nose in somebody else's casebook. A couple of years older than Paul and destined to go places he could throw the bullshit lingo back over the fence when need be.

'I'm not saying your naïve, more a lack of understanding about what this agency does. Your own intelligence service covers a broad canvas whereas the name suggests our focus is purely organised crime and as such look on us as the Special Forces of law enforcement in that we work independently and we work alone.'

'Though when it comes to the Armstrong siblings strictly speaking it's not an organised crime syndicate is it?' Paul replied. 'And the sister has paid you a visit which by our records took up at least a morning of the agency's time. Are you at liberty to tell me what this meeting was about?'

'No, I'm not because I'm not duty bound to do so.'

'Actually you are.'

'Disagree. You can come at me from whatever angle you like but we both know how the other works so you let us in on something first which we may find useful then we'll reciprocate, but at this moment in time the very fact you've requested a visit tells me your worried so the balls in your court.'

A perfect example of why MI5 hated dealing with this bunch. Unlike the London Met these guys were not in the slightest bit intimidated by their neighbours and if anything took great delight in running rings around. For things to progress someone would have to crack and it sure looked like it wasn't going to be the NCA. Share what he had then watch as they take all the credit or keep going on his own and risk seeing Armstrong edge even further ahead in the public opinion polls. Not that the movement and its leader were a threat to national security, as yet, but PTTP was a bandwagon others of more sinister persuasion may seek to infiltrate at which point it could then become a different beast entirely. Unless a spanner was thrown in their works and soon Paul's thus far stellar transitions up through the ranks may come to a grinding halt. Bad enough watching his Fast Fit shares go down the drain but to screw up a career alongside would be one cock up too many.

While the bureaucrats of law enforcement pondered their options across the capital an altogether more resourceful character was frantically working the phones in a desperate search for clues.

No one gets to Charles Grey's elevated position of power without knowing people who know all the right people. Unlike the civil servants who drew their information the hard way as per the training manual all Charles Grey had to do was lift the phone and pick the brains of those well placed within the City's square mile and the higher echelons of government. The city had been awash with rumours for some time about a secretive investor throwing its weight around the capital, its identity as yet unknown. The very same fund whose principle strategist was about to deliver Grey the double whammy of seeing two of his significant shareholders offload their stock onto the open market at the same time causing the value of his company to plummet by twenty five percent within minutes of the news catching the city analysts off guard. Were that not bad enough another kick in the teeth with the lunchtime news announcement that the Power to the People protest group would by 2 pm today encourage their double digit million membership to immediately cease shopping at any branches of his fashion empire. The business that had taken thirty years to erect was crumbling before his very eyes and the ulcer that had finally settled was back with a vengeance.

Somebody in the higher tiers of fund management had to have orchestrated this as the timing of events coming together were anything but coincidental. The price the odd titan of the UK's retail sector makes for lifting their ear off the ground and taking eye off ball. Bad enough the impending collapse in trade but where would the money now be coming from to service the interest payments on his gargantuan debt pile and that was even before suppliers and wages payments were taken into account.

At heart Charles Grey, real name Paul Chandler was a barrow boy done good. The change of name before making it big came at a time when he realised that to move in the circles to which he aspired meant leaving his past behind and modifying the image to one the bankers might look more favourably upon when lending seven figure sums assuming there was family money tied up somewhere in the background to cover the debt. The name he thought carried a touch of gravitas. That he was a glorified chancer who got lucky was known by some, but he still carried their respect. A street fighter who had the drive to succeed in whatever field he'd chosen was born with a nose for the deal. If it smelled right, he was in and if not no hanging around. In this instance his nose was telling him he could smell a rat and a fat one at that. No way on God's earth were the events of the past few hours just a remarkable coincidence on top of which this guy was most definitely not working alone. He had to be in cahoots with someone who knew the inner workings of the stock market or simply he was the front man for something altogether bigger. He knew Armstrong was smart but he was an adversary he'd better get a handle on and soon or else a lifetime's work would soon be in the hands of administrators.

As yet plenty of calls made simply awaiting reply. Isolated and in limbo he did what he always did to take his mind off matters and hopefully quell the ulcer. Needing some immediate stress relief to kick start his recovery plan he made another call.

'Hello Maxine, its Charles Grey here. Is my new favourite girl available?'

Chapter 12

What had started off as a solitary guy struggling to get his voice heard above the parapet of complacency had by a series of fortuitous coincidences and lucky breaks evolved into the kind of social movement no one back in the early days of convening in Harry's living room could ever have thought possible. The real stars of the show and the driving force behind PTTP's spectacular success being the country's retired fraternity where, harnessed in conjunction with the internet may have cost the group founders a lot of their time in the beginning but at least not their money.

As happens in life one man's good fortune is another person's opportunity and although it was now Carolyn orchestrating which financial moves to make the seeds of the plan were actually sown in her partner's mind over dinner back in Abu Dhabi when she mentioned in passing the success younger brother appeared to be having with his fledgling protest group back in Blighty. Ever the opportunist and the only man until now that appeared to have won emotional sway over this most single minded of women a plan was hatched when it became clear Power to the People really had touched some kind of nerve with a disgruntled public and the roughshod practices of their initial target Fast Fit. If he pulled this off the pair could just sit back and allow her brother all-important publicity while picking up the winning chips left going begging in the group's wake.

At first reticent about hijacking her brother's bandwagon, lover boy did as he always managed and talked her around. Either that or be held to ransom with a four day huff and threats to leave which he frequently did when things never went his own way. A tempestuous relationship at the best of times if Mike was influenced by professional sister then Carolyn was well and truly under the thumb with her longer term and similarly qualified partner. A man with a reputation for ruthlessness within the Doha oganisation as well as a roving eye it made no difference to Jonny Castle if his partner's brother were hung out to dry by the British media should news of double dealings behind the scenes leak out. In fact all the better! To have a fall guy in place should the shit hit the fan was what the art of deal making was all about and Mike's loyalty to his fellow sibling appeared to have given Jonny his very own get out of jail card by simply doing as he was now told. So, far so good!

For the country's consumer champion of champions just like his latest opponent Charles Grey his credibility was finally on the line. Two men at polar opposite ends of the financial spectrum but being set up and facing ruination for an as yet unknown outsider's financial gain! Mike's dilemma and for the first time since the movement's inception was that he was advising one thing one thing in public but believing another in private. He simply had no beef with Charles Grey yet his almost messiah like status amongst the party faithful was such that since making the boycott announcement Grey's business sales had practically fallen off a cliff yet here was a guy who just like his father and grandfather before had done it the hard way by building an empire from scratch. The only difference between the two was that the most recent had the drive and self-belief to go further while the other two had settled for what they had. Sure Grey was creative with his accounting practices when it came to paying his taxes but father Jim could be just as forgetful with cash in hand landscaping jobs when it came to recording quarterly sales. Although these oversights were on a much smaller scale compared to Grey's the principle of evading paying one's taxes to Her Majesty's Government remained the same.

Grey himself made great play of the fact that both he and his businessess were UK based, no offshore tax havens for him and that far from being a monopoly he was still a success in one of the most competitive fields around, that of high street fashion. To attack one of the UK's leading entrepreneurs just for the sake of it was not what Power to the People was about but Mike's misgivings by email and subsequent heated exchange were now falling on deaf ears. The once bastion of fairness and moderation that he'd grown up with and been influenced by as a kid had matured into someone Uncle Frank, her mentor, simply wouldn't recognise. An indication of her own single mindedness and determination or a great example of the brainwashing that clouds one's judgement when they fall head over heels and completely in love with the wrong type. Mike was perplexed, Alison less so. And forget about the opulence and sophistication of Doha group HQ, office gossip is the same wherever you go and the chit chat amongst its handsomely rewarded executives was that Carolyn Armstrong was not the only attractive female that was keeping her dashing polo playing partner entertained at night.

Having played his hand there was maybe one card still left up Mike's sleeve. With Carolyn having mentioned her steering certain clients Rachael's way maybe his old friend could shed some light on the next move Charles Grey would shortly make. Initially thought of as an adversary it might not just be Rachael that Grey was jumping into bed with.

It would have been nice if he'd been there to pick her up at the airport, after all she had asked but events like these no longer came as that great a surprise to Carolyn. There'd be the usual plethora of excuses the most common of which his being called away at short notice but always the support of a trusted few at HQ to back the stories up. She'd fallen for him but by the same token hated herself for being so weak. Another Joe but more intelligent although just like her brother devoid of an ounce of emotional intellect!

Sure enough when she finally managed to log onto the airports Wi-Fi the text read that he'd been called away to Riyadh for a meeting but back the following afternoon and the restaurant table was already booked. With the consolation of business class at least offering a half-decent night's sleep she bypassed the opportunity of heading back to her apartment opting instead for a debrief and remaining morning's work and a guaranteed early night when she got home. Not only in the UK that white collar office staff do what they can to slope off early on a Friday and the tradition travelled well which made Jonny's unexpected meeting all the more suspicious as he was Doha's finest when it came to vacating the building on a Friday as soon as feasible after lunch.

As expected he'd covered his tracks as the meeting, schedule and clients all added up. His flying monkeys had served him well. At Doha their executives took care of their own travel arrangements and simply claimed back so on this one salient point impossible to check but everything else seemed in order and yet, the feeling that the rest of the office was party to the missing link but under oath of allegiance to keep it zipped. She already knew some of the rumours and his reputation but in a place like this stories of infidelity were ten a penny. Today somehow felt different. As if the raised eyebrows and smirks behind her back were the code to alert her antennae that not all was as it seemed. Just how blinkered to the obvious had Carolyn actually become?

Most of the time field work was just monotonous. Weekends sacrificed for the sake of shadowing a suspect who knew they were being tailed anyway and therefore deliberately led the tailing ops agents completely up the garden path with the odd subtle gesture just to rub it in.

The Armstrong case felt more like good old fashioned police detective work and it had crossed Paul's mind on more than one occasion whether the first class honours would have been better utilised in getting a fast track up the greasy pole of the police than the long drawn out saga of competing with his academic equals back at MI5. At least here he was granted the autonomy to think on his feet and today yet another addition to his vast repertoire of roleplays. As a client waiting in a hotel room for his afternoon treat to arrive and she'd just this very minute texted to say she was on her way up.

Not the kind of hotel Rachael normally frequented but then not the kind of client her agent Maxine Lafitte would be familiar with either. A three star hotel in Queensway just off the Bayswater Rd more akin to the budget traveler of limited means than someone rewarding themselves for the odd decade or so of hard graft. Still, easy enough to find being a stone's throw from the Tube station and at four hundred pounds accepted for the hour she could now afford to leave the phone on silent for what was left of the working week. Or so she thought.

His heart was thumping as hard as it usually would just before any assignment got underway which Paul himself in this circumstance found quite surprising. Not that he'd never seen a hooker before, more the street walking variety that loitered around Kings Cross but this one now in the lift was more Premier League type. Walking along the corridor it would be Rachael taking it all in her stride as one of the Security Services most promising paced the room the other side of the wall rehearsing his lines.

It did seem slightly out of context that the guy about to open the door was happy to pay four hundred quid for an hour of her time yet stay in the kind of place lucky to get away with charging just a quarter of that for the whole of the night. Slightly odd but literally only occupying seconds of her thinking time! She'd given up trying to rationalise the whys and wherefores of why men did what they did a while back. In booking a place like this it was highly unlikely she'd ever be seeing him again so getting down to business as soon as and she might be lucky in getting away twenty minutes early. Once the deed was done the married ones perversely couldn't wait to get home.

Christ she was hot. About five feet six, brunette with killer curves! Likely at her peak around forty-four she'd obviously adjusted herself the other side of the door and thankfully no chambermaids around to see her undoing a few strategic buttons for maximum impact. All experience and part and parcel of Rachael's strategy to get the testosterone pumping from the off. He seemed quite young, thirty at the most and in pretty good shape. Likely worked out and no sign of the usual nerves that went cap in hand with someone his age. The nerves had gone the minute he opened the door. As if a green light had flashed the job was now on.

Unsure whether to kiss or shake hands Paul just went for the safe option.

'Hi come on in. I'm Simon.'

'Nice to meet you Simon. You look a lovely guy.'

'Thanks. Please, take a seat' as he gestured to the two seater sofa by the window. For a three star hotel at least he had the money to book one of its bigger rooms with what passed as its own bijou coffee annex complete with table sofa and chairs. Maybe she was being unkind as he appeared relaxed without it coming across as fake.

'So, would you like tea or coffee Raquel?'

'Coffee would be nice. Just milk! She looked around but no sign of a stash of notes sitting somewhere prominent to be handed over.'

'So, before we get started Simon would you…ehm…have my fee?'

'Remind me how you like your coffee?' as if brushing her question aside.

'Medium is fine' which he duly finished before bringing cup and saucer across and placing on table. He then took up position on the chair which meant he was sitting directly opposite at which point he retrieved a brown envelope from his inside jacket pocket and placed on the table which he gestured to open.

'Please feel free to look inside.'

'Am sure I won't need to count it all, you look trustworthy enough' as the colour drained from her face in an instant as she scanned its contents.

'You know this man?' he asked as she sat fixated to a particular recent photograph of her and Mike.

'Who are you and what's this all about?'

'What it's about and if you don't mind I'd prefer to call you Rachael, also think I'm right in saying your surname's Compston is that you have a close affiliation with a man who currently runs an extremely effective consumer protest group in the UK. I need your help Rachael but I can't tell what the net result will be but what I will say is that ultimately you'll be doing your friend Mike Armstrong an enormous favour.'

'I need a cigarette.'

'By all means. Don't see any smoke alarms and you can use my saucer as an ashtray. I don't smoke but I came prepared. You smoke these right?' as he threw a packet of Silk Cut on the table.

'I even brought you a lighter. I also think it's time you buttoned yourself up sweetheart. I'm sure you've got great tits but this is not what this afternoon's about and there's no four hundred quid waiting for you either. This is about saving your own skin and that of your friend's.'

'Me and Mike go back a long way' drawing deeply on cigarette hand visibly shaking.

'I know you do.'

'I'm still waiting for you to tell me who you are?' For the first in a long time it was a man that was in control and barely out of his shorts at that.

'All you need to know is my name's Simon and I work for the Government. The same government that you've been withholding paying taxes to from your cash in hand escort work for the past twenty years. Now you can either play ball at which point we turn a blind eye to your lucrative sideline or I make a phone call to a Compliance Officer working at the Inland Revenue, pass on everything I have on you and tell them to mark it down as being a priority one investigation. I know a few Compliance Officers on first name terms and these guys can be bastards at times Rachael. Not just a fine you're looking at here but a realistic jail sentence and how would your two girls feel about that? One's training to be an accountant right?

Won't do her career much good if her employer were to find out her mother's been jailed for embezzlement.

From grey to gaunt in just over a minute.

'So, Rachael here's what we need you to do.'

'I'm in the shit.'

'That's not how it's coming across on TV. It looks like you're about to put yet another tycoon out of business who by an incredible coincidence just happens to be one of my clients. So, who is it that's leaning on my agent Maxine to get me your targets as clients? Is it you?'

'How could it be me? I don't know anything about renting women out in the capital. It's Carolyn. Don't ask me how she does it, but she's got something on this Maxine pimp of yours to steer certain clients your way. You're then meant to pass on the inside information to me that stops me from ruining my family man image.'

'If only they knew!'

As close a throwback to the days of old as you could possibly get! Having arranged to collect Rachael from the station instead of spinning a line of old to his parents about having a girlfriend this time around it was his wife who'd been fobbed off about running late fitting pipe work. No more battered old Mini but an upgrade to slightly past its best white light goods van.'

'Just another day in the life of a high class hooker Mike! One minute Mayfair the next wherever this place is meant to be' as she looked around. With the odd barbed wire perimeter fence to protect the secondhand car lot nearby a fleeting thought to days of old.

'It feels like the back of fucking beyond. A throwback to my prison sentence spent on that horrible bloody Fairfield council estate.'

Not quite as bad as she was making out, an everyday industrial estate where the frantic comings and goings of heavy and light goods vehicles went largely unnoticed. The perfect place for his own LGV to seamlessly blend into the takeaway sandwich bar's car park without any attention being paid as to its occupants were it not for the fact that another fairly inconspicuous hatchback had parked up a hundred yards or so nearby and was watching their every move. This time around no sign of Paul, just a solo operative under orders to come back with some half decent incriminating evidence! The camera motor sprung into action as Mike got photographed carrying a cardboard tray holding two polystyrene cups back to the van.

'So, how many times have you seen him?'

'Grey? Yesterday would have been the third and if you're looking for some inside info I can tell you this much, he bears no relation to the guy you've got your heart set on destroying. If anything he's the complete opposite once you strip away the bravado.'

'He lost his wife a few years back and he's never really recovered which is where people like me come in. He's different to all the rest because he's just lonely. He's got all the trappings but it's just to maintain the image. He's at his happiest either talking about fashion or his animal sanctuary in Dorset that's run by one of his sons. His other two kids work in the business and one of them is a driver. It's just a much bigger version of Armstrong's Mike and he makes sure there are no special privileges. He still drinks in the same pub on a Friday night he went to when he was just a barrow boy. I actually think you'd like him but just like you he's a stubborn son of a bitch so don't bank on this guy going down without a fight. I'll always be on your side Mike you know that, but this could get messy. I know you'll think of something because you always do but whatever it is come up with it soon.'

'I best get you back. What time's your train at?'

'Every half hour so there's no rush. We can stay here just a little while longer if you like', placing her hand on his.

'When all this is over Mike let's do dinner or at least something. I need some normality in my life as at the moment I'm just all over the place.'

'Sure, I'll organise something. I need to be spending more time at home so just bear with me.'

Her hand caressing his face it was obvious to the pair what was coming next. Positioning herself as instructed the whirr of the camera ensured it captured their every move. The kisses as long in length as those of old but this time around not to entice a younger Mike to help her out but to use this middle-aged man to save her skin.

She knew what she had to do. It was just following things through that posed the problem but enough on her mind to ensure there'd be no chance of any sleep on her return to the apartment.

He lived about half an hour's drive away in one of Abu Dhabi's most up market suburbs. A residence befitting his status as one of the city expats' top earners. Another text to inform the meeting had been extended into the evening to include dinner so therefore unlikely to be around later but he'd call in the morning. She guessed he was banking on her having an early night but the whole episode was becoming more clichéd by the minute. What did she have to lose? A few hours forfeited sleep for the sake of clearing her conscience was a sacrifice worth paying. If no one at home then he'd still be none the wiser and she could ease up on her trust issues and if he were then only herself to blame for ending up in this position in the first place. But she'd still want to kill him!

She was a lawyer so therefore a pragmatist at heart. The rose-tinted spectacles about life were lifted the minute she'd found her father dangling three inches off the floor so if she could recover from that and still make something of her life then she could handle being cheated on and that vital moment of truth was literally just around the next corner.

If it's the unexpected that cause palpitations, the sight of not one but two cars in the driveway barely registered a flicker. Her saving grace being that when required she could keep it together. Falling apart could wait till she got home. With no security issues in this kind of neighborhood it was easy enough for Carolyn to park up alongside the Lamborghini then walk through the back gate into the garden which would bring her up towards the pool directly in front of the open plan kitchen area. Just standing far enough back so not directly visible but with a clear view of Jonny in boxer shorts and his leggy blond companion wearing what looked like one of the shirts she'd given him as a birthday present. Talk about rubbing salt in the wound and the blond she'd seen from somewhere at work so obviously an ongoing arrangement exploited to the hilt while she'd been away.

Seated at the breakfast bar and sharing a glass of wine they could pass for any middle-aged couple having recently hooked up were it not for the fact he was meant to be already spoken for. Carolyn's eyesight still good enough to spot his mobile as always close at hand. His attention temporarily diverted from latest conquest by ping of incoming text.

Hi. How's meeting? Having fun? Xxx

She watched from outside with what looked like a gesture to his companion that he's telling her who it's from. Her own ringtone killed as a precaution. Smart move as the response was swift.

It's a drag. Missing you. xxx

Awww that's nice. Tell me Jonny was she any good? Did she squeal or is she the silent type? Nice touch her wearing my birthday gift! xxx

???

The impact of the last was immediate. Having shown sex on legs the last message he's off his stool and opening the patio doors but Carolyn pre-empted that one and stepped well out of sight behind the overgrown shrubbery. Jonny's turn to text.

Don't understand! xxx

A wry smile on Carolyn's face as she wasted no time.

Oh, I think you do. Suggest check CCTV.

Which he duly did and there she was. A cursory glance from Carolyn into the camera before getting back into the car and his diving for cover as this lady was not for stopping as he tried to block her escape. Bawling her eyes out could wait till the front door was closed.

Under normal circumstances the two young men in collar and tie conversing in a car would not arouse too much suspicion but this was not normal circumstance and even though the radio station car park was full to brimming Mike's antennae were still alerted to the fact something appeared not right. Yet another radio interview to spread the word and maintain boycott momentum in what was largely being conveyed by the press as the battle of David v Goliath with a twist. This time around it was no longer PTTP that were the underdog such was its influence all over the UK. Companies and their all-important share prices now lived in fear of being targeted by the group as in the majority of cases the impact was as instant as Charles Grey's Fashion House conglomerate could easily testify.

No surprise then and as if on cue by the time Mike reached his car that the one from the driver's seat in the watching car was already out and making his way towards him.

'Mr Armstrong?'

'That's me and whatever it is your selling I'm not interested.'

'Not here to sell. Just more talking I'm afraid. I'd like to discuss something I have which may be of interest.' At which point the remaining driver had brought their car alongside.

'You guys journalists or just Charles Grey's heavies?'

'Certainly not but I do have a good story for you by way of Rachael Compston, an established London call girl as well as your sister Carolyn and her financial involvement afterwards in businesses your protest group very successfully put out of business. The kind of story that could ruin one's reputation as well as their marriage don't you think?' With Paul opening the rear door Mike was left with little option but to get in as his gut was telling him these guys were anything but Fleet St.

The car felt different without being able to figure out why and appeared to glide of its own accord. Testament to the abilities of the driver who's job was to let the other one take care of much more pressing matters with Mike. They were either police or something higher up. Once out on the main road Paul as with Rachael several days prior clicked into green light professional mode.

'The problem with protests Mike is they tend to go either one of two ways. Nine times out of ten they simply fizzle out but sometimes for other reasons they stick. We could be here all day discussing why but the bottom line is if left unchecked your Power to the People movement could cost the country more that its members might think they gain. It's those large corporations you appear to despise that contribute the bulk of the Treasury's income not to mention the funds that eventually feed through to paying your members private pensions. Thing is Mike, those of greater economic intellect than us think it's time you brought matters to an abrupt halt so we're looking for you to make an announcement by midnight tomorrow at the absolute latest or things might become a bit sticky for you. These should help sway any indecision you might be feeling.'

Just as with Rachael it was passing over of brown envelope time and Mike's turn to face the incriminating evidence from as recent as two nights ago and his brief dalliance with Rachael in the van. With arms embraced and lips practically glued together no doubting how these would be perceived if falling into the wrong hands. Worse still the fact that Rachael was party to all this in the first place as it was her that made the fairly blatant first move.

'Not that we intend doing anything with these you understand but you've been married a long time and have a loving family at home. Now's the time to ask yourself what's more important Mike! You can either do things our way or find yourself a good QC on five grand a day when we raise proceedings on conspiracy to defraud by mass deception. You might get off but think of the stress of it all before you even get round to going to court. Don't think Alison will be best pleased either do you?'

'And what happens to the original photos.'

'Nothing. I'm giving you my word.'

'Even though I don't know who you are.'

'On a personal level Mike you cost me a lot of money when my investment pot of Fast Fit shares went down the tubes so consider yourself grateful I'm doing something I don't actually need to. You did well, you're a small guy that's had his moment in the sun but now time to bow out gracefully while we're giving you the chance. Ok, that's enough', spoken in the direction of the driver.

'Let's take this guy back.'

Having been dropped back at the station car park no further rolling down of windows or pearl of wisdom parting comment. The car simply sped off in silence. Whoever these guys were had just run rings around him...and Rachael.

Ordinarily Mike would have taken the train up to the capital but his success had squandered most opportunities nowadays of travelling with the public en masse. Always someone prepared to invade his private space with their own personal suggestion as to the group's next suitable candidate. Kitchen and fitters and garages easily the most popular given the number of requests received for their demise.

There was a brief chat with Alison before setting off at short notice, essentially a fobbing off exercise that she never bought into anyway but assumed Carolyn was bound to be part of when it came close to anything remotely resembling cloak and dagger. However she'd gotten her wish, he was packing in and whatever it was that had to be done at such short notice she could live with if it meant seeing more of her husband in person as opposed to appearing in print. She knew him well enough to know something dramatic had triggered the change of heart but it could wait. As she frequently reminded the kids, things will always come out in the wash.

Rachael had mentioned Grey had a longtime habit of visiting the same pub every Friday night and it was here at the King George on the Old Kent Rd that Mike had come to pay him a visit. He'd been fine up to the point of actually having to set foot inside the place before anxiety struck and the sudden flashback to days of old and the lion's den that was the outbuilding at the back of the family garden centre and the site of many a beating and partial water boarding at the hands of older brother. The self-doubt that comes from the unknown and sudden realisation of where he was and just what he was actually about to do. If he were to be torn from limb to limb then please God at least make it quick.

One of those pubs as in days of old with a where a keen eye always kept on the comings and goings and Mike's arrival had not gone unnoticed. Sure enough Grey was there perched on a stool in what appeared to be intense discussion at the far end of a crowded bar. As yet unaware of Mike's visit a space opened up between the pair as those standing cleared sufficient room for the unwelcome visitor to come into Charles Grey's line of sight. Casually dressed in an understated kind of way, a far cry from the image of dapper sharp suited tycoon created in support of his Fashion House empire.

A nod from Charles to his small entourage to make themselves scarce and the obligatory cursory glance from each in Mike's direction before departing!

'You've got balls Armstrong I'll give you that. Never expected to see the man hell bent on destroying my business coming into my local boozer.'

'It's only a flying visit. If I'm able to leave in one piece that is.'

'I own the place so it's me that decides what happens inside and out. So, something's happened or else you wouldn't be here.'

'I owe you an apology. I should never have organised a boycott and before the start of trade tomorrow it'll be over.'

'So, who leaned on you then?'

'Let's call it being enlightened.'

'Really well its interesting you say that because during the week you picked up a hooker from the train station who goes by the name of Raquel and while the pair of you had your tongues down each other's throats you failed to notice some geezer in another car nearby snapping merrily away and then just this afternoon another two geezers picked you up in a modified BMW the kind only used by the Met or Security Services. Don't think for one minute these guys don't already know I've also been having you tailed. Now somewhere in all of this there's a vital link I'm missing out on and if you hadn't shown your face tonight one of the guys I've just been talking to is a hack ready to roll what we've got in the Sunday papers. You've just saved your skin, your marriage and your reputation all in one go. Its time you redeemed yourself by telling your millions of followers to get out there and start splashing the cash in my stores otherwise you might just see the nasty side of me Mike.'

'And Raquel?'

'What about her? I'm guessing there's a bit of history there, but she plays her cards close to her chest just as we do. What benefit is there to tell somebody something they don't need to know. For future reference Mike don't get involved in anything like this again. I only ever give people one chance, never a second.'

'Point taken.'

With which a nod to the two heavies on the door to step to the side. Mike actually did make it out alive.

True to his word by breakfast the following morning an online announcement that takes everyone except a certain few completely by surprise.

'Power to the People evolved because of the need to hold companies to account when it came to abusing their power and the ineffectiveness of elected authority to do anything about it. My role was to encourage the disgruntled masses to vote with their feet than rely on those in higher office to do what they are paid for.

A mistake which I now bitterly regret is to have advocated a boycott of the Fashion House retail group. In a nutshell I was misinformed. Fashion House has become one of the country's most successful retailers because of the quality of its management and products on offer, a far cry from those boycotted in the past and as such should be supported rather than penalised. That their reputation has been damaged I can only apologise profusely.

Power to the People has shown that we can all make a difference when our energies are brought together and having achieved its aim the time is now right to bow out and bring this movement to a close.

We can be proud of everything achieved and all that remains to be said is get out there and show your support to those companies that care about their clientele of which Fashion House is undoubtedly one.

Mike Armstrong'

'Very touching' was about as appreciative a comment as Charles Grey could muster as his paid companion sat alongside.

'Just wish I knew what part you played in all of this Raquel apart from the obvious.'

Along the river at Thames House Paul's turn to make his way up to 'C's third floor office for Monday mornings debrief on the previous week's activities. Actually hoping he'd be first in line the schedule was such that he was assigned a derisory third. Irony being that 'C' was just as excited in sharing his own good news as he was.

For 'C' to offer a coffee no matter how stale at least sent the signal that one of his protégés had come up with the goods and he was mighty pleased. Taciturn at the best of times the coffee was even delivered with a smile.

'Paul excellent result. I've already had the Home Secretary's office on the phone passing on its appreciation for a job well done.'

'Thanks, but that was just at my end. Something must have happened at the other end surely with the elusive sister?'

'Ahh, yes. I personally took control of this one as it needed a delicate touch. Transpires her employer the Doha group has been responsible for buying up a few billion or so worth of Government bonds a while back as well as acting as intermediary in some highly classified arms contracts. Not the type of financial entity one wants to fall out with especially as it has come to light that one or two ex cabinet ministers are also on their payroll.

So, it comes to light our very own Carolyn Armstrong has gone and got herself involved with a bit of a maverick at Doha who's even higher up. A fellow by the name of Jonny Castle. He simply got her to lean on brother when it came to boycotting certain companies so that when they went bust Doha could pick them up for a song and make a killing by reselling. So, in the circumstance more about creating a bit of distance between Jonny and Carolyn than falling out with Doha. After all nothing illegal about what they were doing.'

Paul nodding in agreement. He guessed this was the part where it now got juicy.

'Now I a quick call to Vauxhall Bridge where they were kind enough to inform me that a few operatives were also strategically placed in several of the City's most prominent investment centres just to keep us all in the loop that the oil money is still going to where it should be. So, their agent within Doha who has already befriended Castle because of other shady dealings in his own right makes a point of being at Jonny's home when Carolyn comes back and turns up at his house unexpectedly. Caught with his pants down in more ways than one! I'm led to believe Carolyn comes across as a touch arrogant at times and let's not forget she's already paid the NCA two million which she'll now have to beg to get back. Being knocked down a peg or two won't have done her any harm but by the same token given her skill set and connections maybe worthwhile bringing her onboard.'

'Given how much her brother cost my retirement plan I'd rather just forget about the Armstrong name altogether.'

Alison was right. Her husband's protest movement becoming forgotten about faster than even she had anticipated with the Armstrong name to be remembered only in the context on an award-winning garden centre in Waltham but little else.

'At the end of the day Alison was all this about me just clearing my conscience? That kid listening on the other side of the kitchen door as his parents rubbished his prospects. Maybe the timid little mouse as his father so eloquently described him had a bit of bite after all.